A CHRISTMAS GIFT FOR THE EAST END LIBRARY GIRLS

PATRICIA MCBRIDE

Boldwood

First published in Great Britain in 2024 by Boldwood Books Ltd.

Copyright © Patricia McBride, 2024

Cover Design by Colin Thomas

Cover Photography: Shutterstock and Alamy

The moral right of Patricia McBride to be identified as the author of this work has been asserted in accordance with the Copyright, Designs and Patents Act 1988.

All rights reserved. No part of this book may be reproduced in any form or by any electronic or mechanical means, including information storage and retrieval systems, without written permission from the author, except for the use of brief quotations in a book review.

This book is a work of fiction and, except in the case of historical fact, any resemblance to actual persons, living or dead, is purely coincidental.

Every effort has been made to obtain the necessary permissions with reference to copyright material, both illustrative and quoted. We apologise for any omissions in this respect and will be pleased to make the appropriate acknowledgements in any future edition.

A CIP catalogue record for this book is available from the British Library.

Paperback ISBN 978-1-83518-021-1

Large Print ISBN 978-1-83518-020-4

Hardback ISBN 978-1-83518-019-8

Ebook ISBN 978-1-83518-022-8

Kindle ISBN 978-1-83518-023-5

Audio CD ISBN 978-1-83518-014-3

MP3 CD ISBN 978-1-83518-015-0

Digital audio download ISBN 978-1-83518-018-1

Boldwood Books Ltd
23 Bowerdean Street
London SW6 3TN
www.boldwoodbooks.com

This work is dedicated to all the people who have inspired me – friends, family and loved ones. And of course the stories of my lovely mother Joyce Johnson and all the brave women who lived through the struggles of WW2. I couldn't have written this story without them.

1

LATE OCTOBER 1941

'You've got to be kidding!' Mavis scoffed into the receiver of the black Bakelite telephone. 'You're from Buckingham Palace? I didn't come down with the last shower of rain.'

She wasn't about to be hoodwinked by the officious tone on the other end of the line claiming to be speaking on behalf of His Majesty. Any scoundrel could pretend to be someone else over the telephone. Mavis prided herself on being far too savvy to be taken in like that.

'I assure you, madam, this is no jest,' the man replied curtly. 'Please fetch Lady Cordelia Carmichael immediately. I must speak with her.'

Mavis bristled at the man's imperious tone. Who did this man think he was, ordering her around as if she were his skivvy? She considered hanging up on the rude rascal but thought better of it. Perhaps she ought to let her boss Cordelia decide whether this supposed royal summons was legitimate or not.

Her fingers tightening on the receiver, her eyes darted around nervously as she dropped her voice to a whisper, cupping the mouthpiece even though there was no one near enough to overhear her.

'Who are you, anyway? You never said your name.'

There was a momentary pause and Mavis hoped he'd thought better of messing around a busy librarian.

'My name is Mr Jennings, and I am His Majesty's personal secretary. Now, madam, please put me through.'

His tone had an edge to it now, and Mavis finally thought she should let her boss know.

'Very well, please 'old,' Mavis said briskly. She placed the heavy receiver down none too gently and shouted across the library, 'Call for Lady Cordelia Carmichael.'

Several heads jerked up in surprise at Mavis's loud shout. Two women looked at each other.

'What? She's a lady?' one of them remarked. 'She never said. I always said she was a dark horse, didn't I?'

Cordelia was shelving books at the far end of the busy East End library. Her colleague Jane was reading to half a dozen little ones in the children's section. A regular visitor they called The Professor was poring over a weighty tome, scribbling notes, two plump ladies were trying to choose romance books, giggling as they tried to work out how 'romantic' they might be, and others were scattered around reading or, in two cases, sleeping soundly.

Hearing her name, Cordelia came running.

'What on earth are you doing, shouting in the library? And you know I don't want people to know my title.'

Mavis shook her head. 'Never mind all that.' She put her hand over the mouthpiece. 'There's this bloke on the line. Says 'e's the king's private secretary. Mr Jennings or something. Wants to talk to you.'

Cordelia took the phone from her and tucked a loose strand of blonde hair out of the way before putting the phone to her ear. Mavis only took one step away, straining to hear the conversation.

Cordelia listened to what the man had to say, her eyes gradually widening.

'Why, yes, we'd be very honoured,' she began, her voice sounding quite different from normal – shaky, uncertain.

She listened, a frown on her face and blinking faster than usual. 'I see,' she said twice. More listening, then: 'That's excellent, I'll wait to hear more from you. Goodbye.'

'What's happening?' Jane asked, having joined them, alerted by Mavis's cry. 'Is something wrong?'

'Better ask the boss,' Mavis said with a knowing grin.

Cordelia had put down the phone but was still looking at it in a daze.

Jane nudged her arm. 'What is it, Cordelia? What's happened?'

Putting her finger to her lips, Cordelia lowered her voice. 'That was a Mr Jennings from the palace. The king and queen want to visit us!'

Mavis could hardly believe this was true. Could the king and queen really be planning to visit their humble East London neighbourhood library? What a turn-up for the books that would be! Her mind was already racing ahead. Did she have anything good enough to wear? Would someone from the palace teach her what to say? If they actually spoke to her, how on earth did you address royalty? And how did you curtsey? She'd seen women on Pathé news curtseying when presented to the king and queen. None of them had even stumbled, much less fallen over as she surely would. What if she did something terrible and let herself and the library down? She'd never be able to hold her head up in Silvertown again.

Mistrustful as she was, Mavis couldn't help but feel a glimmer of hope fluttering through her veins like a delicate bird in flight.

This might be the most thrilling thing to happen in their little library since the war began. No. Ever.

'Are you joking?' Jane asked Cordelia. 'Why would they come here of all places?'

Before she could answer, their favourite young reader came to the desk, Hetty Gregory. She seemed to grow at least half an inch every time she came in.

'This book was real good,' she said, putting a copy of *Peter Pan* on the desk. 'It's about this boy what flies. He's a bit naughty. My mum would tell me off if I did what he does.'

Barely able to control her curiosity about the royal news, Jane smiled at her. 'I'm so glad you liked it. Why don't you go with Mummy and choose two more books?' She looked at Hetty's mother, Mrs Gregory. 'She's looking really well now, isn't she?'

Mrs Gregory shook her head. 'I was such a fool not getting her vaccination for diphtheria. Thank goodness she seems to have completely recovered.'

The library had displayed a poster about the vaccinations for ages, but some parents still hadn't taken up the offer. Poor Hetty was one of the victims, but at least she had survived.

When they'd gone to the children's section, Jane went back to the others.

'Is it true?' she said, feeling breathless with excitement.

'They are coming,' Cordelia said, unsure whether to be pleased or not. 'But not for at least six weeks. The palace likes to give time to prepare. They'll write to confirm what Mr Jennings said and give us a date.' As she spoke, her mind was already racing ahead, calculating how much would need to be done before the visit. There was so much. And no money to do it with.

At that moment, a reader came in wanting advice about a book for her poorly brother. But Mavis was distracted by the astounding news and didn't notice him speaking.

'Are you listening, Mrs Kent?' the reader asked, her tone unusually sharp. It was Mrs McDonald, a tiny woman who always dressed in dark colours, but, unusually, was wearing a bright red scarf that day.

'Sorry, Mrs M,' Mavis said, dragging her attention away from the exciting news. 'Now, if I remember, your brother likes Agatha Christie. We have a new one of hers, *Hercule Poirot's Christmas*. I know it's only September, but I'm sure he'll enjoy it.'

As she followed Mavis over to the crime section, Mrs McDonald talked about her brother's illness, not stopping once for breath. 'The doc thinks his ticker is playing up. He gets out of breath doing the slightest thing...'

'Well, I'm sure this book will take his mind off his worries,' Mavis said, picking up the book and leading her back towards the desk so she could stamp the book and find out what else the posh bloke had said to Cordelia.

Two more readers came to have their books stamped before Mavis had a chance to hear more about the royal visit. Cordelia had gone to her office, but the door was open, a sure sign she was willing to be disturbed.

Mavis hurried over. 'Are they really coming?' she asked at Cordelia's door, keeping an eye on the desk.

Cordelia pushed her papers aside and came out of the office, locking it behind her.

'Come with me,' she said, her eyes sparkling with excitement.

They stood as far back behind the front desk as possible, trying not to be overheard.

'Is it true?' Mavis asked. 'What else did he say?'

Cordelia's smile was a mile wide as she nodded. 'Nothing else at this stage. But it looks like it's true.'

Mavis's jaw dropped open. 'Well, stone the crows! Royalty in our little library! Who'd 'ave thought it!'

Jane had gone to help Hetty find another book, something Mavis knew she usually loved doing but she could tell she was impatient to get back to the others. Mavis could hardly concentrate on her work as they waited for her to return. She put three books in the wrong place on the shelves and had to go back to correct her errors.

She had to wait fifteen long minutes. Then, as soon as Jane returned to the desk, she said, 'I've bin thinking. I've seen in the papers that the royals visit ordinary places, 'ospitals and schools and things.'

'That's right,' Cordelia said. 'Well, someone's told them of the work we've been doing here, and they know how badly the area has been bombed, so they want to come here! It'll be good for our morale and for the country too after it's in the newspapers.'

Jane looked around at the tired old building. They did their best to keep it looking appealing, but age and lack of investment meant it needed a lot of work to look good.

'I can see what you're thinking,' Cordelia said. 'There's heaps to do, but we've got several weeks.'

Jane giggled. 'Can you imagine old Bert's face when the king says hello? He'll be lost for words for once!'

'So will the king when he gets a whiff of him,' Mavis added, pulling a face. She pinched the bridge of her nose. Was that a headache starting?

'What's that?' old Mrs Totnes said, leaning over the desk. 'I 'eard what you said! I may be old but I'm not deaf.' She turned round to face the main room of the library and shouted, 'Hey, everyone, the king and queen are coming 'ere! Better smarten yourselves up!'

The three librarians looked at each other and groaned. Maybe it would have been better to keep this news secret for a little while. But before they had time to discuss that, Mrs Totnes turned back to them.

'We'll 'elp you get the place smartened up, girls. Folks in Silvertown look after each other. You've all 'elped us often enough!'

2

To their amazement, when the doors opened next morning there was a delegation waiting on the step. Mr Piggott from the hardware shop, Mrs Frinton from the dress shop, George Hubbard who did repairs for the library. But there was a bigger surprise. Bert, the man who always rushed in to read the newspapers each morning. For once, he didn't push past them, but waited with the others. And, was it just possible, he smelled a little fresher?

Jane could've sworn she saw a tear in Mr Piggott's eye, and Mrs Frinton had a spring in her step like nothing she'd ever seen before. George Hubbard, with his paint-splattered coat and bent nose and pencil behind his ear, seemed ready for action, whatever was needed.

'We've come to 'elp get ready for the royal visit!' he declared, licking his pencil and beginning to make notes in his little note-book as he looked around. 'Loads of others'll 'elp if you give 'em 'alf a chance!'

'And we've made a list of things we can do,' Mrs Frinton said. 'You'll be surprised the talents we have, and you'll find us East Enders will muck in and get this place spick and span quicker than a soldier snaps to attention.' She chuckled. 'Fit for a king, it'll be!'

The three librarians and Tom, their volunteer, gaped at the delegation, overwhelmed by their generosity and at a loss to know what to say.

'Come in, come in,' Cordelia said. 'Please don't keep standing there on the doorstep. We are so very grateful to see you.'

She had to swallow back a sob. These wonderful people, each with their own lives, their own losses and hardships, were going to give up their time to help the careworn building.

'But...' Cordelia said. 'Can you spare the time? You all have so much to do with the bombing and everything?'

They had all lived through the Blitz, fifty-seven nights and often days of relentless bombing leaving hundreds dead and countless homes flattened to brick dust.

Mr Hubbard looked at the others, who nodded their agreement for him to speak. 'Let us worry about that, Miss Cordelia. We'll come when we can and do what we can.'

They all crowded round the front desk ready for action, but Cordelia quickly realised they couldn't work while the library was open for business. As well as library users coming and going, it was one of the days for the IIP people, the missing persons bureau. Their task was to help people who were looking for loved ones missing after a bombing. Although library staff were not expected to help them directly, they did provide the room and prepare it for them.

All in all, the renovation team, as Cordelia was already thinking of it, needed somewhere more private to talk. She invited them into her office.

'Tom, would you mind holding the fort for a while, please?' She felt bad excluding him from the discussion but promised to brief him on everything that was decided.

With everyone in Cordelia's tiny office, it was bursting at the seams with eager faces. The space felt crowded with these kind volunteers, herself, Mavis and Jane. What had started as a casual comment about the upcoming royal tour had blossomed into an army of people rallying to help. She thought, as she had so many times before, that the people of Silvertown might not have much, but they had big hearts.

Mr Hubbard leaned against a filing cabinet, while Mr Piggott got his Players out of his pocket, tapped one from the packet and lit it. On the visitor's chair, Mrs Frinton sat upright, smoothing her skirt over her knees, and the rest stood or leaned against the walls.

Mavis pointed to the list hanging on the wall. A long, daunting list of things that needed to be done, which she'd worked on the previous evening. She sighed. 'We've got our work cut out, that's for sure. The place'll need a real good clean from top to bottom for starters...'

'And I've spotted several repairs too,' Mr Hubbard said. The gleam in his eyes suggested he was up for the challenge.

'We'll need a ton of materials, polish and wax for the floors. Goodness knows where we'll find all that,' Mrs Frinton spoke, practical as ever. She looked around and shook her head. 'But we'll have them gleaming somehow for their majesties. Can't let them think we live like slobs in the East End.'

Bert raised an eyebrow. 'I bet them royals think everything everywhere is spick and span. 'Cos you can bet your bottom dollar every place they visit does the same as us lot.' He took a toothpick out of his pocket and began digging it between his back teeth.

'The bookshelves need some work,' Mr Hubbard said. 'A coat of linseed oil and they'll be good as new.'

'We'll have to work out a schedule for storing books while the shelves are drying,' Jane said. She bit her thumbnail. 'We can't have too many books out of circulation at the same time.'

Soon the list on the wall got longer and longer.

Undaunted, Mavis spoke up. 'You lot are blooming marvellous. We couldn't be more pleased to 'ave you working with us.'

'You'll need a bucketload of floor polish,' Mrs Frinton said.

'And half a ton of linseed oil,' Mr Hubbard joined in.

Suddenly, the task seemed overwhelming to Cordelia, despite all the help.

'We've no resources to do all this. The library budget is so tight. Even if we had the money, I doubt we could find all the stuff when everything's in such short supply.'

Mr Hubbard stood more upright, looking as if he was about to salute. Taking a step forward, he said, 'I'm in the trade, Miss Carmichael. I've got a lot of contacts.' He touched the side of his nose with his forefinger. 'Let me see what I can do. Sure to be some half-used pots of stuff here and there.'

There was so much to consider. Disruption to the usual running of the library, volunteer time and scheduling. Too much for this unplanned meeting.

'Tell you what,' Mr Hubbard said to the crowd, 'I'm used to working out plans of action. Have to when you're doing building and repair work like me and my lads do. Why don't me and Miss Carmichael here work out a schedule, then you and any other volunteers can sign up to do whatever you can when you can.'

Mrs Frinton clapped her hands in agreement. 'That's wonderful, Mr Hubbard. I just know you'll do a wonderful job.' She looked at the library workers. 'And you all as well.'

'And I suppose we'll have to work around when you can get materials too,' Cordelia said.

'I used to be a decorator,' Bert suddenly exclaimed to everyone's surprise. As he spoke, he got out his tobacco tin and started making a roll-up. At no time did he look anyone in the eye. 'I'd still need time to read my papers, like, but I could 'elp after that. I 'ave to keep an eye on the time, though. Can't leave my old mum alone too long. She's gone a bit soft in the 'ead.'

In that short time, they'd learnt more about him than they had in all the time he'd been coming to the library. Mavis was so delighted at the change in him and his offer of help that she wanted to hug him, but remembered his lingering odour and changed her mind. Instead, she just said, 'That'd be terrific, Bert. Thanks so much.' As she spoke, she was silently wondering how to keep him working apart from other volunteers, then chastised herself for being ungenerous.

Cordelia having arranged to meet with Mr Hubbard later, the rest prepared to leave.

As Cordelia walked with them to the door, she couldn't believe her luck. It was wonderful to have all these people offering to help to spruce up the library for the royal visit. And it wasn't just for the royals. All the regulars would appreciate having somewhere smart to come when so much of the East End was still in a terrible state. There didn't seem to be a single road with all the buildings intact and even though the bombing was less frequent now, dust still drifted here and there like fine grains of sand shifting in the desert wind – hardly visible unless you stared at it directly.

'How did it go?' Tom asked when the volunteers had gone and Cordelia returned to the desk.

'Spiffing!' she said with a happy smile, shuffling her notes. 'We've got a load of volunteers. Mr Hubbard, he's a builder, thinks he can get us a lot of the materials we'll need.'

Tom looked sad. 'I don't think I'll be much use for the physical stuff because of my gammy leg, but I can make tea and do anything else to help. Just let me know.'

Mavis had come over to them as they spoke and said, 'Thank you, kind sir.' She attempted a curtsey but tripped over her own feet and almost fell over. 'Need a bit of practice at that!' she muttered, turning red.

'Shall I put up a notice for volunteers?' Tom asked. 'I could do it now. There's a lot to do so we need as many people as we can get.'

'That's a great idea, Tom,' Cordelia said, knowing he'd make an eye-catching poster. 'And we can all mention it to visitors. Even if they can't help, they may know others who can.'

By the end of that day, Cordelia was relieved to have a plan of action in place. Mr Hubbard had warned her he'd need a week to get materials for their task, but meanwhile, volunteers could do some deep cleaning. They worked out rotas for work to be done outside normal library hours, scheduled repairs and decorating, and planned how to let readers know where books had been moved to temporarily. Volunteers would work weekends and evenings throughout, moving boxes of books to temporary homes until the newly smartened shelves were dry, as well as completing several tasks Cordelia would never have thought of. Having an experienced builder with his expert knowledge was an absolute godsend.

Yet again, she reflected on the wonderful nature of the East End people around her.

But could they do it in time or would the library not be ready for the royal visit?

3

The days were growing shorter, but London still clung to the last warm breaths of summer on this calm September evening. Mavis said goodbye to Cordelia and Jane and stepped out of the familiar embrace of the library. She planned to stop off at the butcher's shop. If she was lucky, he'd have some liver and she knew she had a couple of spuds and an onion in her kitchen. It wouldn't take long to make herself a meal.

As she strode out, her worn leather shoes tapped lightly on the pavement. She remembered a tip she'd read in a leaflet in the library that you could repair worn shoe soles with part of an old hot-water bottle. Hers had started leaking; it'd be good to find something useful to do with it.

Around her, the city and the river bustled with their unique symphony of sounds – ships' horns, bicycle bells, rumbling bus motors. The smell of roasting chestnuts, even though it mingled with the smells from the Thames, made her mouth water. But she walked on, rarely having money for treats like that. Clutching her cardie tighter around herself, she looked up at the steel-grey sky beginning to be streaked with pink as the sun lowered.

'Red sky at night, shepherd's delight,' she murmured, knowing she could look forward to the next day being fine as well. Flocks of starlings raced overhead. Around her shoes, leaves that were just starting to change colour danced along the pavement, fluttering between ration posters plastered on shop windows.

As she turned into a street that had been bombed during the Blitz, her thoughts turned to her soldier boyfriend Joe. He was as good as his word, writing frequently and with each letter her feelings for him grew stronger. Sometimes she chided herself for feeling like a lovesick youngster.

Up ahead, four boys were playing in the crater that had been caused by a bomb, skidding on the backside of their well-worn short trousers. She was just about to tell them that their mums would have to pay to replace them when one stood up. The hole in his short trousers was big enough to show off his skinny backside. Undisturbed, he loosened his belt, dropped down his shorts, exposing all, then yanked his shirt, which must surely have once belonged to his father, and pulled it down to cover his modesty.

'Got yer pin ready?' a smaller boy shouted, laughing at his friend.

Pin? Mavis wondered why he would need one but soon found out. The lad pulled the front of his shirt down, reached between his legs and joined the front and back together with a safety pin. Like most lads, he didn't have underpants on, so he'd just improvised a pair.

The whole time his mates cackled and laughed at him. 'Don't catch your goolies!' and 'Seen bigger ones on a flea!'

'It's bloody bigger than yours!' he shouted back to one of them, but he was laughing as he said it.

Mavis thought she should tell them off for ruining their shorts, but kids were having such a hard time in the war, they needed to get fun wherever they could. She hadn't the heart to say anything.

Two more streets and then she was at Fred Finch's butcher's on Seagull Lane. There was the inevitable queue outside, women hoping against hope to find something to fill their families' bellies after a hard day's work. One was singing softly 'Whale meat again' to the tune of the familiar Vera Lynn song.

'My old man won't touch that stuff,' another said. 'But I say you can't be picky when there's a war on!'

Mavis recognised some women in the queue. Mrs Essex with her red and black knitted hat she wore in all weathers, and Mrs Green, who was always ready with a smile. But her heart sank a little at the sight of Mrs Jenkins, who was one of the women who attended the sewing circle at the library. She believed she was the only person who knew everything there was to know on any subject.

The butcher's shop had dim lighting, sawdust on the floor and metal hanging hooks that before the war would have been full, but now were sadly almost empty. Across the road, girls were skipping to a familiar song. 'Salt, mustard, vinegar, pepper. Tell me the name of your sweetheart. Is it A, B, C...?' they sang and proceeded to list all the letters of the alphabet. As they skipped, their actions grew more complicated with folded arms, and double jumps, but they never went wrong.

In the butcher's, the women waited patiently, clutching their ration books, baskets over their arms, purses tight in their grasps. The conversation was the usual moans about rationing, the war and worries about loved ones away fighting. Getting bored with it, Mavis decided to change the subject.

'Did I ever tell you about the bloke what used to come into the library and get books on opera?' she asked the others.

'How interesting.' Mrs Jenkins spoke first. 'I've been to the opera many times. What was his favourite?'

Mavis ignored her, continuing to tell her story. 'Well, this man, Mr Wiggins 'is name was—'

'From the Wiggins family in Canning Town? I know a thing or two about them.' It was Mrs Jenkins again. 'The stories would make your hair curl.'

If Mrs Jenkins hadn't been a regular at the library, Mavis might have given her short shrift, but instead she took a deep breath and carried on.

'This was years ago, when I first worked at the library. Well, 'e'd borrowed all our books on opera and we got 'im some from other libraries too. Then one day as I was stamping 'is book, you'll never guess what 'appened!'

'If he's the Wiggins I'm thinking of, he dropped down dead. Only forty-five he was!'

Mavis's patience had worn out. 'Please let me finish and for once in your life you are completely wrong!'

Mrs Jenkins's eyes widened at the rebuke, and she spluttered, 'But...'

'So, I was stamping this book. On *La Boheme* it was—'

'I know that one. It's about a seamstress, Mimi—'

Somehow Mavis lost her footing and stumbled into Mrs Jenkins, knocking her against the wall.

'Ouch!' the woman cried. 'You did that on purpose!'

'Oh, so sorry,' Mavis said without a pause. 'Now where was I? Yes, this lovely Mr Wiggins 'eld the book and burst into song. My boss said it was called "O Soave Fancuilla". It was so beautiful, it took my breath away. Everyone in the library stopped what they were doing and gave 'im a big round of applause. 'E bowed as if 'e was in Covent Garden and left without another word!'

The familiar tones of the air-raid siren interrupted her story, making them all groan.

For a second or two, every woman stopped breathing then looked towards the sky, hoping the German planes weren't too close.

Mavis felt her heart lurch into her throat at the familiar sound, clutching her ration book tightly as she tried to work out where the nearest shelter was.

The queue suddenly erupted into a frenzy of activity, women grabbing baskets and children, shouting to the skipping girls outside to 'come here this minute or else'.

Deciding the reception centre in St Mark's church was the nearest safe place, Mavis began to run towards it. She arrived, wishing she was fitter, at the same time as Mrs Essex and was glad to see that Mrs Jenkins seemed to have gone elsewhere.

Inside, the church was packed. The towering stained-glass windows of the ancient stone building were darkened, covered over with wood for the duration. The oak pews, polished by decades of backsides sitting on them, had been pushed against the walls to make room for rows of mattresses and two baby cots. Candles and several Tilly lamps threw eerie shadows, barely lighting the cavernous space.

People moved around, clutching what they'd brought with them. For Mavis and Mrs Essex, this was only their handbags and baskets, but some others had blankets and what looked like picnics. A low din encircled the vaulted ceiling, punctuated by the occasional sob and cries of hungry or scared infants. The musty smell of old hymnals mingled with perspiration and the smell of fear. An elderly vicar and three WVS women moved between people, offering words of comfort and pointing over to where a table was set up for tea and bread and butter.

Outside, distant booms like rumbling thunder grew closer and closer, and the building itself shook as bombs detonated nearby.

Mavis and Mrs Essex sat together at the end of a pew, squashed but reasonably comfortable.

A boy next to them, a real chatterbox it seemed, soon turned to them. 'Me and my mates worked out 'ow to capture a German,' he said, looking proud.

'Gosh,' Mavis said, trying to keep a straight face. ''Ow will you do that?'

'Well, there's six of us in my gang. Me, John, Andy, Bill, Dave and Maureen.'

Mrs Essex could hardly keep from grinning. 'So you've got a girl in your gang. Will she help you?'

The boy looked around as if not wanting any other adults to overhear. As he did so, his pudding basin haircut swung from side to side. 'See, what we're going to do is...' He held his hands to his lips. 'You mustn't tell anyone. Promise?'

They solemnly promised.

'See, when we see a German, Maureen is going to flash 'er knickers, then—'

'How will that help?' Mrs Essex asked.

'The German'll be so surprised us boys'll jump on 'im – one on each leg and arm – and then Dave will stab 'im in the neck with 'is penknife.'

He sat back, pleased with himself, arms folded.

The two women didn't dare look at each other. 'So it's all planned then?' Mavis asked.

But the boy's earlier cockiness became surprisingly deflated. 'It might not work.'

'Why not?' the women asked in unison.

'That Maureen only wants to stab 'im 'erself, don't she!'

Glad that a WVS volunteer saved them from the struggle of keeping a straight face, Mavis and Mrs Essex made their way over to the refreshments table.

'It's hard to know whether to praise that lad or tell him off, isn't it?' Mrs Essex said.

But she'd no sooner stirred her tea than the all-clear sounded.

'That's a short one,' Mavis said. 'Let's hope not too many people caught it this time.'

But the evening wasn't finished with Mavis yet.

4

The butcher's was closed when Mavis came out of the church. She sighed. She'd really fancied liver and onions, she even fancied she could smell them as she walked. But she continued on her way in a philosophical mood – if the butcher's wasn't closed at the end of the day, it was often closed because it had run out of meat.

She debated whether to have bread and dripping but couldn't face it. It tasted wonderful, all that strong beef flavour, but it took ages to get the slimy grease taste out of her mouth.

Fish and chips it was. Thank goodness they weren't rationed.

May's fish bar on Woolwich Manor Road was her favourite, a bit out of her way but worth it. She stepped inside and May greeted her like a long-lost friend, even though she didn't go there often. May's hair was tied up with a thick cotton scarf and her overall, once white, was thick cotton too. She always wore scarlet lipstick, even though her face was usually slick with steam from the fryers.

The delicious smell of fried fish and potatoes permeated the interior of the cramped shop. Faded wallpaper showed pictures of a variety of fish no one in the East End had ever seen, but most customers realised they were probably eating some unfamiliar fish even if it was called cod or haddock.

Her stomach rumbling, Mavis watched as May deftly dipped battered fish fillets and thick chunks of potato into the bubbling oil. It spluttered and hissed as if fighting back. May's husband, who everyone just called Mr May, wrapped the orders and took the money.

A bottle of malt vinegar and a cracked glass jar of salt sat at the end of the counter. Mr May always offered to sprinkle both on the fish and chips before wrapping them in newspaper, but Mavis was one of the people who preferred to do her own. She loved the pungent acidic smell of the vinegar and sprinkled on a generous helping.

She tucked her meal under her arm to keep it warm and left the shop. Outside a stray cat looked hopeful, but its luck was out. Mavis was too hungry to share her tea.

When she walked in the front door of her house, she kicked off her shoes then rubbed her aching feet, wiggling her toes before she put on her old slippers. The room was chilly, and she kept her coat on as she lit the fire. She picked up some kindling she'd bought from some lads who came round every now and then and put it in the hearth with some screwed-up newspaper, then carefully arranged the coke the boys had 'found' somewhere – she asked no questions – and lumps of coal on top. Cursing her creaking knees, she held up a sheet of newspaper in front of the fire until it caught.

She picked up a couple of things from the doormat and put them on the kitchen table, then got out her plate, knife and fork and bottle of stout before sitting down at her old pine table. It showed the wear of years of meals and crafts she had done with her son Ken when he was a lad. She loved to sometimes trace the scars, as she thought of them, and remember years gone by.

The radio played softly in the background, and as she

unwrapped her fish and chips, putting them on a plate complete with newspaper, she could feel the stress of the day beginning to ease off.

Not paying much attention, she picked up the first paper from the doormat and groaned. It was yet another recipe from the government, this time for Mock Chicken Stew. She read it through.

One pound mixed diced vegetables, 4 ounces lentils, 1 bouillon cube, thyme, salt and pepper. Simmer lentils and vegetables in broth flavoured with the bouillon cube and seasonings until tender.

Mavis grunted. Mock chicken indeed. These blokes what wrote these recipes had a lot of imagination, she decided. She tore the paper into pieces and put it aside to use for the fire.

But when she looked at the envelope that had been beneath it, her fork stopped halfway to her mouth. It looked official, but not a bill.

It could only be one thing. A letter from the children's home where little Joyce lived. Joyce, the girl she hoped to adopt one day. The girl she had rescued from a bomb site where the girl's mother had died.

Her fork fell to the plate with a clatter and her hands shook as she picked up the envelope, turning it over as if she could see through it. She wiped her knife on a tea towel and used it to open the envelope.

Dear Mrs Kent,

I am writing to inform you that Joyce will be able to visit you on the weekend of 10th of next month. She often talks about your visits and is looking forward to seeing you again.

Joyce continues to thrive here at the home. She enjoys draw-

ing, helping in the dining room and looking after the younger children.

Please come to collect Joyce before midday on the Saturday. She can stay until Sunday – please bring her back before seven o'clock. We appreciate you providing her with meals and opening your doors despite rationing and the difficult circumstances people in the East End of London face. It means the world to children like Joyce who have no family that there is someone interested in their welfare. If all goes well, when you bring her back, we can discuss the next visit.

Please let me know if you have any questions. Thank you again for opening your heart and home to Joyce.

Kind regards

J. Anderson (Mrs)

Her heart pounding, Mavis read the letter twice more. It had been so long since she'd first found Joyce, lost and searching for her mother amongst the debris of what had once been her home. When she'd realised the girl had no one, Mavis's heart had gone out to her. Hugging her tight, she had tried to reassure her, but her words had felt hollow knowing the girl was probably now an orphan. She'd walked her to the nearest reception centre, carefully avoiding small fires still burning from the incendiary bombs and debris that littered the roads. Stopping to buy sweets and a comic on the way had cheered Joyce up but Mavis knew that happy feeling couldn't last. Horribly soon she would realise all she had lost.

Mavis had left Joyce in the capable hands of WVS staff, but she couldn't get the little girl out of her mind. It had taken ages to find where Joyce had been moved to, and since then, Mavis had been to the home to visit her several times. Joyce was shy at first, not remembering the way Mavis had cared for her on that dreadful day.

Gradually, though, she began to relax in her company, chatting away about her friends and life in the rambling old building.

Mavis's son Ken was a soldier stationed in Scotland. She'd have to tell him about Joyce. He'd been difficult for several years but since he'd started going out with a lass he'd met in Scotland he was transformed. Now he was the son she'd always hoped for. So far, anyway. She'd wanted a daughter too, but that had never happened. She sent up a prayer that she could become Joyce's mother.

Mavis traced the writing on the letter, her fingers lingering there as her mind flooded with possibilities. She imagined them walking hand in hand to the swings, reading her bedtime stories, helping her to read and write and saying bedtime prayers together.

Mavis held the letter over her heart and whispered to the empty room. 'I'll keep you safe and you'll always be loved.'

5

It was the first day of the decorating, Saturday afternoon. The library closed at one o'clock. Cordelia had asked the staff of Jim's Café to deliver some sandwiches for her, Mavis and Jane to eat as they got ready for the volunteers. She'd already found some photos of Silvertown in years gone by and scoured the markets for cheap frames for them. They'd go on the wall behind the main desk. Timothy, the tailor, had surprised her by offering to make some fabric roses. He'd brought one in to show her, and she was amazed at its beauty. He was going to make seven. Cordelia had found a dust-covered vase in the basement they could go in when it was cleaned up.

As she wound her way through the shelves, she waited for the renovation volunteers to arrive. She loved this time, peaceful after the busyness of the day. The tired building was a bridge with the past, housing books that went back generations. But it was also a hope for the future. Because of the fire in Paternoster Square that destroyed five million books, they hadn't been able to buy many new ones for months. Not that there was money for any anyway, but this event, the king and queen visiting, and the volunteers smartening up the library, made it a place for the future like never before.

She tried to imagine what it would be like when they'd finished. In her mind's eye, she could see the library transformed – not simply through a fresh coat of paint, but through the love and devotion of the volunteers. The tired, scratched shelves and tables would shine again, the corners the cleaner never had time to deal with would be dust-free, the windows would gleam, despite the bomb tape reducing the light through them, and the floor would still be scratched but would shine like new.

Cordelia's thoughts were interrupted by Jane and Mavis, who had been in the basement looking for old curtains to protect the floor and shelves from damage.

'Blimey, these curtains are 'eavy!' Mavis grunted and cursed, lugging a bag of fabric through to the main desk. 'Never thought we'd get them up them stairs. They're gonna make us all sneeze, too. Years of dust on 'em, I reckon.'

'Never mind. We'll shake them out the back before people arrive,' Jane said, always the more optimistic of the two.

Cordelia reached behind the desk and got the list of tasks they'd written. 'Let's go through these lists while we eat our sandwiches.'

'We've made a start this morning, moving all the non-fiction A to E into the back room.' Jane took a bite of her sandwich and swallowed before she spoke again. 'I hope the king and queen won't want to go in the basement.'

'I think we'll assume that they could go anywhere,' Cordelia replied. 'But I'll lock the basement door. I've been advised they are not likely to use the WC.'

'Bums too posh for our library lavvy!' Mavis said with a giggle. 'Bet their shit smells of roses too!'

Loud knocks at the door told them that the first of the volunteers had arrived. Mr Hubbard wore paint-splattered overalls and a cloth cap, also covered in paint. He was pulling a small cart loaded with short ladders, tins of linseed oil, some bowls, cloths, and overalls.

'All ready and correct, ma'am,' he said to Cordelia as he pulled it inside, giving her a mock salute. As he spoke, three other volunteers arrived. The retired tailor, Doreen, a younger talkative member of the library quilting group, and Jamie, a lad who was just too young to be called up. He had a terrible crop of spots on his face and kept trying to hide them by looking anywhere but at the person he was speaking to.

'Thought I'd come,' he said, looking at the floor. 'Been coming here since I was a nipper. Love this place.' As he spoke, he pushed his glasses back up his nose.

'We're right glad you're 'ere,' Mavis said. 'We need some young blood to work with us oldies.' She went over to him and squeezed his upper arm. 'Yep, as I thought, you've got some muscles there.'

He looked as if he hoped the ground would open up and swallow him.

Mr Hubbard clapped his hands. 'Right, you lot. Miss Carmichael and her colleagues here have asked me to organise work today. I'm a builder so it's business as usual for me. Just do as I say and you won't go far wrong.'

'But,' said Doreen, 'what if we don't agree with what you say?' She smiled as she spoke to him, but the smile didn't reach her eyes.

Mr Hubbard looked at her as if she was a silly woman who knew nothing.

'Well, Miss, or is it Mrs, if I may say so, I'm sure you've got lots of good ideas, like most women. Let me know if I'm getting it wrong, and we can discuss it woman to man, like.'

Doreen's eyes opened wide. 'I've learned a lot of new words since I started coming 'ere. One of them is "condescending". 'Ave you 'eard of it?'

But Mr Hubbard wasn't listening.

Two more volunteers arrived just before a full-scale row between the two could get started.

'Oh, look,' Cordelia said, desperate to change the subject. 'Here's Miss Unwin and Mrs Green.' She walked over to them. 'We're very pleased you're here. Mr Hubbard was just saying he's going to be in charge. We've agreed that with him and he's got a list of tasks that need doing.' She thought about Doreen and hoped she wasn't going to ruin the atmosphere. 'But do tell Mr Hubbard if you have any suggestions.'

Miss Unwin simply nodded and made her way to speak to the tailor. Mrs Green put down the bag she was carrying and rubbed her back with a groan. 'I'm not up to much what with me bad back and everything. But I can make tea and dust shelves.' She looked at Mr Hubbard's trolley. 'I'm not climbing no ladders, though.'

'That's fine, Mrs Green,' Cordelia said. 'Mr Hubbard and I have agreed that he will explain the tasks to be done and you can let him know what you'd prefer to do.'

As she spoke, Cordelia kept an eye on Doreen, whose bosom heaved as she listened, eyes darting everywhere.

'Okay,' Doreen finally said, reluctantly. 'As long as you don't try to boss me about. I don't take orders from no man. Get enough of that at 'ome, thank you very much.'

Mavis, who knew everything about everyone in Silvertown, had briefed Cordelia on all the people who were likely to volunteer.

'Doreen 'as a bugger for an 'ubby,' she'd said. 'Excuse my swearing. Knocks 'er black and blue.' She shook her head. 'She's got an 'eart of gold but it's 'ard to find sometimes.'

But now, Cordelia realised she needed to make Doreen feel valued. 'Actually, Doreen, I was going to ask you if you'd undertake a special task for me.'

Doreen turned to her, and Cordelia could see she liked the idea of being important.

'I wonder if you can work on the children's section. I'm sure the king and queen will want to see that. You'll work with Jane. That's her baby, so to speak. Would you be happy with that?'

For a moment, Doreen looked as if she might argue, but Jane stepped in.

'I'd be really glad of the help,' she said, touching Doreen's arm. 'It's so important for the little ones. And their books are much more varied in size than the others.'

Doreen took a few seconds to reply, but finally nodded her agreement.

'Mrs Green, would you mind getting started on that tea now, while everyone decides what to do, and gets started?'

Mrs Green nodded. 'Of course I will. And I made some biscuits, too.'

The volunteers all took off their coats and put them in the office where they would stay clean. The women wound scarves around their heads and aprons over their clothes while the men wore overalls.

'I'm making the tea like you said,' Mrs Green shouted. 'And one thing you lot don't know about me is I read tea leaves. So, if you want to know your fortune, come to see me when you've finished your tea.'

Cordelia was astounded. She wasn't sure she believed in reading tea leaves. In any case, the future was uncertain for all of them. There was still the occasional bombing, the Nazis might invade, and there were still plenty of diseases to slay people. But Mrs Green's suggestion seemed harmless enough.

'Right,' Mr Hubbard shouted. 'Here's what we need to do.' He made a great play of opening his list, shaking it out as if it was the Magna Carta instead of the back of an old piece of wallpaper.

'We need to start at the top!' Doreen said loudly.

'That's right,' timid Miss Unwin said. 'My mother always told me that.'

Mr Hubbard looked around, trying to calm himself. He squared his broad shoulders as if bracing himself for a blow. Then he held up his calloused hand in a gesture of patience. 'Now, now, let's not get in a tizzy, everyone.' He paused and looked around, looking longer at Doreen than anyone else. 'I totally agree with starting at the top, especially when we're cleaning. So I suggest those that are brave enough on ladders, go up and dust the high shelves. No need to take off the books. They're the ones not used much. We've got to cut some corners.'

'But what if the king wants to look at one of those books?' Miss Unwin asked.

'Then one of us will get it for him and dust it as we take it down,' Jane said. 'I really think we should make a start.'

Ladders wobbled precariously as Jamie and Mr Russell worked on cleaning the high shelves and lightshades. Miss Unwin insisted on holding Mr Russell's ladder.

Doreen and Jane began removing books from the children's section, and Tom and Bert worked in that area too, moving the reading tables and rubbing hard against the wood with newspaper, removing an amazing amount of grime from years of use.

'These tables can tell some stories,' Jane said, not expecting a reply, as usual.

But Bert was like a changed man. 'These 'ere tables 'ave told me what's going on with the world for years,' he replied.

Mrs Green came towards them with a bucket of diluted white vinegar. 'Here you are. This'll help. Now, did you save your teacups? Want your fortune told?'

'Daft old biddy,' Bert muttered.

Cordelia hoped Mrs Green hadn't heard him.

'I'm afraid we're too busy at the moment, Mrs Green,' she said.

Mavis turned on the radio and soon they were singing along as they worked. 'I'll Be Seeing You', 'A Nightingale Sang in Berkeley Square', then they started on the old favourites – 'Pack Up Your Troubles in Your Old Kit Bag', 'Puttin' on the Ritz', and 'Pennies from Heaven'.

To everyone's surprise, Mrs Green stood in front of the desk when 'Puttin' on the Ritz' was on and began tap-dancing. Slow and hesitant at first, she was soon keeping up with the rhythm and everyone stopped to watch her, clapping the beat. There was a wild round of applause when she'd finished, and she took a deep bow.

'I was in a dance group when I was a pretty young thing,' she said with a knowing smile. 'The things we got up to!' Then she put her hands on her back as she usually did, and her mouth opened in surprise. 'Well, blow me, me back feels better. I'll 'ave to do the dancing every day!'

But Mrs Green wasn't done yet. She grabbed a broom and began swaying and stepping in time to 'It's De-lovely', using the broom as a dance partner. She twirled around with surprising dexterity to everyone's delight. But in her enthusiasm, she didn't notice the large dust pile nearby until her broom whisked straight through it, sending a cloud of dust and lint at Bert. He was immediately covered like a dirty snowman and he sneezed so loudly he could have competed with the factory whistles.

Mavis held her breath, expecting him to explode, but to her surprise he just dusted himself off and muttered, 'Stupid damn woman!'

When Mrs Green walked back to her chair, Cordelia caught her eye and gave a little wink. She couldn't help feeling a sense of warmth from these wonderful people. Even Doreen had stopped being irritable, laughing and joking with the other volunteers.

When it was beginning to get dark, Cordelia decided it was time to start packing up. Those who could spare the time would be back next day. If she was lucky, some others would appear too.

As some cleared up, a couple of people including Miss Unwin were asking Mrs Green to read their tea leaves. Cordelia overheard a few words she said, something about romance being in the air. But she was busy helping with the tidying and giving hugs and thanks to all the volunteers to hear much else.

Finally, when even Mrs Green had gone, the three librarians walked around to inspect the work done.

Dust had been banished from every corner. Cobwebs that had hung from the high lampshades had disappeared. The treated shelves shone like new. The table Tom and Bert had worked on was completely transformed – the scratches still told its history, but it was smooth and shiny.

Mavis couldn't resist running her fingers across it.

'They can come round to my place any time,' she said. 'They've performed miracles. We're going to be ready for them royals in good time.'

6

Mavis looked around what she now thought of as the sewing room at the back of the library. Like the rest of the building and indeed the whole East End, it had seen better days. She was used to its shabby appearance but now looked at it with a critical eye. There was no way of knowing if the king and queen would want to see any of these smaller rooms, but they had to be smartened up just in case. She took a little notepad and pencil out of her pocket and made a few notes of things to add to the task list.

The room was ready for the weekly sewing group, chairs in place and the table wiped clean. She went to a cupboard and lugged out a bag of fabric scraps. They were heavy and she was impressed by how much local people had donated.

She heard the bustling clatter of the women arriving. She grinned, picturing their delight when they saw the fabric.

Right on time, they entered in a flurry of chatter and greetings. Such strong women. Women who had faced the fury of the Nazis and could still find something to laugh about. Mavis smiled affectionately at each familiar face. There was Ellen with her dodgy hip, limping along with a stick. Her daughter had died ten years earlier of polio. Outspoken Doreen, with the big gap between her two front teeth and who always had plenty to say, but sometimes looked like she was hiding a secret. Miss Unwin, who never told anyone her Christian name, whose fiancé died in the First World War and had become one of the 'surplus women', never marrying. And Mr Russell, who was only sixty-something, but had worked in men's tailoring all his life. His shop had been bombed and he had time on his hands. He was always well turned out, complete with a bow tie; today's was royal blue with tiny white dots.

'You'll be in your element with all us gorgeous ladies!' Doreen teased him.

Mavis had noticed he and Miss Unwin chose to sit together and soon saw little glances between them. Was it finally time for Miss Unwin to become a Mrs?

You're never too old for love, she thought.

'Right, ladies,' Mavis said to the quilting group, who had recon-vened in preparation of the visit of the king and queen. 'I've already had a chat with some of you. As you know, we could do with some bunting to cheer up the place when our royal visitors come.'

Maggie, who must have been at least ninety and was blind in one eye, spoke up. 'It'll 'ave to be red, white and blue. Think we can find enough fabric?'

Like a conjurer performing a favourite trick, Mavis reached for the large sack next to her and upended it. Fabric of all colours and patterns spilled onto the table like an upturned treasure chest, revealing a bounty of creative possibilities. Purple, pink, white, blue, yellow, red, velvet, brocade, wool, cotton, silk and ribbons covered the wooden table. The smells reminded Mavis of her grandmother's attic – mothballs and mustiness.

'I think you all know that the king and queen will be visiting the library soon—'

'When's that then? Can I talk to 'em?' Doreen interrupted.

Mavis held up her hand to let Doreen know to wait and hear her out. 'We don't know when they'll come but it will be at least six weeks away.'

Mrs Jenkins, who'd find fault with the way spiders make their webs, piped up. 'Six weeks! Six weeks! You gotta be bloody kidding. If we only meet once a week, we'll never get it done!'

There was a murmur of dismay amongst the rest of the group. 'Yes, Mrs Kent, how can we achieve such an ambitious target?' Miss Unwin always spoke like a toff, not someone who'd grown up in the East End like the rest of them.

Clapping her hands, Mavis called for silence. 'If necessary, we can have extra sessions, or perhaps have some smaller groups at other times to fit in with what you can manage.'

Miss Unwin looked around. 'Just decorate this room, or the whole building?'

'Certainly the main lending room, and the small rooms if we 'ave time.'

Ellen began picking up the pieces of fabric and inspecting them. 'We'll 'ave to wash that lot before the nobs come in,' she said. 'I'll do it if you like. Just the red, white and blue, of course.'

'You're right, Ellen. We'll have to reject any that ain't the right colours,' Mavis said. 'But that'll only take a mo.' She reached into another bag and produced a bundle of pieces of newspaper cut to identical triangles. 'We can use these for templates.'

'I'm not at all sure they're the right size,' Mrs Jenkins said. 'You should have asked my advice. They need to be at least twice that size.'

Mavis felt her body tighten and gritted her teeth. 'Thank you for your advice, Mrs Jenkins,' she said, hoping she didn't sound as sarcastic as she felt. 'But this is the size we have chosen.'

'But my expertise—' Mrs Jenkins began.

'Oh, for Christ's sake, pipe down, will ya!' Doreen said. 'We'll never get started otherwise.'

Mrs Jenkins huffed loudly, her cheeks going red. She sat back in her chair and folded her arms, glaring at everyone.

No one took any notice of her.

The ladies began to examine the fabric, oohing and aahhing at the nice pieces and rejecting any that were the wrong colour, too small or just plain ugly. They were so excited about the task they talked over each other as they planned how to do the work.

'I 'ope you remembered to bring your own scissors, ladies,' Mavis said. 'We ain't got enough in the library.'

Like soldiers producing their rifles, the ladies all held up their scissors for inspection and then laughed at themselves.

'What are we like!' Maggie said with a laugh, reaching for her magnifying glass. 'Let's show them high-ups us East Enders can make something really top notch!'

Soon they were discussing how many triangles they'd need, what stitches they'd use, and how they would join them together.

'The triangles need to have space between them because—' Mrs Jenkins started.

'Ssshh!' quiet Miss Unwin said, surprising everyone. Back came Mrs Jenkins's folded arms, her chin high and teeth gritted. 'We need to select the fabric and begin cutting.'

Mavis waited until they'd begun working and then left them to it. She occasionally returned and could overhear their conversations:

'Did you hear the Thompsons are taking in some refugees?'

'And my neighbour's got her son and daughter-in-law moved in 'cos they've been bombed. I'd better get some cotton wool for me ears, 'cos there's going to be a truckload of rows with them lot!'

'My Mary's getting married next time her bloke has some leave.

Marry in haste and repent at leisure I always say. They 'ardly know each other!'

One time Mavis went back to find them all collapsed in fits of giggles.

'Okay, share the joke!' she demanded with a smile.

'It's Enid,' Maggie said. 'She said her thread was thicker than her Ernie's you-know-what on bath night.'

'And Maggie only got out her magnifying glass to look at it!' Enid piped up. 'Guess what she said! "It looks like Ernie's willie hair!" As if she'd know!'

'I don't, honest, I don't!' Maggie said, turning red and busying herself threading her needle.

Mavis couldn't resist stitching her own red cotton triangle, eavesdropping on the ladies' lively conversations. Their chatter wandered from rationing woes to family spats to juicy neighbourhood gossip, their voices weaving together to paint a vibrant tapestry of everyday life in Silvertown.

Though she'd never admit it, Mavis felt a swell of pride as she looked around at this mixed bag of women who shared one thing in common. They'd braved the Blitz and were still ready to help others. They embodied the wartime spirit they often read about in the newspapers. The latest one she'd seen in the *Daily Mirror* showed people smiling in the underground shelter. It didn't mention the smells or the mosquitoes, though.

There was less bombing, but it was still ongoing. Would the library still be standing when the royal visitors were due?

7

Jane had longed for the day London felt safe enough to get her daughter back from the farm where she'd been evacuated. It had been a relief to know that she was far away from the Blitz, and yet Jane missed her every day – yearned for her sweet smile, her cheekiness, even her reluctance to eat greens. She particularly missed the special time when she read her a bedtime story and they cuddled up close. Sometimes she even hugged one of Helen's jumpers when she was in bed, telling herself it still smelled of her daughter.

When the Blitz seemed to be over and Hitler had turned his attention to Russia, she decided it was safe to bring Helen home. Everyone expected there would be occasional bombing, but nothing like the relentless day-to-day onslaught they had all had to live through for so long.

So she had been elated as she sat on the train towards the village where Helen was living. She'd brought books as presents for each of the farming family members, carefully chosen for their interests. For Mrs Blackburn, *Lovers Meeting*, a supernatural romance by Eleanor Smith. For Mr Blackburn, *The Story of a Norfolk*

Farm by Henry Williamson. And for the two boys, *Swallows and Amazons* by Arthur Ransome and *The Adventures of Tom Sawyer* by Mark Twain. She had a feeling the boys weren't big readers, they were such outdoor types, but she hoped those books would be exciting enough to keep their interest. She'd also got a couple of comics for them, thinking they were probably more to their liking.

But she'd spent the most time picking a book for her little girl. In the end she'd chosen *The House at Pooh Corner* by A. A. Milne. The books were wrapped individually in brown paper and tied with string. Jane knew not everyone was in love with books as she was, but had no other ideas for what to buy everyone. And she was so grateful for the wonderful care they'd given her daughter.

Little did she know that persuading Helen to come home with her would be truly awful.

Helen had been pleased to see her, showing her around the farm again. So Jane had no indication of what was to come.

'Time to get your coat on now,' she said, looking at the clock. 'Your case is all packed and we've got a train to catch.'

But Helen was having none of it. She had a paddy and lay on the floor yelling like a two-year-old. 'I'm not going! I'm not going!'

'Oh dear,' Mrs Blackburn said. 'I have been telling her she's going home. We've talked about it every day since you wrote to me.'

It almost shattered Jane's heart that Helen didn't seem to want to go home with her. Helen kept crying and kicking her heels.

'I'm staying with my friends, Mr Piggy and Miss Horsey!' she kept repeating. Jane pulled her off the floor, reminding her that the train wouldn't wait. 'You can't make me!' Helen screamed and kicked Jane's leg so hard it bruised. 'I don't want you for my mummy any more! I like it here.'

In the end, it was Mrs Blackburn who soothed her. She took her on her knee.

'You remember we've talked about this. We all love you, but we're not your family. Your family is your mummy who loves you and your daddy who is fighting to keep us all safe.'

'But Tabby...' Helen cried, reaching for the tabby cat, who was sleeping on a nearby chair.

'Tabby will be fine, and I bet there will be a cat living near where you're going.' She looked at Jane as she spoke.

'There is,' Jane said. 'A black cat called Snowy.'

Helen stopped snivelling and a frown appeared on her smooth forehead. 'A black cat called Snowy? That's silly.'

Jane bent down to her level. 'You're right. It's silly, but he loves coming into our home and I know he'll be very happy for you to stroke him.'

It took an hour for Helen to calm down enough to let Jane gather her things ready to leave.

'Come on, Helen,' Patsy the land girl said, holding her hand out to the girl. 'Time for a ride on the horse and cart again. It'll be exciting for you going on the train all the way to London.'

Daisy, the old mare, whinnied softly, her breath coming out in puffs of steam. Patsy stroked her neck affectionately before turning to Helen and Jane.

'Up you hop!' she said cheerily, lifting little Helen up onto the hard bench. Jane clambered up beside her daughter, wrapping her arm around the girl's shoulders. She was dismayed when Helen wriggled her arm away. Her daughter was uncharacteristically quiet, looking down and fidgeting with the hem of her dress.

With a flick of the reins, they were off, trotting down the winding dirt lane, past fields dotted with sheep and cows grazing lazily.

Helen perked up seeing her beloved farm animals. 'Bye bye, Buttercup!' she called out, waving to the brown and white cow.

Jane squeezed her hand tight, wishing this parting were easier for her daughter.

As the cart bumped over ruts in the road, Patsy pointed out landmarks they passed. 'This is where our farm ends. See there? That fence? The bloke who owns the next farm is a right miserable so-and-so.'

They continued on, the autumn sun warming their faces. The sights they saw were quintessential English country scenes, with crops ripening and birds singing in the trees. A light breeze carried the faint scent of hay and manure. Helen begged for Daisy to go faster, she loved the sensation of jogging up and down on the wooden seat and feeling the wind in her hair. Patsy happily obliged. As the mare picked up speed and the cart bumped along, jiggling them on their bench seat, Helen squealed with delight, the wind tousling her hair every which way. Even Jane got caught up in the pleasure of the moment.

All too soon, the small village station came into view up ahead. Patsy slowed Daisy to a stop beside the tiny red-brick building and helped Jane gather their bags before walking them to the platform.

'You take good care of your mummy now, young lady,' she said to Helen, giving her a final hug. The girl clung to her as if she never wanted to let her go.

Jane thanked her for her kindness. Then she clasped Helen's hand tightly and they stepped onto the platform to wait for their train back to London.

Once Patsy and Daisy were out of sight, Helen's mood dipped down again, which made Jane despair. Had she done the wrong thing letting Helen be evacuated in the first place? After all, although so many had been killed, maimed, or made homeless, Jane was still surviving, and their home had been spared. But then, a more sensible part of her brain told her there had been no guarantees of that. She'd just been luckier than a great many others.

Every day when people came in to see the IIP volunteers looking for their missing loved ones, she was reminded of how many had suffered enormous losses. Sometimes their wails of grief and despair echoed through the library, making readers look up, sad-eyed, and shake their heads as they understood what news someone had just received. Cordelia and the team had tried to prevent this by giving the IIP team their own private rooms, but the terrible shrieks, screams and sobs could still be heard.

Yes, she'd been lucky. Her mother, Helen's grandmother, had died, but of natural causes and, unlike so many people, Jane hadn't lost anyone to bombing.

They waited half an hour for the train, the only ones on the platform. When it arrived, Helen pulled back. She refused to hold Jane's hand; her bottom lip stuck out in defiance.

The train whistled. Steam billowed. Doors slammed open. People alighted, lugging their bags with them.

'I won't go!' Helen shouted, bursting into angry tears. Some people looked at them. One woman smiled sympathetically.

Jane had to drag Helen onto the train. It was difficult with her bags but had to be done. The train was full as usual with troops being moved around or going home on leave.

As they boarded the train, Helen constantly struggled to get free of Jane's hand, sobbing the whole time. Jane stopped and bent down to Helen's level. 'You've had a lovely time on the farm. Perhaps we can go there again one day to visit everyone. Would you like that?'

Helen looked up, and her sobs subsided a little. 'Can we?'

Jane nodded. 'Yes, we can come and visit. But now we need to find somewhere to sit, or our legs will be very tired by the time we get to London.'

They were lucky enough to get seats next to the window, although it was a squeeze.

As the train rumbled along, Jane studied her daughter sitting next to her. Despite Jane trying to engage her in conversation, Helen was quiet, her eyes fixed out of the window, her chin resting on her hand. The little girl had bonded deeply with the Blackburn family and the farm animals during her time there. That was clear. It made Jane feel happy that she'd had such a good time, offering her a different lifestyle from that in the East End. But what if her daughter now felt closer to them than to her and never got over it? The thought pierced Jane's heart like a shard of glass.

She took hold of Helen's hand.

'I missed you so much, love,' she said and reached out to stroke Helen's hair. The girl flinched slightly at her touch. 'Did you even think about me while you were gone?'

Helen gave a small shrug.

Jane stifled a sob as she felt the gulf widening between them. She had kept Helen safe, but had it cost them their mother–daughter bond? She ached to reconnect with the giggling, affectionate little girl who used to cling to her skirts and beg for more bedtime stories. Hot tears threatened, and Jane wiped her face with her hankie, swallowing back a tear.

All the way home, Jane tried to keep Helen amused playing 'I Spy', reading aloud, and singing songs they both knew, but Helen's responses were much more subdued than she normally was. The only time she really came to life was when she saw animals out of the window. Then she jumped up and down, naming them.

'Cows!' She pointed, urgently trying to get her mother's attention. 'Look, that one's like Buttercup, all brown and white and that one is more like Violet.'

When they left the fields with animals in behind, Helen's mood became more muted again. Even a little boy opposite in the carriage trying to engage her in play wasn't enough to bring her out of her low mood.

When they arrived home, Jane was relieved that Snowy was waiting on the doorstep – and the cat followed them in, rubbing its legs against Helen as if greeting her. It couldn't replace all the wonderful farm animals but was better than nothing.

That had been two weeks ago, and still Helen wasn't really settled. She'd got used to having animals around and being outside.

Jane talked to her landlady Mrs Simpson about it, worried for Helen's happiness.

'It's a pity the government told us to get our pets put down when the war started,' Mrs S said. 'I let them do that to Toddy, my little mongrel. I still miss 'im, lovely 'e was.' She shook her head at the memory. 'But I suppose the government was right, 'e'd have been terrified during the bombing, poor thing. Still, 'alf a million they put down. What did they do with their bodies, that's what I always wondered.'

'I wish I could take her to the zoo,' Jane said. 'It's a pity they had to close it, though I suppose if it'd been bombed, we'd have had wild animals roaming the streets.'

'Where did the animals go?' Helen asked.

Jane hesitated to answer. She knew some of the more dangerous animals had been put down. Hearing that would be sure to upset her daughter. It had upset her too when she found out about it.

'I don't know, love,' she lied. 'But I expect it's somewhere where they'll be happy and have enough to eat.'

Luckily autumn had been warm, and Helen found some of her old friends to play with outside. Initially, she played in a half-hearted way, as if her energy had been drained from her. But as the days passed, Helen came out of her shell more and more. She ran faster, skipped higher and laughed more often. Instead of sulky 'I won't!' or even 'I hate living here!' she had almost returned to who she had been before she was evacuated.

* * *

The front door creaked open, the noise grating in the quiet evening air.

Jane froze, squinting into the dim light at the silhouette. Her heart raced. For a split second, hope bloomed in her heart – could it possibly be? No, it was inconceivable. She stared desperately, searching for some familiar trait as the man stepped forward. It was only a few seconds, but time seemed to have stopped as she peered at him.

Broad shoulders in an army greatcoat, tousled dark hair sticking out of his cap, a lanky frame. She was sure her mind was playing tricks, letting her see the person she most wanted in front of her instead of reality.

It couldn't be true.

'Jane!' The man's voice was full of emotion and her heart nearly stopped. She'd know that voice anywhere, in her dreams, her every waking moment. 'Don't you recognise me?'

How long had it been since she first heard his voice? All that time ago when they'd met in the Roxy dance hall. She'd been nursing a shandy, trying to make it last because she was short of money. Proud of herself in a new blue and white dress with a sweetheart neck. At first, she didn't see him approaching. Then a friend nudged her. 'Someone wants to dance with you,' she said with a wink.

And there he stood, looking at her shyly, a question in his eyes. Honest eyes. Eyes she instinctively knew she could trust. Not like some of the lads who just wanted to get inside her knickers. Lads she sometimes had to fight off.

She held out her hand. His were rough workman's hands, yet they felt gentle and strong. Hands you could rely on. Even though she'd never met him before, she instinctively knew he was a good man.

'Jane,' he said again, pulling her attention back from the past.

He stepped fully into the light, and suddenly the years fell away. The years of separation, the sad period when he had suffered from battle fatigue. When he was emotionally as well as physically unwell. He was here looking well and healthy.

'George, my George,' she gasped, joy and relief choking her words.

He was home. He was really home.

He put down his kitbag and stepped forward. 'Jane! Didn't you recognise me?'

She wrapped her arms around him, the rough feel of his army greatcoat rubbing against her cheeks. The familiar smell of his cologne, woody and sweet, so dear to her. 'It's really you!'

So excited she could hardly breathe, she pulled him into the room.

'I don't know who that is,' Mrs S shouted, 'but close that door. This isn't a barn. There's a gale coming through 'ere.'

George turned and closed the door, then switched on the light.

'Look who it is,' Jane called out, pulling him into the living room. 'Helen, look, it's your daddy!'

Struggling out of his greatcoat, George bent down and held his arms out wide. 'Come here, darling, I've missed you so much!'

To Jane's horror, Helen took one look at him and ran behind the armchair, pulling the antimacassar over her head. She began wailing again.

Jane went over to her. 'It's your daddy, love. You've been wanting to see him for ages.'

Helen pulled the antimacassar from her face and peeked out from behind the chair. One hand was scrunching up the hem of her emerald-green dress. She stared at the man in front of her, tall and loud, smelling of cold and something she couldn't identify.

This couldn't be her dad. He was that picture beside her bed, a thin man who smiled, his arm round her mum. This man didn't belong in this house of females.

Without moving, she studied his face, unconsciously trying to see her father in this stranger. But time had gone on. Life had etched new lines in George's face and his hair was thinner, its colour fading. The only males she was used to were the farmer and his sons where she'd been evacuated. The farmer didn't acknowledge her beyond rubbing her hair. His sons weren't quite men, and were often mean to her, calling her names, but they spent time with her, playing hide-and-seek occasionally.

She hid her face in the chair again and her mother picked her up, holding her close. 'Your daddy's been gone so long, we'll have to get to know him all over again, won't we?'

George held out his arms again. 'Can you give your old daddy a hug, sweetheart? I've missed you something rotten.'

In response, Helen clung more closely to her mother, arms and legs wrapped round her like a limpet that would never let go.

Mrs S looked from one to the other from her chair. 'Well, this is difficult, me ducks. It's bin so long since she's seen 'im, she's bound to be a bit shy.'

Jane could see George didn't know what to do. He wanted to go to Helen, but he had to be polite and speak to their landlady.

'Helen will be fine in a minute, George. Say hello to Mrs S, then I'll make us all a cuppa.'

Mrs S shook George's hand, then slowly got out of her chair, groaning as she did so. She put down her knitting, a grey and black sock with four needles. 'I may be old and daft, but I can still make a cup of tea. You stay here, George. Get to know your family again.'

'Guess what I've got here?' George said, rummaging in his

kitbag. He put aside some socks, a scarf and a pack of playing cards with a picture of a half-naked woman on the front before looking at Helen. 'Can you guess?'

She stopped sobbing and looked at him but didn't respond.

'Your mummy told me,' George continued, holding the gift inside the bag still, 'that when you had your holiday on that farm, you liked a lot of the animals, but especially Daisy the cow. Is that right?'

Still clinging on to her mother, her face in her neck, Helen nodded.

'I remembered what your mummy said, and I got you a present. Do you want to come here to get it? Just give me a little hug and I'll give it to you.'

His encouraging words had the opposite effect. Helen clung even tighter to her mother and began to sob again. Quietly this time.

'You'll have to give her time,' Jane said softly. She saw the distress in his face and knew he'd been waiting so long for this moment. He'd written time and time again about being together with his family, how the thought of that kept him going through the hard times. He was a family man through and through.

George hadn't given up. He got the stuffed fabric cow out of his bag and saw Helen's eyes light up. 'I got this cow for you. I think it's called Daisy, but if you like you can give it another name.'

Helen held out her hand for it but without letting go of her mother. Of course, from there, she couldn't reach it. She started making whining noises and Jane told her to hush.

George held out the cow and bumped it up and down, pretending to make it walk.

'Moooo, hello, little girl,' he said in a silly voice. 'I think you know my friend Buttercup. Moooo. She has a lot of milk. She's lucky. I'm just looking for someone to play with me and give me a cuddle.'

Helen reached out again but still wouldn't let go of her mother.

'Do you know,' George said, 'when I was a lad, I lived here in Silvertown. At the end of our road was this old lady, Mrs Banks her name was. She was little and bent over like a tired mule. She always wore men's trousers and boots. None of us wanted to get close to her because she was likely to give you a clip round the ear. She had this house that looked like it would fall apart any minute.'

He stopped talking to see if Helen was listening. Her eyes were still fixed on the toy cow, but her sobs had stopped. Jane nodded to him to continue.

'Well, this Mrs Banks only had a cow and a pig in her garden. Can you imagine!'

Finally, Helen spoke. 'Were they friends?'

George nodded, the tension beginning to leave his face. 'They were. The pig had his own pen, but the cow, I think her name was Bessie, she used to visit the pig all the time. Me and all the other kids used to love watching them.'

Helen leaned towards Jane and whispered in her ear, cupping her hand in the way children do.

'She wants to know what the pig was called,' Jane told George.

He rubbed his chin. 'I'm not sure I really remember, but I think it was Porky.'

He held out the toy cow again and Helen tentatively got off her mother's lap and walked towards it. All the time she watched George as if he might bite. The few steps from one to the other seemed to take forever and the adults watched her anxiously. Then George leaned forward and handed the toy to her. Helen snatched it and ran back to her mother, clutching it tight.

'I've got some pictures of places I've been. Why don't you and your mum come and sit on the settee with me, and we can look at them?'

The kettle whistled and Mrs S returned to the kitchen where she began putting everything on a tray.

A few minutes later, she appeared in the doorway carrying it. It wobbled dangerously and Jane hurriedly took the tray from her.

'Thanks, ducks,' Mrs S said. 'Getting weak in me old age. I'll let you be mother.'

While Jane poured the tea, George opened his kitbag again and took out a bulging envelope with postcards and photos in it.

'Let's go and have a look,' Jane said, picking Helen up and sitting down next to George. Helen wriggled slightly so she wasn't touching him.

As luck would have it, the second postcard had a cow on it, in the background quite small, but there nonetheless.

'Like Daisy!' Helen said, taking the card from him. She looked into his eyes for the first time. 'Is it for me?'

He smiled and touched her arm. 'Of course it is, sweetheart. You keep it.'

Quite soon, Helen was rubbing her eyes.

Jane looked at the clock. 'Your bedtime, young lady. Let's take your new toy and postcard and get you upstairs. Want to kiss your daddy goodnight?'

Tentatively, Helen leaned towards him and gave a quick peck on his cheek. In return, he pulled her to him, breathing in her little girl smell and kissing her head. 'Goodnight, my love. See you in the morning.'

She wriggled free but didn't seem distressed at his hug. It was a start.

Jane picked up the farm book she'd been about to read earlier and followed Helen up the stairs.

'Goodnight, Mrs S, goodnight, Daddy!' Helen called.

Jane came back into the room. She smiled at him and put her finger to her lips. 'Sshh. She shouldn't wake up, but let's make sure she's properly asleep.'

He took her hand and kissed it. 'Mrs S went up for an early night to leave us alone.'

She grinned and squeezed his hand tight, her eyes twinkling. 'We won't be down here for long. Helen's a heavy sleeper once she's properly asleep. I'll pick her up and put her in the box room. I've got it ready.'

8

'Where are we?' Joyce's voice was shaky as she and Mavis walked along their street, holding hands. 'Is this where my mummy lives?'

Mavis was filled with sorrow. Joyce's home had once been in a road just like this before being smashed to smithereens at the height of the Blitz. Mavis had found the poor child wandering lost amongst the debris, looking for her mother, who was trapped lifeless under the rubble.

For a minute, Mavis was unsure how to respond. Would talking about the girl's mother upset her or would refusing to do so make her feel as if her mother was lost to her, even in her memory? She wondered how staff at the children's home where Joyce lived handled issues such as this one.

'This is like the street you used to live in with your mummy, but it's not the same one,' she said, squeezing the girl's hand.

'Before she went to heaven to live with Jesus?' Joyce's eyes darted around as if trying to see her mother somewhere.

'That's right. She's up there with Jesus. I wonder if she can see you now. See how much you've grown and what a lovely girl you are. She must be very proud of you like I am.'

They had reached her door and Mrs O'Connor next door hastily came out to see what was going on. She was a kind woman who, like Mavis, was willing to help anyone in need. But the disadvantage was she never stopped talking, and taking a hint that the person she was speaking to had had enough was beyond her.

'You staying with your Aunty Mavis for the weekend, then?' she asked Joyce.

Joyce looked from her to Mavis, unsure what to do.

'Yes, just for the weekend,' Mavis answered for her. 'Is your granddaughter going to be around? We'll be fairly busy, but perhaps she'd like to come in to play with Joyce for a while, or they could go to Sunday school together.'

At that, Mrs O'Connor took her opportunity to launch into a long tale about how much trouble her daughter had with a mean landlord who kept putting up the rent but never did repairs. It was a familiar story in the East End.

Mavis cut across her. 'Sorry to interrupt you, but we both need a wee, and it's been a long journey. We'll see you soon.'

She fumbled with her key, keen to get inside before Mrs O'Connor could start another tale.

The house was cold, and she saw Joyce shiver. 'Keep your coat on, love. I'll light the fire and we'll soon be warm as toast.'

Joyce was looking round the room at the shabby but clean settee, and the little table that served as a dining table but was also used for everything else. She ran her hand over the cream crocheted antimacassars on the settee and on the multicoloured rag rug in the middle of the room. Lace curtains, yellowing with age, but spotless, framed the window at the front overlooking the street.

Mavis was busy setting the fire but kept looking over her shoulder. 'Are you okay, love? I'll get you a drink in a minute.' She pointed to the settee. 'Have a look under that cushion, the blue one, there's a little treat for you there.'

Wide-eyed, unused to treats in the children's home, Joyce slowly took the few steps to the settee.

'For me? What is it?' she asked, her voice so quiet Mavis could hardly hear her over the sound of the fire beginning to catch.

'Go and have a look, see if you like it.'

Cautiously, Joyce moved the cushion aside to uncover a newspaper-covered parcel tied with a strip of old fabric.

She struggled with the knots and Mavis got up to help her, letting her unfold the paper.

Inside was a pretty pink flowered dress. It was second-hand, bought at the market, but as good as new.

'Is it mine?' Joyce asked, excitement making her eyes shine. 'For me? Honest?'

Mavis took it from her and held it up against her. 'Yes, it's for you and upstairs you'll find a cardigan you can wear over it.'

Without warning, the happiness in Joyce's eyes dimmed. 'Someone'll nick it,' she said.

It was probably true. The children at the home had so little, they did sometimes take things belonging to the others.

'Tell you what I did,' Mavis said, turning the dress inside out. 'I embroidered your name twice in the seams. So, if it goes missing, the people at the home will be able to find it and know it's yours.'

Joyce smiled and wrapped the dress up again. 'I'll take it back home with me,' she said.

Mavis wanted to say that her house could become Joyce's home but hesitated. The adoption process was long and difficult. She was determined not to promise what she couldn't be sure of.

'Let me get you a drink of milk,' she said instead. She reached up to a shelf near the fireplace and took out three children's books that she'd bought from Rathbone market. 'These are for you as well. We can read them together.'

Joyce sat on the chair nearest the fire, opening her coat, but not yet warm enough to take it off.

'I can write my name,' she said proudly, turning the pages. 'This book is about a cat. It looks funny.'

'I'll read it to you if you like,' Mavis said as she went to the kitchen to pour the milk. 'Would you like to make some biscuits when we've 'ad our dinner?'

Before Joyce could answer, a hammering on the door made the little girl jump in terror, her tiny frame instinctively curling into a ball as she looked around with anxious, wide eyes.

Mavis looked at her in astonishment then realised it was natural for her to be spooked by loud sounds. She'd been in an air raid when her mother died.

'It's just the rent man,' Mavis said, getting out her purse. 'I won't be a minute.'

'Mummy used to hide from the rent man,' Joyce whispered, still looking worried and biting a nail.

Mavis opened the door, picking up the coins she had ready on the mantlepiece. The man facing her looked as weary and stoop-shouldered as ever.

Joyce's mother wouldn't be the only one who hid from him. People in the East End lived from day to day with never a penny to spare. Many, like her, had seven jam jars in the kitchen, each marked with a day of the week. On payday, they divided their food money, putting a seventh in each jar. Mavis never let herself spend more than the allowance for one day even if her stomach rumbled and her shoes needed new soles.

She handed over the money and a smile transformed his care-worn face.

'Bless you, Mrs Kent,' he said. 'I know I can always depend on you. More than I can say for a lot around here.'

He doffed his cap and went on to Mrs O'Connor's house. Mavis silently wished him luck getting away in less than five minutes.

'Right,' she said, turning back to Joyce. 'I made us some shepherd's pie before I came to collect you. I'll pop it in the oven and while it warms up, I'll show you round and we can read a book together.'

Sitting down with Joyce, she let her choose her first book. It was about a ginger cat called Sammy who gets lost and has to find its way home. On the journey the cat meets a bird, an elephant and a friendly dog. Mavis did a good job of using exaggerated voices for the different characters, and soon, she and Joyce were both giggling at the cat's adventures.

'He's a silly cat, isn't he?' Joyce said, then her stomach rumbled audibly. 'Is dinner ready yet? At the home we have to wait for the bell to ring. Sometimes I get really, really hungry.'

Mavis closed the book and stood up. 'I don't have a bell, but I can tell from the smell our pie is ready.'

That afternoon, they baked biscuits, using scarce rations that Mavis had saved.

'Can I take some home with me for my friend?' Joyce asked.

'Of course you can, sweetheart,' Mavis said with a smile.

* * *

The rest of the weekend was taken up with going for a walk to George's Café for a bun, doing a jigsaw puzzle, and several bedtime stories. Joyce was happy to go to Sunday school because that's what they did at the home, walking in crocodile fashion along the road. Luckily Mrs O'Connor's granddaughter, Annie, was going too, so Mavis took both girls and waited to bring them back, sitting quietly at the back of the church reading *Jane Eyre* for the umpteenth time.

It was difficult to keep a straight face listening to the girls' conversation on the way back.

'The vicar said we should thank God because we get sweets and some people don't get them,' Annie said.

Joyce looked at her in amazement. 'Will you pray for me then? We don't get no sweets where I live.' She paused. 'Do you think Father Christmas lives in heaven? He has lots of presents.'

Annie looked at her as if she'd gone crazy. 'No, silly. He lives in Iceland. It's very cold there. My mum says it's lucky he's got a big fat gut to keep him warm!'

They were walking past the corner shop Mavis often went to. 'Come on, girls. I'll buy you some sweets,' she said. 'Not many, though, I don't 'ave enough ration coupons left.'

The girls held hands and ran ahead into the shop, their eyes wide at the choice of sweets in big glass jars.

'I'm gonna have sherbet dabs,' Annie said. 'They're my favourite.'

Joyce frowned and looked at Mavis for help. 'What's my favourite, Aunty?'

Mavis felt a swell of compassion for the little girl. She probably had had a favourite when her mother was alive but in the home there would be no chance to try alternatives. 'I don't know, love. Why don't you just choose one and try it?'

Joyce chose a gobstopper, and her eyes went big as saucers as she tried cramming the giant sweet into her tiny mouth, her cheeks bulging like a hamster. Both girls giggled so much they almost spat the sweets out.

Her mouth full of gobstopper, Joyce could hardly speak the rest of the way home, but the girls managed to wonder if Noah had provided sweets for the animals in his ark. Then they talked about Jesus feeding the five thousand.

'Do you think he gave them sweets?' Annie asked Mavis.

Mavis suppressed a smile. 'I don't know, sweetheart, but I bet 'e would have done if 'e had any.'

All too soon it was time for Mavis to take Joyce back to the home. As they got ready to catch the bus, she thought how much she'd enjoyed the weekend.

'She won't always be good,' Jane had warned her. 'They say children behave like angels at first when they get a new home, but then play up.' She bit her lip. 'I suppose they're just testing their new family to see if they'll get rejected again.'

'Poor Joyce wasn't rejected, though,' Mavis said. "Er mum died.'

Joyce slept for much of the way back to the home, exhausted from all the new experiences. Mavis loved that she cuddled up to her as she slept. Once or twice when the conductor called out the name of a stop, she would half wake, bleary-eyed.

'Are we there yet?' she would ask and then promptly go back to sleep.

'How did the weekend go?' Mrs Anderson asked when Joyce was back with the other children. 'Did you have any trouble with her?'

'Not a minute,' Mavis answered with a smile. 'We 'ad a smashing time. We did some cooking, went for a walk, a jigsaw, and she went to Sunday school with another little girl.'

Mrs Anderson reached for a folder with Joyce's name on the front. 'If we did go further with this, Mrs Kent, who would look after Joyce when you are at work?'

Mavis remembered trudging round three nurseries, looking for the one she was happy with. The last thing she wanted was Joyce to be miserable anywhere. 'I've found a good nursery, attached to the local church. I expect you know the government 'ave started a load of 'em up to encourage us women to do our bit for the war. But I've got a question.'

Mrs Anderson looked up from the form she was reading. 'What is that?'

'Well, Christmas isn't too far away. Can she come and stay with me then? I won't 'ave much in the way of presents to give 'er, no one 'as, but I promise 'er a real good time.'

Mrs Anderson sat back in her chair and steepled her fingers. 'That's a lovely idea, Mrs Kent, and we have almost completed all the necessary paperwork. There is one more thing, though. We need to come to inspect your home and make sure it's suitable.'

Mavis's breath caught in her throat. Like most people in the East End, her home was modest. Joyce would have to share her bedroom and she had no luxuries.

As she walked to catch her bus back home, Mavis's heart fluttered with hope and trepidation. She imagined Joyce's face lighting up as they made Christmas decorations from old magazines and saw the cosy bedroom again. But Mavis also pictured the faded curtains, the saggy settee and chair. She could only clutch her hands tightly and hope that love would prove enough.

What would she do if it wasn't?

9

Cordelia tucked a wayward strand of her hair under her new uniform cap and ran along the road. She'd joined the Women's Voluntary Service as a volunteer and was late for her first shift. She felt a mixture of excitement and worry as she hurried along, her sensible shoes tapping on the paving stones. She used her shielded torch to see her way along in the blackout, her hands stinging as the cold metal found its way through her woollen gloves. The beam of her torch danced across the pitch-black streets, illuminating cracked pavements and bombed buildings. As she walked, shadows stretched down lanes like long ghostly fingers, making her jumpy.

Muffled voices floated from behind the walls of homes settling down for the night and a distant wail of an ambulance siren punctured the stillness, a haunting war cry in the darkness. But up ahead, a sliver of warm light peeked through the blackout curtains of the community hall's windows.

She'd been assigned to Canning Town, the next borough to Silvertown where her library was. It meant she could grab a quick bite to eat when she finished the day job before going to her new role. She'd only signed on for three evenings a week, but if she liked it, thought she might do more.

As the community hall came into sight, she felt her heart sink to find her new centre organiser, Mrs Donaldson, standing outside looking at her watch. Was she going to be one of those sergeant major types who relished pointing out faults just to assert her authority? Cordelia quickened her pace, ready to apologise. But as she approached, Mrs Donaldson's face softened into a smile.

'Good evening, you must be Miss Carmichael. Is it okay if I call you Cordelia? We don't stand on ceremony here.' She held out her hand and gripped Cordelia's firmly. 'I'm delighted you've decided to join us. There's always more to do than time allows. We only have two other volunteers this evening, but I'm sure you'll all have a jolly time.'

She led the way down a narrow hallway with pictures of Canning Town in years gone by on the walls. Cordelia liked the idea and decided to add more pictures of Silvertown to the walls of the library. As she followed Mrs Donaldson, she was relieved to be out of the cold, and unbuttoned her coat and removed her scarf. Ahead, she could hear laughter and music playing on the wireless.

'I hear you're in charge of the library in Silvertown,' Mrs Donaldson said. 'You must be a clever young thing. I hope you won't find the work here too boring.'

Cordelia smiled. 'I get enough excitement every day at the library, so something like packing boxes for the troops sounds perfect.'

'This is where you'll be working,' Mrs Donaldson said, opening the door. It was a small side room. The cream paint on the walls was beginning to break up in places and the scuffed wooden floor showed the tread of many feet over the years. In the middle of the room, four small tables had been pushed together to make a workbench, mismatched wooden chairs placed around it. On top were boxes of goods the volunteers would pack for the troops – corned beef, cigarettes, boiled sweets, socks, scarves, soap, a random selection of things for entertainment such as playing cards, harmonicas, dice.

'I've got an urgent appointment, so I'll be back in a minute,' Mrs Donaldson said, looking apologetic. 'You'll be in good hands here with our very experienced volunteers.'

Cordelia looked around. In a corner of the room, a few faded Union Jack bunting flags lent a small splash of colour, and a picture of the king hung over the fireplace. A handmade sign reading 'Care packages for our boys' in large, cheerful letters hung over the door. Although the room was shabby and worn, it brimmed with life.

'Bless You' by the Ink Spots was playing on the wireless.

The door opened and to her surprise in walked Doreen, who was one of the volunteers helping to smarten up the library.

She was wearing an overall and had a bright patterned scarf on her head bandana-style with the loose ends tied in a bow at the top of her head. With her curvy figure she looked like a film star.

'Hello, luv,' Doreen said. 'You're the boss at the library, aren't you? Never expected to see you 'ere.' She stopped midway through putting a tin of corned beef into a box and spoke to the other volunteer who had walked in behind her. 'Ann, this is Miss Carmichael. She's the boss at the library at Silvertown. I almost got into a bundle with a builder bloke when I was there last week.'

Ann's jaw dropped open. 'A bundle! What was you doing there then?'

"Elping smarten the place up. 'E was a plonker. Mind you, 'e knew 'is stuff really. But the king and queen are coming. Didn't you 'ear?'

Ann's face took on a wistful look, her eyes glazing over with longing at the thought of seeing the royal couple. 'Wouldn't it be just magic to meet them?' she said.

'Yeah,' Doreen said. 'But I'd never know what to say to them if I did.'

'Mind you,' Ann went on, 'my mum can't stand the queen. Says she's up herself going places with her airs and graces.' She put a slip of paper in the box in front of her. 'And she's right, you know. The queen only goes and says she understands people what have been bombed 'cos they had a few windows broken in the palace. I ask you. She's got to be kidding. We ain't got nowhere else to go. It's the reception centre for us unless we've got family to take us in. They've got loads of places.'

Her words made Cordelia hope that there would be no demonstrations when the king and queen visited the library.

The kettle that Doreen had put on before Cordelia arrived began to whistle. 'Let's 'ave a cuppa before we start, shall we?'

Cordelia hung her coat up on a coat hook next to the door. 'Can I help?' she asked as Doreen got out the big brown teapot and spooned tea leaves into it. She took three china cups and saucers out of a cupboard and plonked them down on the side table so hard they rattled.

'We take it in turns,' Ann said. 'And if you miss your turn, Doreen never lets you forget it!'

She went pink as she spoke and picked up a packet of cigarettes to put in a box.

'How d'you like your tea then?' Doreen asked Cordelia. 'And what do we call you 'ere anyway?'

Cordelia was stumped for a minute. Would it affect her role in the library if she used Christian names?

'My name's Cordelia, but in the library I'm Miss Carmichael,' she said eventually. 'And I like my tea medium strong, please.'

'Oh, I didn't introduce ya,' Doreen said. 'This is young Ann. She works at the sugar factory and 'er lad is away in the army somewhere.'

Cordelia wondered if that was why Ann gave up her spare time to fill the boxes. It was certainly why she'd chosen to do so. She missed Robert so much, his smile, his warmth, his love. Other than writing letters and sending him the occasional book, there wasn't much she could do to feel close to him. But filling the boxes for the forces would make her feel closer. And maybe, just maybe, a box she filled might find its way to him.

'Hello, Miss... I mean Cordelia. Nice to meetcha.' Ann's smile was wide and open. She had a small smudge of lipstick on her tooth.

Mrs Donaldson came back into the room. 'Ah, I see you're all getting settled. I'm sure I can leave you two to show our newcomer the ropes,' she said. 'I'll be back in a while.'

Doreen gave her back a mock salute, and after Mrs Donaldson had left again, she turned back to Cordelia and Ann. 'Actually, she ain't that bad. A lot nicer than my boss at the marmalade factory. *She's* a right tyrant. You'd think they paid 'er by the jar. She goes apeshit if we're as much as a minute late. Docks fifteen minutes. She even times our toilet breaks!'

'Tough luck if you've got the runs then!' Ann chipped in with a grin. She took the tea Doreen handed her and put one spoon of sugar in. 'Everyone thinks we get free sugar for working at Tate, but we don't. Not a bad place, though.'

'It's a bit smelly like our place,' Doreen said. 'Last summer we had wasps just outside one of the windows. They must've fancied some marmalade and 'undreds of 'em came in all at once. We all screamed and ran out faster than we run to the shelter when the siren goes!' She was gesticulating wildly as she spoke and her bracelet flew across the room. She could hardly speak for laughing at the memory of the wasps. 'With none of us seeing to it, loads of jars of jam ended up on the floor and did the wasps love it?'

The door was flung open and an elderly man wearing a brown

cotton coat over his clothes walked in. He staggered under the weight of a massive box he was carrying. 'More fags for the boys,' he said. 'Where d'you want them, sweetheart?' He winked at Doreen.

She grinned and blew him a cheeky kiss. 'Over there on the floor, Charlie. I 'ope you 'aven't been 'elping yourself to any.'

'Honest as the day is long, me,' he said heading to the door. 'I'll love you and leave you, ladies.' And he was gone.

'Well,' Doreen said, looking at Cordelia. 'It's pretty clear what we 'ave to do. We fold up the boxes then fill them with all this stuff. One of each for every box. Then we use that string there to tie them up tight.' She waved her hands over the boxes of goods like a magician. 'And Ann likes to add a little something extra!'

Ann looked up from what she was doing and went pink again.

Cordelia was baffled. What could Doreen mean? What extra could she put in? The boxes were all the same size and weight.

She would soon find out.

Ann took a bundle of papers out of her handbag. 'I write little notes and put one in each box. Cheers 'em up.'

Cordelia's eyes widened. 'But what do you write on them?'

As she sorted through the papers, Ann pushed some towards Cordelia. ''Ave a look. All sorts.'

Picking up the papers, Cordelia began reading the brief messages:

I put an extra sweet in here, but it's not as sweet as you! Xxx

The chocolate may have melted but my heart still melts for you.

Some had lipstick kisses on, with the message:

Roses are red, violets are blue, the kiss on this paper is just for you!

'One of the volunteers who used to come here used to put her address on the notes,' Ann said, watching her. 'You'll never guess what. One soldier only went to her house. And it was love at first sight. They got married the next week!'

Cordelia and the two women finished their tea and set to work filling the boxes, working in an assembly line, each packing two or three things in a box, then passing it along. They sang along to the wireless as they worked, which was very different from Cordelia's experience in the library, where they tried to keep things as quiet as possible. She found she enjoyed the relaxed atmosphere and the lively chatter.

Cordelia fell into easy conversation with the other two, sharing titbits about families and lives outside the task at hand. Ann was full of how wonderful her boyfriend Ernest was – tall, handsome, kind, good with children and a good kisser. Cordelia couldn't help but think he sounded too good to be true. But she hoped she was wrong.

'You want to watch out there, girl,' Doreen said. 'Or he'll be in your knickers lickety-spit, and then you'll be in the club.'

Ann looked shocked and went pink again, putting the wrong thing in the next box. 'He... he wouldn't,' she finally said.

The conversation brought back memories for Cordelia of the boy she went out with in Cambridge, another student. She was always having to tell him to keep his hands to himself. He had a peculiar way of looking offended, like a child deprived of his sweets. The world was so unfair, she mused. The blokes pushed the girls but often didn't take responsibility for using condoms. Then if the girl got in the family way, they cleared off, leaving her life in pieces.

'Well, my old gran said they always will and they're never too old 'til they're in their box. You know what'll 'appen. These blokes know all the tricks – "I might be dead before I see you next", "I'll pull out in time"...'

'I think you'd better stop,' Cordelia said. 'This is a bit much for poor Ann. But Ann, she's right in saying you need to be very careful.'

Ann kept her head down and concentrated on wrapping a bar of soap inside a hand-knitted scarf in black, grey and brown. Given a choice, Cordelia would have thrown the scarf away as it was too depressing.

An air-raid warden shouting 'Turn off that damn light!' saved Ann from having to reply, and all three of them instinctively looked at their curtains. They were just as they should be.

'Not us, this time,' Doreen said. 'Bloody little 'itlers, them wardens.'

The time flew past, punctuated with laughs and singing that easily avoided the tedium of the task. The only small worry that marred the session was that Cordelia thought she saw Doreen slip a pack of cigarettes in her bag. The trouble was, the action was so quick she couldn't be sure she hadn't misinterpreted what had happened. She would keep it in mind, though.

At the end of the shift, Cordelia surveyed the big stack of completed parcels with satisfaction. Her fingers were sore and her back ached, but she didn't regret this new role for a second. Every parcel sent a reminder to the troops that they hadn't been forgotten, that the folks at home were thinking of them. And it reminded them of what they were fighting for, not just victory but to return to their families and English joys like well-cooked meals, warm socks, and hugs from their loved ones.

When their shift was finished, they began tidying up. 'I think we've done the lads proud this evening,' Doreen said.

Ann nodded. 'Wouldn't it be lovely if one went to my Ernest?'

'Do you send him anything?' Cordelia asked.

'I do, but it's mostly socks and things like that. I'd like to send him something a bit different.'

Doreen grinned as she put on her coat, buttoning up the big brown buttons and pulling the collar up. 'Send 'im a picture of you in the altogether. 'E'd like that!'

'Give the poor girl a break,' Cordelia said. 'She's not going to do any such thing. But what is he interested in? Robert, my boyfriend, likes mystery books, so I send him one of them sometimes.'

She smiled as she remembered the last one she'd sent him. *Artists in Crime* by Ngaio Marsh. She had enclosed a letter in with the book and, like Ann, had put a lipstick kiss at the top. As she usually did, she read the book first so they could talk about it in their letters. And sometimes, going against all her librarian training, she did little doodles in the margins in pencil. But she never gave any clues as to who the murderer was.

Ann began speaking again, bringing her back to the present. 'I dunno what he likes really. He likes to watch the dogs down at White City. I can't see why. I think it's boring watching dogs running around and around.'

'Me too,' Cordelia said. 'But I know one book that he might like. It's called *Odds On* by Michael Joseph. I haven't read it, but it's supposed to be exciting.'

Ann's face dropped. 'I dunno if I could afford it, though. Money's tight at the moment.'

'Try the bookstall on the market,' Cordelia said. 'They might have it.'

They were all getting ready to leave, coats on, when Mrs Donaldson returned. She looked at the pile of boxes they'd completed.

'Well done, girls. Just think of the pleasure our boys will get when they open them. You'll have made someone's day. Thank you all so much.'

Bidding goodnight to Ann and Doreen, Cordelia stepped out into the cold night air. Her eyes took a minute to adjust to the darkness after the light of their workroom. It was a clear night, with a bright moon. What they called a bomber's moon during the Blitz. It reflected on the Thames, making it easy for the bombers to find their way. She sent up a prayer of thanks that they now had only occasional bombings. But something that had happened worried her.

Was Doreen a thief? Cordelia didn't feel confident enough about what she'd seen to tackle her or report her to Mrs Donaldson. Her mind was going round in circles as she wondered what to do. But finally she decided she would just have to keep her eyes open in future.

Apart from that incident, she was happy that her evening work would bring pleasure to some troops. Just like the work in the library, this voluntary work gave her a sense of purpose. But as she sat on the bus, her recurring worry forced its way into her mind once again. Visions of Robert getting killed or suffering one of the dreadful diseases in North Africa he'd mentioned. He'd only written about malaria and cholera, but she had looked up diseases found in places like his and been horrified. Dengue fever, dysentery, typhus, sandfly fever, heatstroke, and TB. Any of them could kill or leave the sufferer with lifelong difficulties.

When she got off her bus, she quickened her pace down the deserted streets, trying to outrun the worries about what Robert might be facing. All she could do was keep writing and keep him in her heart until he was back home with her.

As she approached her flat, Cordelia glanced up at the black sky, dotted with stars. Somewhere under those same stars was her beloved. 'I'll be waiting for you, Robert,' she whispered.

10

Two evenings later, it was impossible to miss the bruise on Doreen's arm when she reached across the table for another box.

'Whatcha do to yer arm, Doreen?' Ann asked, continuing to fold the lid on her box without thinking. 'That's a nasty bruise you got there.'

The three women had only started their shift half an hour earlier. The frigid air in the room made the skin on Cordelia's arms rise and she got up to put more coal on the fire.

She turned and saw Doreen's arm, just above the wrist. From her angle she could see what Ann couldn't. Not just the bruise at the front of her arm, but the finger-shaped bruises on the tender inside. The mark round her wrist looked like a grotesque bracelet, all the telltale colours: brown, mottled green and dull purple.

Before she could say anything, Doreen pulled her sleeve back down. 'I caught it on the mantlepiece,' she said. 'Damn near fell on my face.'

There was an awkward silence between them, broken only by the sound of paper being put into the boxes and the fire crackling.

The women kept their heads on their work, not looking at each other.

Cordelia's throat tightened at the thought of what must have happened to this bold woman. Her hands clenched so tight her fingernails dug into her palms. Anger flared up in her chest at the treatment Doreen must be getting at home. She wanted to shout and scream for the woman who was becoming her friend but forced herself to be calm. The last thing Doreen needed was to be embarrassed in front of Ann. The younger woman had much less experience of life.

As she worked, Cordelia began putting together things she'd noticed about Doreen before. Her boldness often seemed forced, as if it was her way to overcome sadness. And she rarely discussed her home life unless asked directly. And when she helped that time in the library, she had several times stopped to clutch her ribs, joking that she had heartburn.

The awkward atmosphere was broken by Mrs Donaldson coming in, bringing a cold breeze with her, along with her usual smell of lavender perfume.

'Are you three lovely helpers okay here?' she asked.

As usual she looked immaculate, not a hair out of place. Cordelia remembered reading in a novel about a woman who was obsessed with looking perfect all the time. She always took off her skirt and hung it up on the back of the toilet door when she did her business so it wouldn't get creased. Cordelia smiled at the memory of that character and wondered if Mrs Donaldson did the same.

'We're all fine,' she said, her voice sounding more cheerful than she felt.

'Give me a shout if you need anything,' Mrs Donaldson said. 'I'll leave you to it.' As before, Doreen saluted to her back.

The trio began filling the boxes again, working automatically, their hands knowing what to do without needing to think about it.

It left plenty of time for chat. Ann was full of a letter she'd had from her boyfriend and how she'd managed to get the book Cordelia had recommended cheap at Rathbone market. 'It's a bit tatty, but all the pages are there. I checked.'

'I see you wear a wedding ring, Doreen,' Cordelia said. 'Is your husband away fighting? You haven't mentioned him.'

There was a pause while the other two women glanced at each other. Then they hastily picked up the next things they had to pack.

''E had an accident on the docks,' Doreen finally said, a sheen of sweat appearing on her forehead. 'Terrible, it was. Done his back in. Never worked since. Not a day.'

Stories about dock workers' injuries were commonplace in Silvertown. It was hard manual work, often with little regard for the safety of the men. She'd heard of men being crushed under massive boxes being unloaded, or between the boats and the dockside, or even drowning when knocked into the Thames by the cranes. The stories she'd heard often made her shiver.

An uneasy silence followed Doreen's reply, just the sound of the boxes being filled to break it. Although Doreen had pulled down her sleeve, Cordelia's eyes kept being drawn to her arm. Women being hit by their husbands was not unusual in the East End. Alcohol, poverty, and desperation made people act in ways they might not have done otherwise.

'Have you two got any plans for the weekend?' Cordelia asked, trying to lift the atmosphere. 'I'll be at the library Saturday, but I'm hoping to see that new film sometime. You know, *The Ghost of St Michael's*. It looks really funny.'

Ann clapped her hands. 'Me and my mate are going to the dance at Tate's Saturday. I won't tell me boyfriend, though. What 'e don't know won't harm 'im. Not like I'm going to get up to anything, am I?'

'Make the most of it,' Doreen said, shaking her head. 'Things change when you go down that aisle.'

Her voice was so bitter that Cordelia felt for her. Whatever was happening in her life was taking its toll.

'What about you then, Doreen?' she asked. 'Got anything nice planned?'

A grunt was her first response, then Doreen muttered, 'Same as usual. Housework, shopping, cooking, laundry, mending his lordship's socks.' Then under her breath, so quietly Cordelia was unsure if she'd heard it properly, 'Getting rid of the bottles.'

Cordelia could see the signs. Doreen's shaking hands as she packed the boxes and her nails bitten to the quick showed her emotions as much as the harshness in her tone.

When Ann went to the WC, Cordelia plucked up courage to speak to her.

'Doreen, I've seen that bruise, and it looks like someone grabbed your arm really hard. Is everything okay at home?'

Without looking up, Doreen continued putting items in the box as if she hadn't heard. But as the sound of Ann's footsteps rang out in the quiet room, returning down the hall, she muttered, 'Everything's just tickety-boo.' Her tone said it was the end of the subject.

11

Jane's nostrils flared and for a minute she thought the smell was coming from one of the many factories lining the docks nearby. The people of Silvertown lived side by side with an endless array of unpleasant manufacturing smells. There was the rich, sweet smell of melting molasses from the Tate & Lyle sugar refinery, the pungent smell like rotten eggs from Johnson and Phillips chemical works, the fatty smell of vegetable oils from Dunkirk margarine factory. The terrible acrid stench of rubber cement and melting tyres from Silver's rubber works and more beside.

But then she recognised it. The smell was inside the library, not outside.

Fire!

Jane and Tom looked at each other, alarm making their eyes wide.

'Incendiary?' Tom asked.

'Can't be,' Jane replied, feeling panic nonetheless in case one had somehow landed in the library. But there had been no bombing for a while, so it was unlikely.

She nudged Tom. 'Some idiot has started a fire somewhere. I'll go and see what's happening.'

She rushed behind the desk to the tiny kitchen area and filled a jug with water.

'Do you want me to call the fire brigade?' Tom called after her, but she was already too far away to hear him.

She ran down the book stacks and rushed towards the back corner of the main reading room. It wasn't hard to follow the smell. As she feared, tendrils of smoke curled up from one of the rubbish bins near a table.

'Fire!' she shouted breathlessly, sending several readers leaping up in alarm. One man even dashed for the exit, convinced an incendiary bomb had struck the library. Others moved towards the desk.

Billowing clouds of smoke began to pour from the bin.

Dropping to her knees, Jane doused the contents with water, which produced angry hisses as it met the burning paper inside. When she was sure it was safe, she picked up the bin gingerly. The fire was out, but small wisps of smoke drifted up, giving off an acrid smell.

Turning, she noticed a sheepish-looking soldier whose ears were bright red. He shuffled the papers in front of him, unable to meet Jane's gaze.

'I'm so sorry, miss,' he stammered. 'I didn't think... I must've flicked my ciggie without looking and missed the ashtray. I never meant...' His voice trailed off and he looked at if he might cry at any moment.

Jane felt a pang of sympathy for the man. He looked barely old enough to shave, never mind fight for the country. His face crumpled with embarrassment, and he began to wring his hands nervously.

'I promise I'll never smoke in the library again, miss. My girlfriend keeps telling me off. Says it's not good for me.'

Jane hadn't the heart to lecture him. 'I'm glad you owned up,' she said instead. 'And it's a good idea to stop smoking. Doctors are beginning to think it's bad for your chest.'

'I will, miss. Thank you, miss.'

Still carrying the bin, she returned to the desk, where Tom was waiting anxiously.

'Is that it?' he asked. 'No need for the fire brigade?'

'Hang on a minute,' Jane said, wanting to be rid of the stinking, soggy paper. She took it outside to the communal bin and banged it on the side to dislodge the last pieces.

Back inside, she went to the desk and saw the soldier was just leaving.

'What did you say to him?' Tom asked. 'He looked like a dog with its tail between its legs.'

'I wasn't horrible to him. He felt bad about being careless with his cigarette. I thanked him for owning up.'

Hetty appeared from the children's section clutching her latest book.

'I'd like this one, please,' she said with her sweet smile.

'Of course, sweetheart,' Jane said, taking her library card and stamping the date page inside the book. 'I hope you enjoy it. Will we see you on Saturday?'

Hetty's eyes glowed. 'Yes, I'm coming. I've got a boyfriend now, he's the same age as me. I'll ask him to come. But he can't read as good as me yet.'

When she and her mother had gone, Jane returned her attention to Tom and the matter of the burning bin.

'I think we should remove all the bins. This happens about once a month and it could be a whole lot worse. What do you think?'

Tom nodded. 'Good idea and perhaps we can find more ashtrays too. It's a pity we can't stop people smoking but I don't suppose that would be allowed.'

'You're right. That would be wonderful.' She paused for a second. 'Oh, my goodness! Did the smoke mess up our lovely new paintwork? I should have looked.'

Grabbing the trolley full of book returns, she almost ran back to where the soldier had been. Screwing up her eyes, she looked at the wall and ceiling but there were no noticeable marks. She relaxed. They might not be allowed to ban smoking in the library, one of the few pleasures people still had, but perhaps they could find a way to discourage it. It was important that the library looked spick and span for the royal visit.

12

The bus ride home from her next WVS shift seemed a blur to Cordelia. She rubbed away the condensation on the window and looked outside, but there was little to see in the blackout. Even if there had been, she was too distracted to notice them.

She took Robert's latest letter out of her bag and read it yet again. Unusually, he sounded in low mood. Parts of his letter were blanked out by the censors, but he'd written about a sandstorm.

The desert has its own dreadful way of testing our resolve. Yesterday a massive sandstorm descended that totally blotted out the sun. We wrapped scarves around our faces and took shelter wherever we could, behind tanks and lorries, in tents. But even so the stinging sand covered us in a thick choking blanket, getting in our eyes, our mouths, and our ears. So difficult for patients who were only just clinging on to life. The heat is bad enough even for the healthy. It is often 120 degrees in the middle of the day. This place is unforgiving, and I look forward to getting some leave. We aren't allowed back home but get sent some-

where else for a break. I don't think that will happen for a while
though.

She thought how unlucky he'd been to be sent so far, when
the bulk of British soldiers were somewhere in Britain. But she
shook herself. It was no good wallowing in self-pity. She was alive
and so were all she loved. That was more than many people
could say.

As she neared her stop, her thoughts became engrossed with
memories of Doreen's bruises, and she didn't register where she
was. Luckily, when they got near her stop, the conductor recognised
her and nudged her.

'You're a million miles away tonight, miss. Be careful out there
in the dark!'

She stepped down from the bus and turned on her shielded
torch. Like most people, she automatically looked at the ground for
fear of tripping over fallen masonry or other debris. Her shaking
hands took three attempts to open her door. She needed a cup of
tea, but instead poured herself a generous glass of whisky before
she even took off her coat. The amber liquid warmed her chest. It
did nothing to ease her thoughts, though.

Restless, she walked up and down her living room, her spirit
caged. She replayed the events of the previous evening over and
over in her mind. Could she have done anything else to help
Doreen? Had she asked about the bruise in the wrong way? Was it
any of her business to get involved? If only she had... but she
couldn't... could she perhaps...

She lit her fire, still too restless to settle, and then, without
conscious thought, tidied the cupboards in the kitchen. They were
already tidy, but she needed to do something with her nervous
energy. As she worked, she lit a cigarette and almost burned her
clumsy fingers with her lighter. Finally, she made a cheese and

tomato sandwich and poured herself another whisky, spilling a dribble down the side of the glass.

She settled herself at the table and propped her latest novel in front of her, *Mr Finchley Takes to the Road*. It was the third in the series and the storylines and funny characters usually made her smile. The day before she'd enjoyed it. But not this time. She read the same page three times. She hadn't taken in a word.

Putting down her book, she picked up a women's magazine, knowing it would be light reading and wouldn't need much concentration. But when she got to the agony aunt page, she changed her mind.

Dear Agony Aunt,

My husband returned from duty a changed man. He used to be gentle and loving but now his temper is short. He has frequent angry outbursts, and he's even hit me a few times. I'm scared for myself and my children who shouldn't have to witness this. What can I do?

Worried Wife

Cordelia knew the type of answer she would read. No matter how badly they were treated, women were expected to support their men and not think of themselves. This reply was no different.

Dear Worried Wife,

These are difficult times that can make any of us behave out of character. Give your attention to providing a calm, comforting home life to soothe your husband's troubled mind. Gently reason with him when he loses his temper. Do nothing to provoke him further. With your patience and prayer, his spirits should lift in time. Keep your own spirits high – our men need us to be strong to support them. My thoughts are with you and your children.

Infuriated, Cordelia ripped the page out of the magazine and tore it up. What nonsense. No wonder she saw so many women in the East End looking careworn. It wasn't just poverty that did that, in some cases it was being beaten as Doreen was or being kept short of money by husbands who spent all their time and money in the pubs.

Mavis sometimes told her about women in similar situations she had helped. One had reported her husband's violence to the police. They made it clear they weren't interested, saying it was a 'family matter'. Her vicar had been no more help, saying she should pray harder. In the end, Mavis helped her pack everything while the woman's husband was in the pub. She escaped to her sister in Wales. He'd been outraged when he came home to an empty house and no dinner on the table. He'd gone all over, knocking on doors, including Mavis's, trying to find out where his wife was. But Mavis was the only one who knew, and she wasn't going to tell him.

Shaking her head at the memory of the story, Cordelia grabbed a piece of paper and a pencil. Anger swirled in her chest like a gathering storm. She'd make a list of things she could do or say to help brave, hard-working Doreen.

* * *

The next two shifts with Doreen and Ann were agony for Cordelia. It was obvious by the careful movements Doreen was making that she was in pain. A certain way she slowly bent to pick up a dropped packet of cigarettes, her face contorting as she rubbed her ribs, a tiny split in her lower lip, all gave away what had happened.

Each time Ann was out of the room, Cordelia tried to speak to her. 'Doreen, please let me help you...' she began. She was immediately stopped by Doreen sharply holding up her hand and avoiding her eye. The second time, Cordelia ignored that gesture.

Her heart pounded in her chest as she seized the opportunity to speak.

'I can see what's happening, Doreen, and I understand you don't want to speak about it.' She paused and looked at her. There was no response. Doreen still avoided her eye, her shoulders slumped. 'But please remember I can help. You can stay with me until you find somewhere to live. I'll help you.'

But her pleading died on her lips.

Doreen finally looked at her. Dark rings circled her eyes. Her usual bold manner gone. Tears fell down her cheeks. She gave a small sob then looked back at the box she was packing.

'I can't...' she began to say, then stopped herself.

Bouncing back in the room, Ann didn't notice the atmosphere. She chatted about the latest dance she'd been to and the gorgeous hunk she'd kissed. Apparently, he was tall, dark and handsome, a dead ringer for Clark Gable. 'I couldn't believe 'e wanted to dance with little old me!' she gushed. 'But I was strong. Only one kiss, I said. 'E kept pleading with them big brown eyes, but I was determined,' she went on, blissfully unaware of Doreen's pain. ''E tried to get his hand up my top, but I soon put a stop to that.' She giggled. 'Got to keep meself pure for Ernest, ain't I?'

She became uncharacteristically quiet for a moment, and it seemed as if the room chilled. Cordelia looked up and saw how Ann's face had dropped. She blew her nose as if to cover up her feelings.

'What is it, Ann?' Cordelia asked. 'Is something wrong?'

Ann bit her lip and shook her head. 'I was just thinking of the last geezer who walked me home after a dance... That's all I wanted him to do. I wasn't offering anything else, was I? I thought he was a gentleman, but...'

'But he wasn't?' Cordelia asked.

'No, 'e wasn't. Not at all. It was dark when we got to our door and I 'ad to fight 'im off. If my big brother 'adn't 'eard me shouting... well... you know...'

Not for the first time, Cordelia thought how comfortable her life had been. She'd had one romance go wrong, badly wrong, but nothing like these two women had experienced.

'Get a police whistle!' Doreen said, her voice harsh. 'That'll make them run, the bastards. And knee them in the crown jewels. That'll give you time to run away.'

Ann clapped her hands. 'Good idea, Doreen, I'll get meself a whistle tomorrow.'

As if that was the end of the conversation, she walked to the wireless, turned it up and began singing along to 'Bless 'Em All'.

'Love this one,' she said, her usual cheery personality back again.

If only Doreen's problem could be fixed that easily, Cordelia thought. She felt helpless in the face of the woman's suffering. She knew the woman was trapped. It was likely she had no savings, few people in Silvertown did. And Cordelia guessed she felt she owed her husband her support because of his injuries.

When Ann was out of earshot again, Cordelia made one last desperate appeal.

'Doreen, no one deserves to be hit, especially not you,' she pleaded. 'Please consider my offer. You can stay with me while you find somewhere to live.'

Doreen lifted her eyes, rimmed red from crying. 'It's... impossible... He'll find me, and it'll be worse than ever.' Her fingers twisted the sleeve of her cardigan. 'He said he'd kill me if I tried to leave him.' Her thin body trembled.

Cordelia reached out and squeezed Doreen's hands. 'I'm here for you if you change your mind.'

Just then, Ann burst back in. 'That's better, I was busting for another wee.' She went over to the kettle. 'Let's 'ave a cuppa.

Anyways I was telling you about this gorgeous 'unk. The one what looks like Clark Gable.'

She rambled on in her innocent, youthful way but the other two women weren't taking in what she had to say.

Their minds were on much more dangerous things.

13

Afraid his leg would stiffen up, Tom got Mavis to take his role at the desk and walked slowly through the stacks to stretch his leg. He loved walking around the library, watching the patrons choose their books, or sit reading. But one man caught his eye. He'd come in five minutes earlier and gone straight to the stacks without coming to the desk first as people usually did.

In the middle of the day, most users were elderly. Later, mums would come in with their children and others would pop in after they'd finished work. But this man looked out of place, he was none of those things.

Tom stopped mid-stride, his eyes narrowing as he watched the man. There was something about the way the skinny chap in the beige macintosh carried himself that made Tom suspicious. All the librarians were alert to theft ever since Cordelia and Mavis had dramatically caught one some time earlier. It was an experience they swore they'd never forget.

The man's eyes shifted around the room, never focusing on one spot for more than a few seconds, and he didn't seem to be looking at the books. Instead, his cigarette hanging out of the side of his mouth, he seemed to be eyeing up the patrons. His movements were jerky too and once or twice he picked up a book, flicked the pages without looking at them and then replaced it. He was obviously planning something.

Gripping his stick tighter, Tom decided to follow the man as best he could. He needed to confirm what he was up to before confronting him. The man kept looking round. Was he checking if he could be seen by Mavis and Jane?

With bated breath, Tom watched as the suspicious man sidled up to Bert. He moved close enough to be able to speak in whispers, impossible to be overheard.

Keeping hidden, Tom strained to see what was going on between them.

The man slyly withdrew a small package from his coat and passed it to Bert, who placed it under his newspaper. Bert nodded, then slipped the man a ten-shilling note and got some coins in return.

It was a black marketeer operating in the library!

He was selling cigarettes!

None of Tom's working life had prepared him for this sort of situation. Should he tackle the man? Go to get the police? Wait by the door and grab him when he tried to leave?

Wishing he could walk easily, Tom followed the man, feeling like a clumsy detective. It was impossible to walk silently with a stick.

The man continued to look around surreptitiously and then went over to another library user who was smoking. The same exchange happened.

It was enough to be sure.

Spotting Mavis nearby, Tom subtly signalled to her to join him.

'This man there, the one in the trench coat, he's selling black market ciggies. Bert just bought some,' he whispered. 'I'd see him off, but I can't run with this damn stick.'

Nothing if not brave, Mavis placed a steadying hand on his shoulder.

'Leave it to me,' she whispered. 'I've seen 'im around before. I've handled bigger crooks than 'im when I worked behind a bar.'

Tom was alarmed. The last thing the library needed was a scene.

'We need to handle this delicately,' he said, knowing that Mavis didn't do delicacy.

She simply squared her shoulders, raised an eyebrow, and marched towards the unsuspecting black marketeer. Tom thought he'd be frightened if he was the spiv.

'Oy, you!' she said, looking the crook in the eye. 'I see what you're up to, mate, and you've come to the wrong bloody place.' Mavis made no attempt to keep her voice down and everyone nearby turned round to see what was happening.

The man looked up, startled, then looked her up and down as if assessing his chances if he tackled her.

'Don't even think about it,' she said, her hands on her hips. 'I've dealt with bigger narks than you. Now, go on, 'op it or I'll call the Old Bill.'

She pulled a police whistle out of her pocket and made as if she was going to blow it.

'Always a copper around 'ere,' she said.

The man looked from her to Tom who now stood beside her, holding his stick as if it were a weapon.

'You heard what she said. Go on, clear off.'

The man sneered at them, then spat on the floor.

'I bet you're not above grabbing a pair of stockings, either of you,' he hissed. Then he wrapped his coat around himself and strode off towards the door. 'You ain't seen the last of me!'

Mavis went over to where Bert was reading his newspaper. 'Bert, I'm disappointed in you, buying illegal fags 'ere. This is an honest place.'

In response, Bert pulled a packet of Senior Service out of his pocket, a more expensive brand than his usual Woodbines. Opening the pack, he offered Mavis one. 'Yeah, but I can resist everything but temptation. Or a bargain!'

'We all like a bargain,' Mavis replied. 'But do your dealing some-where else or I'll 'ave to forbid you from coming 'ere and we don't want that any more than you do.'

Suppressing a smile, Mavis went back to the desk. And some people thought working in a library must be boring!

14

The black eye was the last straw, the purplish swelling harsh against Doreen's pale skin. Doreen had attempted to cover it up with make-up and by pulling her hair over it. Despite that, it was obvious.

Ann took one look at it and squealed. 'Cor, Doreen, you been in the wars. What 'appened to you?' She laughed. 'Don't tell me you walked into a door, neither!'

Was she really that naïve? Cordelia wondered. Did she understand what she was saying? She noticed Doreen flinch at Ann's words and could see the pain and humiliation on her face.

Cordelia thought back to her own parents. Her father could often be distracted by his responsibilities and sometimes short-tempered. He had never hit any of the family, though, and yet again she thought how lucky she was.

'No, not a doorpost,' Doreen mumbled. 'I fell over in the black-out. Hit my face on a kerb.'

If it wasn't for the previous bruises, Cordelia might have believed her. The blackout was responsible for many accidents, some of them fatal. When her boyfriend Robert worked in the accident department, he had often talked about patients he'd seen who had suffered terrible injuries because of the darkness.

No, she wasn't fooled by Doreen's explanation.

She'd talked to Mavis about the situation one recent grey day at the library. Mavis knew everything that went on in Silvertown, and she'd immediately shaken her head when Cordelia explained Doreen's bruises.

'Can't say I'm surprised. Word on the street is 'e was a changed bloke after that accident at the docks.' She stopped speaking to tie her worn shoelaces, then groaned and rubbed her back as she straightened up again. 'Don't know if 'e had a knock on the 'ead or something. Doesn't work, but 'e goes down the Baker's Arms every night so I 'ear. Gets bladdered.'

Her words played on Cordelia's mind as the three women continued packing boxes for the troops for the rest of their shift. Even the wireless playing in the background couldn't lift the mood in the room. If it was true, Doreen's husband must be drinking away all her hard-earned money. She was quieter than usual, and the atmosphere was strained. Not even Ann's endless chatter made things better.

'What'll I write in a note for this box?' she asked several times. 'How about "Roses are red, violets are blue, I'm gorgeous, I bet you are too"? Then "Remember to write to your mum, she loves you". And "Keep your pecker up!"' She chuckled at her own jokes, not noticing the others' silence.

No matter how many times Doreen ignored Cordelia's offers of help, she was going to have a conversation with her about it.

She waited until their shift finished and kept Doreen talking until Ann had gone.

When Doreen walked towards the door, Cordelia blocked it, arms wide, face determined. Her mouth was dry, but she promised herself that this time she and Doreen would have a conversation about the poor woman's situation.

* * *

'This is where we get off,' Cordelia said when their bus slowed, its brakes hissing as it pulled up to the bus stop. Doreen hadn't spoken a word all the way from the community centre. She clutched her small cardboard suitcase tight, her eyes firmly fixed on her scuffed shoes. Now she stepped from the bus, her eyes darting about as if she expected to be captured at any moment.

On a nearby corner, the newspaper vendor was shouting, 'Roosevelt proclaims war on Germany! Read all about it. The Yanks are coming.' It was the news everyone was hoping to hear. Britain was on its knees after two years of bombing and shortages, but the two women were too worn out to take in the news.

Each had worked a full day then done the shift for the WVS. Feet aching, they set out on the darkened streets, the only lights being from shielded torches and car headlights. As they walked, they heard a piano being played in one house, a row going on in another, and a baby crying in the third.

They almost bumped into an air-raid warden checking each house had followed blackout instructions.

'Go careful, girls,' he muttered as he passed them.

Cordelia could see from Doreen's tense body language that she felt uncomfortable. She'd been reluctant to accept Cordelia's offer of help and Cordelia hadn't known if she would agree to stay in her flat.

But the suitcase Doreen had brought with her that evening told Cordelia that she had finally decided to leave her violent husband.

Cordelia put her arm through Doreen's. 'I expect this is difficult for you,' she said. 'But I've got a spare room. Just a box room really, but the bed is comfortable. If you're anything like me, you'll feel a lot better after a good night's sleep.'

They continued through the echoing streets, arm in arm for support. Someone cycled by, swerving this way and that to avoid potholes and cursing loud enough to wake the dead. The Crown and Cushion sounded as if it was doing a roaring trade as they passed, despite the shortage of beer.

'Not far now,' Cordelia said, leading Doreen around a corner to her road. It was one of the few in Silvertown that had had no bombing.

Fumbling in the dark, she got her key out of her bag and let them both in the outer door, up a flight of stairs then into her flat.

'Make yourself comfortable,' she said, taking her coat off and turning to light the fire. 'This place soon warms up. I'll make us some tea.'

Doreen hovered in the doorway, looking round at the living room. By the standards of Cordelia's family, it was simple and sparsely furnished, but to Doreen it was luxury she'd never experienced in her life. Slowly, as if she couldn't believe she should be there, she put down her case and took off her coat.

'It's very nice here,' she finally said, her voice trembling. 'Me and Albert live in two rooms in a grotty house.' She sighed. 'Not much choice with so many places bombed to smithereens.'

'Would you like a cuppa, or some wine?' Cordelia asked.

'Um, you got any beer?' Doreen reddened.

Cordelia looked in a cupboard. 'I've only got one bottle, I'm afraid. I hope it's okay. You can have it. I'll have something else.'

She reached into one of the kitchen drawers for an opener, popped the top off and handed it to Doreen with a glass.

'I'm afraid I can only offer you a sandwich. Cheese or ham. And I've got some nice pickle to go with it. I get it from Rathbone market.'

'Sounds just the ticket. I'm putting you to a lot of trouble.' Doreen twisted her hands together as she spoke. 'Cheese'll do me, please.'

A few minutes later, they were sitting at the small kitchen table, sandwiches and drinks in front of them.

'Thanks for inviting me,' Doreen said, not looking Cordelia in the eye.

'I'm just so glad you're here. And I've never asked you,' Cordelia said, picking up her sandwich. 'Do you have any children?'

The corners of Doreen's mouth turned down. She looked wistful and toyed with her glass.

'No. I'd'a liked a couple, but it just never happened. Dunno why. Too late now.' She paused and her bottom lip trembled. 'I got in the family way a couple of times but couldn't keep them. Lost both of them at three months. Slipped away before I ever got to hold them. Me mother-in-law, witch that she is, said it's 'cos I work too hard.' Her jaw clenched before she continued. 'Like we'd have money for the rent or food if I didn't work, silly bugger.' She shook her head. 'Don't suppose I'll 'old a babe of me own now.'

Reaching over, Cordelia held her hand for a minute. 'That's so sad. I can't imagine the pain you've been through. Well, both of you.'

'Huh! You'd think so, wouldn't you? But me old man never wanted none. Never got an ounce, not a single ounce, of sympathy when it 'appened.' For the first time, she looked directly at Cordelia. 'You gonna 'ave any?'

The question made Cordelia think instantly of Robert, working there in North Africa. Tending to the sick and injured in awful conditions. His letters made light of things, telling funny stories about his colleagues and the awful food, but she could read between the lines.

'I don't know. I've got a special man in my life, but we won't be able to think about that until after the war.'

Doreen swallowed the last bite of her sandwich. 'If it ever ends. What if them bloody Nazis invade, and we all have to live under Hitler's thumb? Some Jews I know're already shaking in their boots. Plenty in the East End.'

When they'd finished, Cordelia put the kettle on.

'It's getting late. Shall we have a cuppa before bedtime?'

She turned and saw that Doreen was taking off her wedding ring. She thrust it in her handbag and snapped it shut.

'Shoulda done that years ago.'

Over tea, she told Cordelia that her husband, Albert, was okay until his accident.

'He was never God's gift, but no worse than most in the East End. Gave me me housekeeping every week. Less his booze money, of course. Didn't matter what 'e earned, 'e always 'ad enough for beer. But after the accident...'

'He changed?'

She nodded. 'I feel terrible even moaning about him. It's not his fault. That accident did something to his head. It changed 'im.' She looked up. 'Can I have a glass of water, please?'

She continued to speak as Cordelia fetched the drink.

'I should probably stay with him. It's not his fault... But 'e gets so mad if I don't bring him ciggies every day...'

Cordelia put the glass down firmly, spilling a few drops on the tabletop.

'He could have got help,' she said. 'I don't think you should blame yourself. Anyway, you've got plenty of years ahead of you. You can't stay in a dangerous relationship for the rest of your life.'

Doreen sipped the water, thinking about her guilt and how many of the people she knew would condemn her for leaving Albert. So many women put up with terrible lives. And worse, they often criticised others who tried to escape them. To find a better life without fear and injury.

'That's what I think. So I've thought and thought and I've made a big decision.'

Outside, a car backfired, making them both jump, then smile at their nervousness.

'I think we get a bit nervous about any loud noises these days,' Cordelia said. 'It's no wonder really.'

Doreen reached down to her suitcase, put it on her knee and opened it. 'I couldn't bring much with me, but I made a carrot cake. Perhaps we could have some with our cuppa now.'

Inside the case, Cordelia could see a photo of Doreen and Albert together, and sadly, a baby rattle.

'So you've really left him then?'

'I 'ave. I told you I've made a big decision. I'm going to... Tomorrow I'm going to... I'm going to join up!' She slapped one hand on the table. 'I've decided. I'm going to join the ATS.'

Cordelia couldn't have been more surprised if Doreen had said she was flying to the moon. 'But don't you have to get a letter of permission from your husband before they'll take you?'

Reaching into her handbag, Doreen took out the wedding ring she had just removed from her left hand.

'I'm never wearing this again and I'm not telling them I've ever been married, neither. None of their bloody business, excuse my swearing.' Doreen twisted her handkerchief, choosing her words with care. 'Joining up's the only way to escape from Albert. Once he realises I've gone, 'e'll come looking for me. Even if I 'id away somewhere else in London, 'e'd keep 'unting me. I'd be looking over my shoulder all day long. This gives me a chance to start fresh, be someone new.' She glanced at Cordelia, her eyes shining for the first time. 'I never 'ad much schooling. The ATS'll learn me some new skills, do work to 'elp us win the war. And my wages'll be mine to spend, not wasted down that damn pub.'

Doreen paused, her smile fading.

'I wish me'n Albert could've got old together, but living like we have is killing me. I've almost forgotten who I am.' She reached for Cordelia's hand and squeezed it briefly. 'They say when one door closes, another opens. I keep reminding meself of that.'

'Goodness, so you won't be staying with me long,' Cordelia said, struggling to fully absorb this news. 'But of course you can stay as long as you like.'

'It'll only be a few days. I've been and talked to them at the recruiting office. Once you're signed up, they take you real fast. I'll go off to some training camp. Bed and all meals provided. Sounds like heaven to me.'

15

'Oh dear, did I say her name was Maggie?' Mrs Shaw said, frowning as she tried to remember. 'I get so muddled up these days.'

Jane was helping with the IIP team, assisting people who sought news of their loved ones missing after bombing. Mrs Shaw was her first customer and because of her confusion, this appointment seemed likely to take all morning.

'Could her name have been Margaret?' Jane asked, aware of the queue growing by the minute. 'Do you know where she lives?'

'It was Dock Road, I think.' The old lady paused. 'No, that was my brother, he's long gone. It must be Connaught Street.'

As she was speaking, Jane was checking the lists of people whose whereabouts were known. Was it only an hour ago that she had been asked to volunteer?

'Do you think you could help us, Jane?' Mrs Walton, the IIP coordinator had said as soon as the library opened. She looked at Jane imploringly. 'You know about our work, I'm sure. We are the Missing Relatives Bureau. Our task is to help locate people who have gone missing for one reason or another.'

Jane nodded. She had seen the IIP volunteers post up lists of people whose whereabouts they knew. Those lists showed whether the person was dead, missing or moved to a known address. The same lists were in a book on a table in the area and in lists in front of each volunteer. The idea was that people confident enough to look the information up for themselves could do so. But not everyone in the East End was literate, especially older people. Jane's own landlady could read and write, but it was a struggle for her. And other people were too scared to look in case the news was bad. They needed the support the volunteers could offer.

'You get people coming in who are looking for their loved ones, don't you?' Jane said.

Mrs Walton nodded. 'That's right, and today two volunteers can't come so that only leaves me. It simply won't work. The queue would be halfway down the road and if someone gets upset...'

'I've heard that happen.' Jane remembered seeing an elderly man saying he might as well be dead. He'd just learned that his only child had died. It was common for people to be talking about what they learned as they walked through the lending room on their way out of the building. Some were joyful with relief, while others had no news or the news they dreaded.

'I don't mind helping, but I'm not trained or anything.' As usual, she was underestimating her own abilities.

'But I've seen how you manage people in the library. They're not always easy, are they? I've admired how you handle things.' Mrs Walton looked around. 'I see all your colleagues are in today so even if they can only spare you for an hour or two it would be so helpful.'

Jane's stomach had twisted with anxiety as she considered the IIP task. Part of her longed to help the poor souls seeking any shred of news about their missing loved ones. She knew if it were her own family, she would be frantic for answers. But she worried she might not be strong enough to cope with the anguish of those who got the worst imaginable news. How would she able to maintain composure while giving such dreadful information? Would she be able to hold back her own tears? Worse still, what if she made a mistake that gave false hope or led to more pain? The weight of responsibility felt unbearable.

But Jane remembered the words of her kind landlady: 'Do all the good you can every day.' She knew it would be the right thing to do, no matter how difficult. She wanted to provide warmth and care when people needed it most. A listening ear might be all she could offer, but that could count for a lot and the truth was she often had to provide that in the library. Despite her swirling concerns, Jane agreed to the request.

'But I'll have to check the others can cover for me.'

'That would be wonderful,' Mrs Walton said. 'Our work is so vital for people. It must be awful for them not knowing what has happened to their loved ones.'

Half an hour later, she had her first 'customer', Mrs Shaw. She wore a brown wool coat, skilfully patched in several places. On her head was a knitted brown and white hat. The wrinkles on her face spoke of a lifetime of hardship.

'I'm afraid I can't find a Maggie or Margaret at either of those addresses,' Jane said, keeping her voice gentle. 'Could it be another niece you're thinking of?'

Behind her, a burly man was tapping one foot and checking his watch, but Jane had been told to ignore people in the queue and concentrate on the person in front of her.

Mrs Shaw put her hankie to her mouth. 'Oh dear, oh dear. I'm in such a muddle...'

'Mrs Shaw,' Jane said. 'Would you like to go and sit in the library while you think about it? Or in the café along the road? You can always come back in a few minutes.'

The elderly lady nodded and stood up, grunting, and leaning

heavily on her stick. 'You're a very kind girl,' she said, bending over and patting Jane's cheek. 'I'll go and get a cup of Rosie Lea and come back.'

When she'd gone, the burly man took her place.

'Josie Turner,' he said, his voice harsh. Jane wondered if he was always so unpleasant or if worry had made him like this.

'Do you have an address?' She turned her lists back to the beginning.

'Three Albert Road. She's me girl.'

Jane checked her records, looking by name and by address. 'I'm so sorry, but we don't have a record of her.'

'What!' he started, but she held up her hand.

'The latest bombing was only last night, as you know,' Jane said, struggling to keep her voice firm when it wanted to wobble. 'We get information from a number of places and sometimes it can take a few days to reach us.'

He put his hands on his hips. 'So I gotta come back, I suppose. I'm a working man, you know. It's costing me to come down 'ere.'

Jane could just hear the laughter of children inside the library. It was story time, and Tom was clearly making sure they enjoyed the book he was reading to them. The sound made her think of her Helen and wish she could be with her instead of giving people bad news.

'I'm sorry, Mr... Oh, I don't know your name.'

The man thumped his fist on her table, making it shudder. 'You're no bloody 'elp at all.' And with that he stormed out, almost pushing over the woman behind him.

Jane took a sip of water from the glass on her desk and breathed deeply to compose herself before smiling a welcome at the next woman in line.

'Bet you could do without blokes like 'im,' the woman said, struggling to smile through her worry. 'I'm looking for Jim Taylor,

Canning Town Road. He's my brother and I'm so worried about him. 'Is place 'as been flattened, not a stick standing. My last relative 'e is, I got no one else.'

How could the IIP volunteers do this day in, day out? It was heartbreaking. But as Jane flipped through her records, her mood lifted.

'I've found him! Here he is. He's gone to the reception centre in Canning Town. It's Barking Road School Centre. You should be able to get a bus there.'

The woman looked as if she might faint with relief and the friend she was with put her arm round her.

'There,' she said. 'I told you he'd be okay. Right as ninepence like always.'

The hours passed in a blur as Jane remained stationed at the IIP's missing persons' desk. Each enquiry blended into the next, though she gave her full focus to every person. There was the elderly gentleman searching for his son, whose name Jane finally located on a hospital casualty list. Relaying the tragic news felt like a punch to her own stomach. She'd paused, blinking rapidly to clear the tears that stung her eyes, before she continued in a quiet, steady voice.

Later, a sister desperately seeking her little brother broke down when Jane had no details to offer, only hollow apologies and promises to keep trying. The girl released a harrowing sob, folding herself over as her friend stroked her hair, helpless to console the anguish.

Not all was sorrow, though – she had the honour of confirming survivors too. Like telling an anxious wife her husband had safely turned up at an aid shelter. The woman's face had flooded with relief, her shaking hands covering her mouth as joyful tears trickled down her cheeks.

Still, after delivering the fourth death notice that day, Jane felt darkness creeping in. The hours passed in a haze of cigarette smoke and quiet misery. Each tragic confirmation felt like a blow, the searcher's raw grief piercing Jane's heart.

Nearing lunchtime, she desperately needed a few minutes' break.

'Excuse me, I need to go to the ladies',' she whispered to Mrs Walton.

Mavis saw her going in and waited for her to come out.

'You look white as a sheet,' she said. 'Come and sit down for a minute, catch your breath.'

Her sympathy was almost too much when Jane was just about holding herself together.

'Tell me something funny,' she said. Anything to get her thoughts away from giving bad news.

'Well,' Mavis said, struggling to keep a straight face. 'An hour ago I 'eard a strange scuttling sound. I thought it must be rats or something.'

'What was it? Was it rats?'

Mavis shook her head. 'It only turned out that blinkin' Bert had brought 'is favourite ferret with 'im. Damn thing escaped and got into old Mrs Watkins's big bag. Must 'ave been looking for a snack, I reckon.'

Jane's mouth dropped open. 'Goodness. She must have been horrified.'

'Not a bit of it. Seems her old man used to keep 'em and she just took it out of 'er bag and stroked it!'

The story was just what Jane needed. She walked back towards the IIP section feeling she could manage whatever news she had to give.

By the end of her shift, she had given four people the worst news possible, while four more were left with agonising uncertainty. Even with the number of people she gave good news to, exhaustion overwhelmed her. Her mind was full of images of weeping mothers, stoic fathers and orphaned children.

Mrs Walton thanked her profusely when they finished.

'This is heartbreaking work, I know, but it is so valuable to the people who come in, even if the news is bad.'

Jane was still struggling to calm the feelings she seemed to have absorbed from the people she'd seen. 'I couldn't do this every day like you do. You and your volunteers deserve a medal.'

As they were tidying away their papers, Jane overheard Mavis's voice from the next room and remembered an earlier conversation.

'Mrs Walton,' she said. 'My colleague is hoping to adopt a little orphan. Her mother died in some bombing, and she has nothing at all of hers. Mavis would love something to give her to help her remember her mother. Is there any way she could find out if there was anything?'

Mrs Walton shuffled her papers and put them in a box, closing the lid tight.

'She might just be lucky. Undertakers remove any jewellery or other objects, and they are sent to the local authorities for storage. She could try there.'

It was a long shot, but Jane knew Mavis would try anything to help little Joyce.

When Mrs Walton left, Jane should have gone straight into the main library which didn't close for a couple more hours, but she needed to be alone to deal with all the emotions she had experienced.

Stepping outside, she turned her face skyward, letting the cool air spread over her. She raised her arms and imagined stars raining down on her, washing away the sadness. She said a silent prayer for all those seeking answers she hadn't been able to provide, hoping that the next day the information they sought would be available.

Tomorrow would bring new searches, new sorrows. But now,

this moment was hers alone. Despite the hustle and bustle of the East End around her, Jane breathed in the air and exhaled her pain.

Then, shoulders back, she turned back towards the library, looking forward to closing time when she could return home to her daughter and give her a hug that would heal the day's sorrows.

16
_____

'I've done everything you asked to get people to support the drive for clothes and toys for East Enders,' Cordelia's mother said. 'Of course, I haven't told your father. He believes everyone should be able to look after their own affairs.'

Cordelia's father blustered his political opinions to anyone who would listen. Cordelia imagined her father's reaction. His face crimson. Blood pressure spiking.

'He'd have a stroke if he knew,' she said.

She looked at her mother fondly. The majority of their manor house had been taken over by the army for use as a convalescent home. Cordelia's father was still furious about it, but her mother was transformed. Initially only planning to read to blind soldiers, she'd become quite involved with the hospital.

'Do you know,' her mother said, 'helping at the convalescent hospital has opened my eyes to so many things I wasn't aware of before.'

She opened her handbag and, taking out a cotton hankie, wiped her face as if expecting a tear.

Cordelia was already aware of her mother's changing attitudes but was curious to know exactly what she'd learned.

'What sort of things, Mother?'

Her mother's face turned pink. 'Well, you know we live quite a... how shall I put it... restricted life. Only meeting people like us and so on.'

As she wondered how to express what she wanted to say, she looked out of the window at the clouds scudding quickly by and the trees swaying in the wind.

'I suppose, if I'm honest, and I'm ashamed to admit this, I've always thought some people, those who weren't wealthy, were inferior somehow. Uneducated or lazy.'

Cordelia had to bite her lip as she listened to her mother. How often had she heard those sentiments expressed over the dinner table or tea? How often had her parents frowned on her if she tried to put across another point of view?

'Now,' her mother continued, 'I've realised that a lot of the men are very bright and very motivated. They simply haven't had the advantages people in our class have had.'

Cordelia struggled to stop herself from clapping as she heard these words. Finally, her mother's eyes were being opened.

'And,' her mother added, 'seeing the men get free medical care when the rest of the population doesn't made me realise we need some sort of universal scheme.'

So many graves in the cemeteries in Silvertown and Canning Town were testament to the effects of poverty. With harsh working conditions, poor homes and no money to pay doctors, many died before their time.

'You're right, Mother. We're very privileged. Even living in a small part of our home, we have so much more than many people.'

From Cordelia's point of view, the wing of the house they now occupied was much more reasonable, much cosier than rattling about in the whole property, never using half the rooms. She glanced out of the tall mullioned windows where pale winter light fell on the thick oriental rug in front of the fireplace. The view from here couldn't be more different from the view anyone in Silvertown would experience. A graceful garden, much of it given over to growing vegetables, a background of tall trees, birdsong and rabbits and even the occasional deer appearing shyly to look around.

Her mother opened her handbag and took out a long piece of paper, the diamonds on her bejewelled hands glinting in the light of the lamp on the elegant side table beside her.

'I put up notices round the village as you suggested, but I had some ideas of my own.'

As she spoke, her face glowed with pride. Married to a wealthy landowner, she had never been expected to do much more than be a wife and run the household.

'That's great, Mother,' Cordelia said, the aroma from black tea and a hint of cinnamon drifting up from her cup as she lifted it to her lips. 'I'm so grateful for all that you're doing. The people of Silvertown will be too.'

Her mother put on her glasses, pushed them up her nose and read from her list. 'I got the vicar to read out the request for good-quality toys and children's clothes in church.' She paused. 'I had a word about a contribution to the roof appeal, and he read out my exact wording three times. He also spoke to the mothers' meeting.'

She sighed, smoothing her dress.

'It's been very difficult for your father to adjust to the army taking over so much of the house. He still grumbles about it frequently. If he knew half of what I've been doing, he'd be very cross.'

Cordelia could imagine her father's response: 'That is not suitable work for a lady in your position. I insist you stop this minute!'

A smile played on her mother's lips. She leaned forward

conspiratorially. 'I must admit I've surprised myself. These changes have shown there is more to me than even I thought.' Resolve hardened her voice as she continued. 'I've decided that your father will just have to accept the work I'm doing. It's given me more satisfaction than I've had for a very long time.'

At that moment, Mrs Taylor, the family cook, knocked on the door and entered, smelling faintly of rosemary and stewing lamb.

'What time would you like luncheon?' she asked. She smiled at Cordelia as she spoke.

'Perhaps in about an hour,' Cordelia's mother replied, barely looking up from her list. She waited until Mrs Taylor had gone before she spoke again. 'Once upon a time, she'd never have come in here herself. A maid would have done it. But they've all gone off to work in factories and the like. I ask you, why would they do that? The work must be very unpleasant and noisy.'

Cordelia bit back a response. Working fourteen hours a day for a rich family with exacting standards who never gave a word of praise was probably much worse. Paid less too.

'Things are changing, Mother,' she said. 'It's a blessing you have smaller premises to look after.'

She thought about the lives of the women of Silvertown. Many worked in the factories that skirted the Thames, others did a range of jobs once done by men – farm work, civil defence, postal workers, bank clerks, construction, bus driving.

'Women are working more now, just like during the Great War,' Cordelia said. 'Do you remember my friend Rosalind?'

Her mother frowned as she tried to place the girl. 'Oh, yes, could be charming, but rather spoiled, I always thought. Flighty.'

Cordelia didn't like to say so, but she agreed with her mother's summation. Rosalind had always had money to splash around and used to be very insensitive about how she did so.

'Well, Mother, she's a bus driver now. And she does it every bit as well as a man.'

Her mother pushed her glasses up her nose again. 'Ha! Tell your father that. He'd be very upset. Anyway, where was I? Oh, yes. I went to the headmistress of the village school.'

Cordelia had never been allowed to go there. Instead, her parents had a governess for her and her brother until they were old enough to go to boarding school. How she'd envied the children when they drove past the school, out playing with each other, laughing and running about. None of the restrictions to behave like a young lady that held her back from truly having an enjoyable childhood.

'Yes,' her mother continued. 'Mrs Essex must be eighty if she's a day, but she still keeps that school running like clockwork. She has held a special assembly and asked the children to donate their cast-off clothes and toys.' She looked at her hands as if appraising them. 'She phoned me only yesterday to say I'll be delighted with how much they will bring to the village hall tomorrow. Perhaps my biggest success is asking all my friends to donate any clothes their children have grown out of. They are excellent quality, of course.'

As she spoke, they could hear the sound of singing coming from the hospital part of the building. Noticing Cordelia's interest, her mother inclined her head in the direction of the singing.

'Matron believes it helps to strengthen the men's lungs,' she said. 'And it's quite a pleasant sound, so I don't complain.'

The little clock on the mantlepiece chimed the hour.

'Anyway, my dear. We must go and get ready. I've got a team of volunteers preparing the village hall, but of course I want to help. I assume you'll be coming too.'

'I wouldn't miss it for the world.'

Little did they know that things wouldn't go as smoothly as they expected.

17

Cordelia could hardly contain her excitement as the family chauffeur drove her and her mother down the winding country lanes towards the village. As they went through the countryside, it was alive with autumn colours. The trees they passed showed off their leaves of crimson, gold and yellow. Gusts of wind sent the leaves into a merry jig, pirouetting and leaping until, exhausted, they collapsed onto the cold ground below. Soon, the woods gave way to open fields divided by ancient hedgerows where sparrows hopped and looked for tasty treats. In the distance, farmers rode their tractors over fields already empty of their bounty and geese honked overhead as they left the country for warmer climates.

'Can you smell that bonfire?' her mother asked. 'It'll soon be Guy Fawkes Night.'

Her words reminded Cordelia of that special night in November when villagers built a big bonfire on the village green, and children begged for old clothes to make a straw-filled Guy to burn atop it.

'We can't have a bonfire in the library, of course,' she replied. 'But Tom is very creative, and he's got something special planned for 5 November. I'm not sure what yet, but he's promised local children will be involved.'

As they neared the village hall, Cordelia was astonished to see the bustle of activity outside. There was a big banner pleading 'Donate your toys and clothes here!' and children were playing hopscotch and skipping, full of life and energy.

'Mother,' she said, her eyes full of gratitude. 'Look what you've done! You're a marvel.'

Her mother smiled. 'It's wonderful to feel I'm doing something useful for the war effort, even if it is only reading to the soldiers and arranging this event.'

Cordelia had often felt sorry for her mother when her father was being difficult, when he was exploding about something the government had or hadn't done, or when a tenant was late paying their rent. Cordelia had sometimes noticed how skilled her mother was at calming him down, but for the first time she realised how much this must have cost her – a woman who never said what her views were on such things, or contradicted her husband when he was red in the face with rage.

And she had never wondered before if her mother would have liked a different life. She was an intelligent woman, there was no doubt about that, and ran the house like clockwork. But if she had been born later, perhaps she wouldn't have married when expected to do so. She might even have had a career of her own.

'Mum, you must give yourself credit for all you've achieved. I'm so proud of you.'

Her mother leaned over and squeezed her hand. 'Thank you, darling. You're very kind to say that.'

As they pulled up outside the village hall, Mrs Essex, the elderly headmistress, hurried towards them. 'We are so very glad to see you, Lady Carmichael and Lady Cordelia. We have had a wonderful response to our appeal.'

The vicar stood chatting with the postman, who had a large parcel under his arm. A gaggle of Girl Guides in their smart uniforms directed people who had come with donations to the right part of the hall. Inside, the chatter of so many people competed with the jolly tunes being played on a piano at the back of the hall. On the stage were two vases full of crimson winter berries that must have been plucked from the hedgerows.

Looking round, Cordelia gasped. There were trestle tables lining the walls and every one was covered with donations – toys, clothes, jigsaw puzzles, games and books. Local people milled about, admiring the collections and adding last-minute items.

'We also got donations from two nearby villages,' her mother said, seeing Cordelia's gaze.

Cordelia went to a table where a variety of hand-knitted gloves and scarves lay. She ran her hand over a bright blue scarf, imagining the sound of clicking needles as industrious hands made the lovely garment.

Suddenly, the noise of the kitchen hatch being thrust open caught everyone's attention. The smell of freshly baked cakes drifted through, making Cordelia's mouth water.

'Right, ladies and youngsters,' a plump woman wearing a felt hat called out. 'Tea and cakes. Come and get them!'

Cordelia knew that Mrs Taylor and another local woman had been busy for days making the cakes, so they would be delicious.

'I can hardly believe my eyes,' Cordelia's mother said, placing a gloved hand on her daughter's arm. 'Most of these people have very little, yet they have contributed so much.' She paused and looked wistful. 'I wish your father were here to see this.' Then she shook her head. 'I probably shouldn't say this, but he would probably find something negative to say about it.'

Mrs Essex appeared beside them with a tray carrying cups of tea and a small selection of cakes.

'Why don't you have a sit down and have this?' she said. 'Mind, everyone'll want to come and talk to you.'

At that moment, the pianist, who had been playing gently up until then, struck up a loud chord and the village choir launched into a rousing rendition of 'Pack Up Your Troubles in Your Old Kit Bag'.

'Come and see everything when you've drunk your tea!' Mrs Essex said. 'It'll give you a chance to say hello to all the helpers.'

By the end of the tour, seeing so many wonderful donations, Cordelia's heart was full to bursting. Some children had brought simple toys whittled by their grandfathers – little cars, spinning tops and wooden dolls dressed from scraps of fabric and wool. Other wooden contributions were beautifully made animals, so realistic they looked as if they could walk off any minute. Then there were half a dozen little kits each containing a wooden dolly peg and enough wool and fabric scraps for the recipient to make their own doll. And most valuable of all were clothes of all sizes. All had been worn previously and many were repaired here and there but they would be gratefully received by the East Enders.

There was a little stage at one end of the hall that was used for the very occasional theatrical production, but more often for giving prizes for the best vegetables in show. Mrs Essex stepped onto this raised platform and clapped her hands. The noise in the room lessened.

'Can I have your attention, please, everyone. You have all done such a wonderful job and I've asked Lady Cordelia to say a few words about how these donations will be distributed.'

Her heart pounding, Cordelia mounted the four steps and turned to see the whole hall full of people waiting to hear from her.

'The first thing I must do,' she said, her voice ringing out to reach all corners of the room, 'is to give you thanks for your incredible generosity today. When my mother and I first talked about this event, I have to be honest and say I wondered if such a small village could make such an impact.'

A voice from the back shouted, 'We're small but we're big too!'

'You are indeed,' Cordelia said. 'And you've shown you've got big hearts. Your kindness has surpassed even my wildest dreams. People in the East End have suffered so much. It is one of the poorest boroughs in London and the one that suffered the most in the Blitz. Hundreds died and many more lost their homes and all their belongings. The toys, clothes and other items you've donated will go a long way to brightening Christmas for the children of Silvertown. But there is some exciting news—'

She was mid-sentence when the crowd was suddenly parted and a tall, thin woman wielding an umbrella strode through.

'Let me through, out of my way!' she cried. Her footsteps heavier than expected because of her size, she stomped up the stairs onto the stage. Her grey woollen stockings gathered round her bony ankles.

Before Cordelia could react, the woman pushed her aside and stood in the centre of the stage.

'Thank you, dear, I'll take over from here.' She turned to the audience. 'You all know me, I'm Mrs Grundy, chairwoman of the Ladies' Benevolent Society, and I've been left more or less alone to organise all of this.'

She waved her arm about to demonstrate the donated goods.

Cordelia stood still, amazed at the woman's interruption as she launched into a lengthy, rambling speech about proper etiquette for donations. She criticised the way blankets and sheets had been folded and those who donated well-worn items.

It was all lies.

It was insulting.

But Mrs Grundy was interrupted.

'Get off the stage, you old hag!' a farmer wearing a cloth cap shouted. 'Let Lady Cordelia speak.'

But his words didn't have any effect. Mrs Grundy just continued.

'Do you seriously think we should send our tattered rubbish to the poor people of Silvertown? They probably own better than some of the donations I've seen.'

The murmur in the crowd got louder as people shuffled.

'Dreadful woman.'

'How dare she!'

Cordelia had heard enough. She stepped forward. Gently, she pushed the woman aside. The hall became quiet again. She gave her mother a nod. Without speaking, her mother understood her meaning. Placing herself between Cordelia and Mrs Grundy, firmly she edged the woman to the side of the stage.

'Thank you for your input,' Cordelia said. 'But as you know this wonderful event has been a joint effort involving many people from the village. They have done a sterling job.'

The hall erupted in applause as Cordelia resumed her speech. Mrs Grundy stomped back down the stairs, huffing loudly. She stood right at the front of the crowd, where Cordelia could hardly miss her, her arms folded across her chest.

'I won't take up much more of your time,' Cordelia began.

'How are you getting this lot to London then?' Mrs Grundy asked, her penetrating voice reaching all corners of the hall. 'It won't fit in that posh car of your father's.'

A gruff voice spoke up from just inside the door.

'That's all arranged. I've got my lorry here to take it all back.'

Mrs Grundy put her hands on her hips and turned to the man. 'And who, may I ask, are you?'

Cordelia answered, speaking to everyone. 'This is the wonderful Mr Hubbard. He's a builder from Silvertown and has been helping the library prepare for very special visitors. Now he has kindly given up his day and his petrol allowance to collect all your generous donations. Let's give him a big round of applause.'

When the clapping died down, Mrs Grundy shouted out again. 'What's this special event then?'

Cordelia wanted to jump off the stage and throttle the woman. Her hands would easily fit round her scrawny neck. For a second, she imagined doing exactly that, seeing Mrs Grundy's eyes open wide, her tongue protruding and her face going beetroot red. The feeling she got as she imagined this was visceral, and her fingers twitched. But then she shook her head and brought her attention back to her speech. Shame filled her mind and she had to drag her thoughts back to continue.

'I'm delighted to let you all know that the king and queen plan to visit our library.' There was another spontaneous burst of applause. 'Our library is well used by local people but was in dire need of some care and attention. Mr Hubbard has led a hard-working group of volunteers to make it look fit for the royal visit.'

He grinned at her and took an exaggerated bow.

'But now,' Cordelia continued, 'I'll let you get back to your tea and cakes. And thank you all again. The people of Silvertown will really benefit from your kindness.'

She and her mother left the stage to more applause. But she hadn't gone five feet before Mrs Grundy sidled up to her.

'You'll need to know how to speak to royalty. You must let me educate you.'

Cordelia had had enough. 'I can manage quite well, thank you.'

She very pointedly turned her back on the woman and walked away.

Throughout the rest of the event, so many people came up to talk to Cordelia that she thought her throat would dry up. So much kindness from people who had very little. Just like the people in Silvertown.

As they were about to leave, a little girl came and looked at Cordelia, biting her nails and looking scared.

Cordelia bent down to her level. 'What is it, dear? Did you want to speak to me?'

The girl was holding a home-made fabric cat. It was black with yellow beads for eyes and the fabric was so worn through there were tiny holes in it here and there.

'Please, miss, is it all right if I give you Tiddles?' She held out her toy, stroking it as she did so. 'He wants to help other children not feel scared. I cuddle him if I'm scared of thunderstorms.'

Cordelia gave her a hug. 'I think Tiddles will help a lot and I can think of one particular little girl who will love him as much as you do.' She took the cat and stroked it as the girl had done before tucking it under her arm. 'You are very kind and thoughtful.'

As Cordelia and her mother got back into the car to return home, Cordelia mused that she had learned a lesson. Goodness can be uncovered even in difficult times. She held her mother's hand for the first time as an adult.

'We've done something wonderful today, Mother. And it's all down to you.' She paused and looked through the window. 'When that dreadful woman, Mrs Grundy, was standing there glaring at me, I... it's embarrassing to admit it, but for a moment I imagined strangling her.'

Her mother laughed out loud. A rare sound.

'So did I! But I was going to hit her with a candlestick.'

For the first time ever, they giggled together like schoolgirls. It filled Cordelia's heart with love and hope for the future.

Her mother squeezed her hand. 'Today has been such a pleasure,' she said. 'And I've decided. I'm going to keep talking to your father about improving the cottages we own.'

Cordelia had seen her glancing through the windows at the cottages. Some still didn't have electricity and several needed works done outside – unsafe chimneys, and damp patches.

It seemed her mother's new experiences were not only giving her a confidence boost but making her question things she had accepted for her whole life.

But would her father listen?

18

The rap of knuckles on the front door made Mavis jump, even though she'd expected her visitor all morning and looked out of the window a hundred times. She smoothed her best dress and hair before opening the door to find Mrs Anderson's tall, imposing figure filling the doorway.

'Hello again, Mrs Kent,' she said. 'May I come in? You are expecting me, I hope.'

'Come in, come in,' Mavis said, butterflies in her stomach almost freezing her ability to speak normally.

While Mrs Anderson was taking off her grey tweed coat, Mavis tried yet again to see her living room through the eyes of the head of the children's home. She knew that many homes in the East End were in much worse state than hers. Some she'd visited when she'd been called on to deliver babies, lay out bodies or help with other tasks had damp that stained the wallpaper black, or no electricity, or old stained mattresses on the floor that she knew were shared by several children. Although she was normally house-proud, today her home was especially spick and span for the visit. She'd dusted as if royalty were coming to inspect, scrubbed the front step and put whitener on it, plumped up the cushions, and polished the table with diluted tea.

'Why don't you make me a cup of tea while I look around,' Mrs Anderson said. 'And a biscuit if you've got one.'

She threw her coat over the settee and got a clipboard and pencil out of her black bag. From the kitchen, Mavis tried to surreptitiously see what she was doing. Mrs Anderson seemed to have a checklist and was writing ticks on the right-hand side of her paper. Each time she did so, Mavis felt her stomach contract with worry.

'I've only got one bedroom,' Mavis said as she brought in the tea tray with her best china on it and placed it on the little table. 'When Joyce stayed 'ere we shared a bed, but if she comes 'ere to live I'll get rid of the double bed and get two singles.'

Mrs Anderson waited until Mavis poured the tea from her old brown teapot. Then she sat down and picked up a cup.

'Lovely,' she said. 'Just what the doctor ordered.' She paused. 'What facilities do you have? Any inside toilet?'

That was a luxury few in the East End had. 'I'm afraid not. Just the one outside and I share it with Mrs O'Connor next door. We are both very rigorous about keeping it clean.'

Mrs Anderson wrote something on her clipboard. 'Bathroom?'

This wasn't going well. Mavis's home was much like many in the area, better than a lot, but still without things that wealthier people would consider normal.

'No, no bathroom. I've got a tin bath that I fill up and have a cosy bath in front of the fire. Or there's the bathhouse at the end of the street.'

More writing on the clipboard.

'Now, before I inspect the bedroom, tell me again about your job and any support you would have. That's important because if you became ill or indisposed in some other way, we need to be confident someone could step in to look after Joyce.'

Mavis had anticipated that question.

'As you know, I'm a librarian. Not qualified or nothing, but I've got a lot of experience. I do everything you'd expect librarians to do. And that includes seeing to some difficult people what come in from time to time. But there's three of us and a part-time volunteer. We're a good team.'

Mrs Anderson scribbled more notes on her clipboard. 'And support?'

In the East End, kids were in and out of each other's homes regularly and their mums helped each other out all the time. But a lot of kids had been evacuated and many families had either been killed in the bombing or moved away to somewhere safer. Quite a few mums had brought their kids back home during the phony war, though, so there were still a fair number out and about. Mavis was so well known in her street, she could call on half a dozen mums to help out if necessary.

'Mrs O'Connor next door and me 'elp each other out. She's got a granddaughter the same age as Joyce. There's other neighbours I could ask too.'

They talked about war news and events at the children's home, then Mrs Anderson inspected the bedroom. Not once did she make a comment on what she'd seen.

Finally, she returned to the living room and put her coat on again.

'The board for the home makes the final decision about your application and I'm sure they will write to you soon,' she said with a smile. 'Thank you for showing me round, Mrs Kent.'

Mavis rested her head against the back of the door when Mrs Anderson left. She felt totally drained, as if the effort of being on best behaviour had taken all her energy.

She poured herself another cup of the cooling and stewed tea and sat replaying every moment of the visit in her mind. She tried to second-guess how Mrs Anderson felt about her faltering answers to her questions, wishing she'd said this or that. Anything to make her suitability clearer.

She spent the next few days in a state of high anxiety. She longed for a letter from the home yet was terrified they might decide her home wasn't good enough. She busied herself at the library so much Cordelia had to tell her once or twice to take it easy and sit down with a cup of tea for a few minutes. At home, she wrote long letters to Joe.

During one of these times, there was an unexpected knock on the door.

The man had his cap in his hands and was twisting the brim. 'Can you help me, luv?' he asked. 'I'm Fred George, live in the next street. Me old mum just popped her clogs. She was a hundred and two and ready to go but I need someone to lay her out. Someone told me you do that. Can you help?'

As distractions go, it was a sad one, but done respectfully Mavis knew it comforted the bereaved family. She picked up her apron, put on her coat and followed Fred to his house. His mother, who he called Ma, but whose name was Lizzie, was still in her bed.

'Do you want to stay in the room while I do this?' Mavis asked. 'Or is there anyone else who would like to help?'

Fred's eyes opened wider. 'Not me, luv. I ain't doing it. Never seen me mum starkers in me life and I ain't starting now. Me daughter Carol will be here any mo. She'll want to help.'

'Well, while we wait, bring me a bowl of warm water, some soap if you've got any and a towel.'

He saluted and went back downstairs, humming 'Amazing Grace' as he went.

While she waited for the water, Mavis pulled back the bedcovers from the top sheet and placed a chair nearby to put things on. She'd just finished when Carol came in.

'Hello, love,' Mavis said. 'Your dad says you'll 'elp me get your gran ready. Is that okay? Can you manage it? It's 'ard to lose someone you love.'

Carol took off her coat and put on an apron. 'She went years ago. Soft in the head, you know what I mean. Just sat in the corner staring into space.'

Once Fred had brought the water, they began by washing the old lady.

'Always be respectful,' Mavis told Carol. 'No need to leave her completely naked. Do one bit at a time.'

Carol shuddered when she saw her grandmother's wrinkled skin. 'I hope I die before I get that old,' she muttered.

Someone had put pennies on Lizzie's eyes and Mavis was grateful not to have to do that.

'Looks like the stiffness 'as gone,' she said as she moved the old lady's limbs. 'She must've died a few hours ago.'

As she talked Carol through all the stages, she put a strip of cloth in place to hold Lizzie's jaw closed.

'You can take that off in a few hours,' she advised. 'What'll we dress her in? People often like to use the best clothes.'

Carol looked at the few bits of clothing in the narrow wardrobe. She picked out a black dress.

'This'll swamp her. She used to be bigger, but it's the best there is.'

When they'd finished, Mavis asked if Lizzie had been religious. 'Some people like to have a cross of some sort in their hands. What do you think?'

'I think she'd rather hold some flowers. I'll find some.'

'You did good,' Mavis said, watching as Carol took off her apron, folded it up and put it in her bag. She looked relieved that it was all over.

Downstairs, Fred was full of thanks. 'What do we owe you?' he asked, hands in his pockets.

'Nothing, love,' Mavis said. 'I'm glad I could help.'

The look of relief on Fred's face was easy to see and he didn't try to insist.

'Tell you what. We got chickens. Let me give you some eggs.' He carefully put four in a bag and handed it to her. 'Ma would've been glad to be so well looked after.'

As she walked home, perhaps Mavis should have felt sad, but she was comforted by the knowledge she'd helped Fred and Carol. Nodding to several people she knew as she walked along, her thoughts soon returned to Joyce and the letter she was waiting for.

Then, on the Friday, it arrived. A stiff envelope with the emblem of the children's home on the front. Mavis's hands trembled as she sat down and opened it. It was from someone called Mr Hatter, who signed himself as the head of the board for the home. She scanned the contents, barely taking in each word. Then she gasped, hand flying to cover her mouth with delighted surprise. It was approved!

She sprang up from her chair, the letter falling to the floor, forgotten. Then, still unable to believe what she'd read, she picked up the letter and scanned it again.

Dear Mrs Kent,

I have received Mrs Anderson's home inspection report and am pleased to let you know you have met our requirements for adopting Joyce. While your home lacks some modern amenities, I was pleased to read that Mrs Anderson noted the clean, cosy atmosphere and your obvious affection for the child. She believes Joyce will thrive with your care.

With the inspection approved, we will now proceed with the remaining legalities. This will take a while.

I have noted your request to have Joyce with you for Christmas and think this is an excellent idea. She can come to

you on 24 December for a week. Christmas is a time for family,
and I feel sure you will make it a happy time for little Joyce. I have
met her on several occasions, and she is a delightful child.

    Mrs Anderson will be in touch to explain the further details.

    Yours sincerely,

    G. Hatter, Esq.

'They said "Yes!"' she shouted to the empty room.

Mavis clutched the letter to her heart and did a little jig on the spot. It was there in black and white. She had been found worthy.

Mavis imagined little Joyce's lovely face lighting up when she discovered they would spend Christmas together. The child had been through so much already in her life. Mavis vowed she would ensure Joyce never wanted for love again. Modest though it would be, she would do all she could to make Christmas magical, one Joyce would always remember. She would fill it with love as she had for her son Ken. What a pity he wouldn't be able to get home from Scotland for Christmas. That would have made her happiness complete.

She couldn't wait to tell Jane and Cordelia her news.

19

Gasping with relief that she had caught her train, Cordelia flopped into the last seat in the train carriage, willing her heart to calm down. The train was cold, not much warmer than the air outside, and London was often a few degrees warmer than the countryside. She pulled her coat more closely round herself, fished a well-worn novel out of her small case, then shoved the case on the overhead rack with a thud.

'You just made it then,' an elderly grey-haired woman opposite said. 'Me too. I only got here a couple of minutes ago. I'm going back home to York. What about you?'

The woman may have only been there a couple of minutes, but she already had her knitting on the go. A scarf, navy and grey. Cordelia, no expert at knitting, could tell the wool had once been some other garment. The crinkly look of the wool gave away it had been carefully unpicked. She briefly wondered who had worn it. The old lady's husband, perhaps.

'I'm going to the north of Scotland,' she said. She hoped by avoiding further information, the lady would realise she was feeling unsociable. The four other people in the carriage – a parson, a middle-aged man who looked like a travelling salesman, a young woman wearing scarlet lipstick and what seemed to be her boyfriend – were all wrapped up in their own lives, ignoring her and the woman opposite. Out in the corridor, several soldiers stood chatting and smoking.

'Excuse me,' Cordelia said to the woman. 'I didn't get much sleep last night. I'm going to close my eyes for a while.'

'You go ahead,' the woman said. 'You'll not hear another word out of me!'

As Cordelia sat back with her eyes closed, she attempted to clear her mind. The train chugged along the tracks, its rhythmic rumbling soothing her frayed nerves, but her mind kept returning to the previous night, just a few hours earlier. The phone's harsh ring had woken her up. She could hear the sound now, urgent and ominous. She rubbed her temples, remembering the dread that had filled her stomach as she reached for the phone. No one called at that time unless something serious had happened.

As she'd got out of bed, her mind went through all the possibilities – her parents, her friend Rosalind, Mavis, Jane and Tom. She picked up the phone and tried to say her phone number, but her mouth was dry with fear.

'Hello? Hello? Is that you, Cordelia?' an elderly voice, thready and creaky said, only just audible over the crackling line. 'I can't hear you. Speak up!'

Cordelia knew immediately who it was. Her great-aunt. 'Yes, it's Cordelia, Aunt. Has something happened?'

She wasn't exactly sure how old her great-aunt was, but Bess had to be well into her eighties. But if there was something wrong with her, surely someone else would be phoning, not her. 'Is something wrong, Aunt?' she asked again, speaking louder.

It had to be Jasper, her brother. She didn't know anyone else there. But he was fit and healthy, even if he'd managed to dodge being called up. She assumed he was even healthier now he was in the fresh air instead of in smoky nightclubs drinking all night. He'd certainly looked very unhealthy just before he left. Pale skin, dark rings round his eyes, limp hair.

The line crackled again, and she didn't catch what her aunt said. 'Can you repeat that, Aunt? I couldn't hear what you said.'

'It's your brother. You know, Jasper. Your brother. He's ill.'

Cordelia felt as if she'd been punched in the stomach. She and her brother had been close as children, but as they grew into their teens, she had become the academic one, going to the University of Cambridge. He had got in with a bad set and ended up drinking heavily and finding himself in a lot of debt which he couldn't pay back. The debt collectors had threatened not just him but also Cordelia. It had been a fraught and terrifying time. Jasper had been useless, with no solution to his dangerous problem. She'd come to an agreement with Great-Aunt Bess. She would pay off Jasper's debt. In return he would leave his beloved London with all its temptations and move to the north of Scotland. There he would learn how to run her farm until his debt was paid off.

As the train picked up speed, it began to rain, and the pitter-patter of the raindrops joined the rhyme of the wheels, acting like a sleeping draught. Cordelia had only been asleep a few minutes when the changing sound of the rain woke her up again. The rain-drops pelted the window like millions of tiny frantic fingers trying to get in. The wind had picked up, rocking the carriage in irregular gusts. At times, the water cascaded in steady sheets, a deluge, a flood. In between these moments, it lightened to a tapping, the droplets forming rivulets on the glass that warped the blurred view outside, first giving the outer London houses a science-fiction look, then later making the countryside look like an impressionist paint-ing. Condensation gathered on the window and Cordelia rubbed it off so she could see outside.

The train began to slow and then ground to a halt at a station. Cordelia couldn't see where they were because the government had ordered all station signs to be removed in case there was an invasion. She wasn't worried, though; she knew she wouldn't be changing trains for a very long time.

'I feel sorry for those poor people who've been waiting on the platform in this weather,' the woman opposite said, seeing she was awake. 'They must be like drowned rats. I hope it eases up before my stop.' She held up her knitting. 'I'm making this scarf for my grandson. He's just joined up and we've no idea where he is.'

Jolted out of their romantic haze, the young couple suddenly leapt up and ran to the corridor to get off the train, pushing soldiers aside as they passed. Two of the soldiers in turn, seizing the opportunity, took the vacant seats as the train slowly began moving again. They said a cheery hello to everyone and promptly lit up their Woodbines, the smoke soon creating an unpleasant haze in the carriage.

'That's better,' one of them said. 'Me plates of meat needed a rest.'

'I was just saying my grandson has joined up,' the knitting lady said to the men. 'I'm Mrs Smith, by the way. But everyone calls me Aunty.'

The nearest soldier took his cigarette out of his mouth. 'I'm called Skinny. Can't see why.' He was far from skinny, unusually fat for these war times of rationing. 'I work in the kitchens feeding the thousands,' he added.

A deafening clap of thunder and a flash of lightning made them all jump.

'Blimey O'Reilly,' the other soldier said. 'That must be right overhead. No wonder the gravy train is so 'ard.'

Cordelia heard Cockney slang every day. She knew the locals used words that rhymed with the word their slang was replacing, but she'd never heard of 'gravy train'. Not in that context. Then the penny dropped. It meant rain.

The train had slowed down, so through the windows they could see what had happened.

An almighty flash of lightning had hit a tree just ahead of them. It had split in two and burst into flames.

Skinny's jaw dropped open, his cigarette staying balanced on his bottom lip. 'Would you Adam and Eve it! I've 'eard of that 'appening but never seen it.'

No sooner had he spoken than the train stopped with a jolt so sudden they were almost thrown off their seats. Cordelia's anxiety rose with the intensity of the storm increasing. Rain lashed the windows relentlessly. Howling wind rocked the carriage so violently she had to grasp her seat. Thunder crashed deafeningly. Lightning illuminated their pale, nervous faces.

'I'm not usually a moaning Minnie,' Aunty said, 'but this is getting dangerous.' She grabbed Cordelia's hand, but neither felt reassured.

Cordelia thought of the swollen river under the viaduct they were on. Debris must be piling against the bridge. What if it gave way, plunging them into the swirling torrent...? She shook herself. She couldn't let those terrifying thoughts win. Jasper needed her. She pictured his face, so full of vitality and mischief when they were young. So good-looking all her friends wanted him to ask them out. She had to get to him. To help him recover.

'Oh, deary me, deary me,' Aunty said, letting go of Cordelia's hand and picking up a stitch she'd just dropped. 'I hope we won't be stuck too long. My hubby will be waiting for me. He's eighty-one and not quite all there. My neighbour's been keeping an eye on him for me.'

Thirty minutes later, the conductor stuck his head in their carriage.

'Trouble up ahead,' he said. 'Not sure how long we'll be.'

And then he was gone, leaving them all none the wiser. The storm seemed to be abating but its noise in the carriage was still so loud they had to raise their voices to be heard.

'Well, I don't know about you lot, but I'm getting a bit peckish,' Aunty said. She dug in her quilted bag and took out a pack of sandwiches. 'I haven't got enough to share, but I've got some boiled sweets if anyone wants one. Why don't we have something to eat to make our minds off this blinking storm?'

Minutes later, they were all sharing what they could.

'This is nearly as good as getting our parcels from home,' Skinny said.

His words caught Cordelia's attention. 'I volunteer for the WVS and help put those parcels together. I'm glad you like them.'

There was a pause while the soldier unwrapped a boiled sweet and put it in his mouth. 'Do we! I had a little bag of dried fruit last time. First time I'd had that for ages. And there was a note wishing me well. A lipstick kiss on it too.' He patted his pocket. 'I've still got it. It's my good luck charm.'

Cordelia remembered Ann's notes she put in for the troops and wondered if the one Skinny had received had come from her. The thought made her smile.

'I tell you,' his friend said, 'those parcels make a smashing change from bully beef and overcooked spuds. I miss me trouble and strife's cooking something rotten. She makes the best toad in the 'ole in the world.'

Skinny nodded. 'And mine cooks great cakes when she can get all the stuff. Makes 'er own jam too. Hard with rationing. But that Lord Woolton's pie is enough to make you go on 'unger strike. I bet that bloke never 'ad one for 'is dinner in 'is life!'

The train suddenly jolted and moved a few yards. Then stopped and moved a few more. Then stopped again. This happened about a dozen times. Each time it happened, they looked at each other, trying to cover their alarm.

Then they ground to a halt again.

'If this goes on much longer, I'm goin' to get out and walk,' Skinny said. 'Bit of rain won't put me off.'

Cordelia wiped the condensation from the window and peered out. 'I don't think you will,' she said. 'We're on a viaduct. We're stuck. We can't get out.'

The train jolted forward once more, inching forwards through the hammering rain. Everyone in the carriage seemed to be holding their breath. Were they going to move again?

Without warning, the engine spluttered and the lights flickered out, leaving them in the murky darkness of the feeble emergency lights. A baby in the next carriage began to wail.

Cordelia gasped, gripped by a sense of disaster. Would they make it to safety? Was this how their journey would end?

She thought again about her brother. What if this delay meant she was too late? He might be dead already. All she could do now was wait in the gloom and hope to get the answers she needed soon.

20

Hours later, the train limped into the next stop.

'All out!' the stationmaster shouted again and again, waving a red flag.

'All out?' Aunty repeated. 'But we're nowhere near my station.'

They all hesitated, as if this was some type of trick. Then the stationmaster knocked on their window, making them all jump. 'All out! Now!' he repeated, then strode off to the next carriage.

They gathered their belongings and stepped down on to the platform.

The rain had stopped but the air felt laden with water just waiting to fall again. Cordelia shivered; glad she'd put on several layers of clothes in readiness for the temperature in the north of Scotland.

'What is it? What's happening?' she asked the stationmaster as he returned their way.

'Track's subsided because of the rain,' he said. 'Should be fixed by the morning.'

Skinny took his fag out of his mouth. 'You gotta be kidding.

Where are we supposed to sleep tonight then? Don't say a hotel 'cos I ain't got no readies.'

By now there was a small crowd around the stationmaster all wondering the same thing. He looked at them as if they were a nuisance.

'You can sleep in the waiting room,' he said, indicating behind him. 'It'll be a bit of a squeeze, though. But if you go into the village you'll find somewhere.'

The two soldiers looked at each other. 'Come on then, let's make it to the waiting room.'

With that, they were off with a cheery goodbye.

Aunty stood clutching her quilted bag, looking lost. 'Oh, deary, deary me. I don't think my arthritis will stand a night in the cold on a hard floor.' She looked down at her feet. 'I can't afford a hotel neither.'

Cordelia linked her arm through the elderly woman's. 'Tell you what. Let's go and find a room somewhere. We'll get a twin room. I'll pay. How does that sound? You can buy me a drink.'

Aunty looked at her as if she were a fairy waving a magic wand.

'Are you sure, dear? That'll cost a fair bit, a hotel room.'

Cordelia hitched her bag over her shoulder. 'Lucky I'm made of money then,' she said with a laugh. 'Are you able to walk if we need to find somewhere?'

Aunty nodded. 'As long as it's not too far and not uphill.' She looked around. 'This looks okay, not too steep.'

The Yorkshire village was quaint, with cobbled streets and stone cottages. Small front gardens showed the remains of summer blooms, now cut back for the winter. There weren't many people around and it wasn't long until blackout time.

'Let's try the Black Bull pub over there,' Cordelia said.

Mrs Smith hesitated. 'I don't know what my Fred would say, me staying in a pub. I've hardly ever even been in one.'

Cordelia tugged at her arm. 'Your Fred wouldn't want you sleeping on the streets like a tramp, would he? Let's hope they've still got a room free.'

The pub smelled of beer and cigarettes and was dimly lit with oil lamps, their light reflected on the polished if battered wooden tables. A threadbare dartboard was against the wall opposite the bar and a rowdy game was going on with much teasing and jostling. The blackened fireplace, which had an old rag rug in front of it, cast a warm glow over the room, making the bar warm and welcoming.

It was a relief to be out of the cold and rain.

As they walked in, the locals all paused what they were doing and stared at them. Cordelia was reminded of those cowboy films where a stranger walks into a bar, dramatically pushing through the swing doors. Everything in the bar stops – the honky-tonk piano music, the chatter, the clink of glasses. Every person turns to look at the newcomer.

Luckily, no one had a gun.

She could feel Aunty tense next to her.

'Is it going to be okay?' she whispered.

In response, Cordelia walked to the bar.

'Good evening. Our train has broken down. Do you have a double room for the night please, or two singles?'

The barman held up his hand to tell her to hold on a minute and finished serving a burly man wearing a donkey jacket and a flat cap.

'Now,' he said, turning to Cordelia. 'You need a room for two people. Hang on, love, I'll ask the missus if we can squeeze in two more. Already had some people just come in.'

As if someone had clicked a switch, conversations started again, although the men at the bar still looked at Cordelia. Not at Aunty, she noticed. She'd often found that after a certain age women seemed to become invisible to men. Cordelia herself felt very out of place in her expensive city clothes, as if she'd dropped in from another world. The pub was filled with village people wrapped up for warmth more than fashion.

'Did the train crash then?' a tall, thin man further along the bar asked. 'You two don't look like you've been in a crash.'

The two women both shook their heads.

'It didn't,' Aunty said. 'Problem on the track, they said. Rain, they said.'

The landlord came back, beaming. 'The missus says if you don't mind going up in the attic, we can fit you in. That do you? I'm Mr Holland, by the way.'

Cordelia looked at Aunty. 'Is that okay with you? Can you make it up to the attic?'

Mrs Smith rubbed her knees. 'If you carry my bags, I dare say I'll manage.' She looked at Mr Holland. 'Can we get something to eat here?'

Before he could answer, his wife appeared. She was a classic country woman, plump with rosy cheeks and fair wavy hair.

'If you're happy with a cheese sandwich and a bowl of vegetable soup, we can manage that. That okay? If it is, you sit and have a rest while I get it ready and put the sheets on the beds.'

Grateful for a bed for the night, the two women sat down near the fire.

'Where you two from then?' an elderly man with a wooden leg asked. 'You don't sound like you'm from round these parts.' The leg, unbelievably old-fashioned, looked like something a pirate might have.

'Nor do you, John!' someone shouted.

'Take no notice of him. Where did you say you'm was from?'

The two women began to take off their coats and warmed their hands in front of the welcome fire.

'London,' Cordelia replied. 'I'm on my way to the north of Scotland and Mrs Smith here is going to York. If the trains get going again, that is.'

The man took a long drink of his pint and put the glass down with a thud. 'London, you say. Never bin there. Sounds like an awful place. Full of bombs and things. We don't have nothing like that around here.'

'You should thank the good Lord for that then,' Mrs Smith said. 'My cousin lost his house and...'

Excusing herself, Cordelia went to the bar and ordered two halves of shandy for herself and 'Aunty'.

While the drinks were being poured, Cordelia went to the phone at the end of the bar to call Bess, her aunt. She was worried that the delay to her journey would mean she wouldn't be in time to see her brother while he was... she didn't dare even finish that sentence to herself. Surely he would get better.

But the phone line was dead.

The landlord pushed her drinks along the bar to her.

'Out of luck? Often happens in a storm. Sometimes it's out for days. In the morning you could try the phone box in the village. It might be working.'

Thanking him, she balanced the full glasses and negotiated her way between tables and a group playing dominoes. She ducked her head to avoid the brass beer mugs hanging from the ceiling and didn't see that the old man, John, had shifted in his seat. His wooden leg was directly in her path. Arms flailing, she staggered forward as the mugs slipped from her grasp. Beer sloshed over the rims, splattering the small round drinks table and the scarred wooden floorboards, spraying the amber liquid around as they smashed into many pieces.

The pub went silent again and all eyes turned to her. She could feel herself going bright pink.

The burly man, who was sitting nearby, muttered, 'Bloody Londoners!'

'I'm so sorry,' she began, ignoring his remark.

'Don't worry me none, girl,' John said, wiping his leg. 'But you'd better mop that up before someone has an accident.'

But the landlady beat her to it and was quickly there with a dustpan and brush as well as a mop and bucket.

'Everyone out of the way!' she said with a good-natured grin. 'Let the worker through!' She turned to the one-legged man. 'I bet you did that on purpose. I know your games!'

When the landlady had finished wiping the wooden seats as well as the floor, Cordelia and Aunty sat down.

'Replacement drinks and your food'll be with you in two shakes of a nanny goat's tail,' Mrs Holland said.

The food was delicious. Doorstep sandwiches made with home-made bread, slathered with fresh butter, thick chunks of cheddar cheese and beetroot relish. And the soup was the best Cordelia had ever tasted. Better even than the expensive restaurants she'd often been to.

'Mmm,' she said, sitting back and patting her stomach when she'd finished.

'I suppose you'm used to rationing down there in the big smoke,' John said. 'We'm lucky around these parts, farms and things. We don't go hungry.'

'That and the black marketeers like you,' the burly man muttered.

Faster than Cordelia could have imagined, John whipped round. 'You weren't above having some stockings for your missus, was you!'

'Now, now, boys,' Mr Holland said, who was nearby checking the empties. 'No arguments here or I'll throw the pair of you out. It's started raining hard again, so if you know what's good for you, you'll act nice.'

Both men mumbled into their beer but let the argument go.

'I'm ready for me bed,' Aunty said. 'Is it too early for you, Cordelia? It's been a tiring day.'

Cordelia nodded her agreement. She'd often thought how tiring travelling was. Most of the time you were simply sitting, moving from A to B, yet somehow it used up unreasonable amounts of energy. If she found she wasn't ready for sleep yet, she would read or simply think about Robert or all the plans for the library.

Mrs Holland, the landlady, was near the bottom of the stairs as they headed to their room. 'Just keep going up, ladies, you can't go wrong. You're the only people in the attic.'

'How many other people are staying here tonight?' Cordelia asked.

'Six altogether, all men,' she replied. 'Squashed into two rooms. Said one in each would sleep on the floor. Couldn't turn them out in this weather, could I?'

Aunty began the slow ascent of the steep stairs, pulling herself up with the banister and groaning as her knees protested.

Cordelia followed with the bags. 'Take your time, Aunty. We're in no rush.'

The attic room was small with sloping ceilings covered with pink rose-patterned wallpaper. There were two narrow single beds, each with a crocheted bedspread of many colours. In one corner stood a small table with a bowl, a jug of water and two glasses. There was a tiny fireplace with a newly built fire in it, though it hadn't done much to warm the room.

Aunty looked around. 'Well, I've had worse bedrooms. I've got to warn you, though, I always need a pee in the night. Two sometimes. I'll try not to disturb you.' She lifted up the bedcovers. 'No guzunder there. I'll have to go to the bathroom. Probably just as well, me knees won't take me squatting to use one.'

The room was so small, they had to be careful not to bump each other as they got into their nightclothes. All the time, Aunty chatted about her family – who had been bombed, a new baby born just a week earlier, and two funerals she'd attended in the previous fortnight.

'Too close for comfort, if you know what I mean,' she said. 'They were the same age as me. It wasn't the war that took them. It was old age.'

Once they'd turned off the light, Aunty was asleep within seconds.

Meanwhile, Cordelia lay there listening to the rain lashing the walls of the pub, rattling the loose windowpanes. The thin cotton curtains gently drifted as a draught found its way round the window frames and blackout curtains. She lay thinking about everything they needed to do to prepare the library for the royal visit and Christmas. They planned to have an event where Tom would dress as Father Christmas and give invited children the gifts donated by the villagers from her mother's area. Tom was still struggling to move around on his stick, but he'd only have to sit for that event.

She was still deep in thought, wishing she could sleep, when the pub closed. Noisy customers called their goodbyes to each other, one drove off, but most seemed to walk home.

Cordelia wriggled in the bed, trying to get comfortable on the old, lumpy mattress, and pulled the covers up around her chin to keep out the cold. Through a gap in the curtains she could see the sky, clouds scudding quickly past. Beside her, Aunty began to snore very gently, and once again, Cordelia envied her ability to fall asleep so quickly in an unfamiliar place.

Finally, just as she was drifting into sleep, a sudden sound jolted her awake. Moving shadows across the sloping ceiling caught her attention. A car must be going past. But it wasn't going *past*. It stopped under her window.

The front door opened with a squeal. Heavy footsteps thudded across the wooden floor.

Cordelia froze, her pulse racing. Who would be arriving this late? Surely everyone from the train would have found a bed for the night by now. Men, she decided – she was sure it was men from their heavy footsteps. And then they began to speak in urgent, hushed tones. She couldn't make out the words from so far above, but she was sure something sinister was going on.

To her horror, she then heard footsteps on the stairs, coming up. Had she locked the door? Could she even get there before the men reached the room?

She saw shadows under her door and the footsteps were right there. Inches away. She froze, clutching the bedcovers as if they might protect her.

A scratching sound. A muffled grunt. The door handle creaking, slowly turning. It creaked as it was turned but didn't give way. She must have locked it after all.

'Not that room, idiot!' a harsh voice said. 'You've come up too far.'

There was a muttered swear word and the footsteps retreated. Cordelia didn't dare move. Whoever these men were, they wouldn't want any witnesses to their nefarious actions. Her mind ran riot. What could they be doing? Burglars? Murderers? Rapists?

Then she heard something being dragged from the car towards the pub. She went to the window, making sure she was far enough back to avoid being spotted. Through the dim light, when there was a gap in the clouds, she could see what the men were moving. It was a beer barrel being rolled along. Two minutes later, the men returned to the car and unloaded several big sacks. The whole time they were looking around as if expecting to be challenged.

Cordelia got back into bed, shivering. Pulling the covers over herself again, she ran through the evening spent down in the bar in her mind. One conversation stood out. John, the one-legged man, was a black marketeer. That must be it. These must be goods to be sold on the black market. She relaxed a little. As long as the men didn't know she'd seen them, she was safe.

And she wouldn't have minded a new pair of stockings or a lipstick.

21

The musty smell of books hit Tom in an instant and the ancient ladder creaked as he made his way to the top of the 'bonfire'. The bonfire wasn't tall, but tall enough that he couldn't reach to put the Guy on the top without the ladder.

The ladder was old and made him nervous, but he persisted. It had to be finished today. The ancient wood, rough against his palms, groaned. Dust motes floated in the air.

He was about to step down when it happened. The rung he was standing on broke in two.

Tom's agonised cry pierced the hushed library air as he crashed down in a tangle of broken wood and flailing limbs. His ankle shattered on the unforgiving floor and excruciating white-hot pain raced up his leg as the room spun dizzyingly, white spots spinning before his eyes. He'd bitten his lip as he fell and tasted blood. It was thick and iron-rich like a penny left too long on the tongue. He tried to clutch his rapidly swelling ankle, breath coming in ragged gasps, but it was too painful to touch.

Jane knelt beside him. 'Don't move, Tom,' she whispered, her voice hoarse with shock. Her face was paper-white as she looked at the grotesque angle of his foot.

A cluster of readers had raced over and stared down at Tom's crumpled form, surrounded by the materials he'd used to build the Guy Fawkes bonfire near the circulation desk. Crumpled paper, pieces of fabric too small for use and moth-eaten, torn-up clothes lay everywhere.

The broken ladder had fallen, almost knocking over a child waiting to have his books stamped. He promptly burst into tears, his wails reaching the furthest corners of the library. His mother dithered for a few seconds then slapped his leg.

'Stop crying, you're not hurt.' She picked up the book and put it in her big cream handbag. 'We'll bring it back next time,' she called over her shoulder. No one was listening.

Mavis came dashing over, eyes wide with shock. 'What on earth—'

She sucked in a sharp breath at the sight of Tom's leg.

'I'll phone for an ambulance!' she said, spinning round and nearly stumbling in her haste to reach the telephone.

Tom simply bit his lip and struggled to sit up. The small movement was too much. Sharp pains shot up his leg again.

'No, don't!' Jane commanded. 'We'll get a pillow for your head. Stay still until the ambulance people come.'

His face damp with sweat, Tom collapsed back on the floor.

'I should have asked one of you to hold the ladder,' he gasped. 'It must be as old as the library. My fault. And it's my dodgy leg.'

It was late October and Tom had been preparing a mock bonfire to commemorate Guy Fawkes Night. The mock bonfire hadn't been big, but high enough for his fall to be serious.

But with the blackout, Guy Fawkes celebrations outdoors were banned. That didn't mean the library couldn't celebrate it, though.

And they planned to have a small get-together of regular patrons on the day.

Urgent voices and footsteps swirled around Tom. Through the haze of pain, he heard Mavis's garbled telephone conversation with the ambulance people.

Jane shooed the onlookers away to give Tom some privacy while they waited for the ambulance. It wasn't long before they heard the siren coming closer.

All Tom could do was grit his teeth and focus on surviving the throbbing pain that threatened to make him faint.

Then he made out Jane's voice. 'I can hear the ambulance, Tom. They'll be here very soon.'

The doors were flung back with force as the ambulance men ran in.

'Looks like you've gone and got yourself in a bit of bother,' the taller one said, as if Tom had just knocked over a cup of tea. 'We'll soon sort you out. It'll mean a trip to the hospital, mind.'

The two men, seasoned professionals, soon assessed the situation.

'Go and get a splint,' the tall one, whose name was Norman, said to his colleague. He then bent down to talk to Tom, and as he did so his grey hair fell over his forehead. He brushed it back as if that happened a hundred times a day.

'I'm tempted to try to take your shoe off before your foot swells even more.' He was watching Tom's face as he spoke. 'But it'll be very painful. At the hospital, they'll probably cut it off.' He saw Tom's alarmed look. 'Your shoe, you daft 'alfpeth, not your foot. But when they cut it, it'll be no good unless they chop your leg off too!' He chuckled at his own ill-judged joke.

His friend ran back in with a splint. It was just two bits of wood and a long bandage.

'Now,' Norman said. 'If we splint your ankle and foot, I've got to be honest. It'll hurt like buggery while we do it, but it'll stop it moving.' He heard the onlookers gasp. 'But once we've done that, we can move you without much more pain.' He looked around. 'It'll be short-term pain for long-term gain if you get my meaning.' His hair fell over his eyes again. He looked at Tom. 'What do you think? It's what me and my mate here recommend.'

More people came into the library and stopped in the doorway, looking at the scene with wide eyes. Mavis went over and asked them to come back later. Then she closed the doors.

'I'm so sorry,' Tom said, his voice shaky. 'I should have asked one of you to...'

'No apologies, Tom,' Jane said, taking his clammy hand. 'Let's get you to the hospital.' She looked at the ambulance men. 'Is there anything we can do to help?'

Norman raised his eyebrows and pushed his hair back again. 'Maybe a cloth to bite.'

He gathered together the splint, bandages and a piece of cotton. He knelt down beside Tom's leg, his brow creased in concentration.

'Okay, mate, this is the rough bit. Ready yourself. It'll soon be over and you'll feel more or less tickety-boo.'

Half scared to look, the two women held their collective breath as Norman positioned the splints on either side of Tom's swollen ankle.

'Ready, mate?'

Tom put the rag between his teeth and nodded, his face rigid with fear.

Norman confidently took Tom's foot in his hand and deftly manoeuvred the bones back in place. It was over quickly but the sound of bone rubbing on bone made everyone flinch. Tom couldn't hold back a muffled scream.

Taking a deep breath, Jane held his hand again.

'You're doing great, Tom,' she said. As she spoke, another ambulance went by, its siren splitting the hushed silence in the library.

Tom clenched his jaw, hardly breathing as Norman secured the splints firmly with the bandages.

'Right, mate. Worst is well and truly over. I bet that feels a lot better, don't it?' With a final gentle tug of Tom's foot to ensure everything was in place, he sat back on his heels. 'Time to get you to the hospital. Looks like a clean break so you might even be home before bedtime.' He looked at his colleague. 'Go and fetch the wheelchair, will you?'

Getting Tom in the wheelchair wasn't without pain. He yelped a couple of times but with the support of the two ambulance men, he was safely in the chair.

As the ambulance bumped over the old London streets, Tom gritted his teeth. Jane, who'd volunteered to go with him, held his hand.

'Won't be long now,' she said. 'It's not far to the hospital.'

They'd broken the library rule and left Mavis alone there, but there was nothing else to be done.

At the hospital, Tom was pushed to the accident ward with Jane hurrying along behind them. Although the hospital was busy, the Blitz was over, otherwise Tom would have had to wait hours to be seen. As it was, he only waited twenty minutes before a nurse called his name and he went into a curtained-off cubicle to be examined.

'Someone will be along to see you shortly,' the nurse said before quickly making her way through the curtains.

Jane made small talk to distract Tom, whose eyes kept being drawn to his ankle. Despite the splints, the swelling looked alarming.

'Well, if it isn't Tom Hudson! I thought I recognised your voice.'

The curtains were pushed open and a pretty nurse with

chestnut curls walked through. Her starched apron made soft whispers as she moved.

'I haven't seen you for ages, Tom. How have you been?' She laughed. 'Apart from breaking your ankle, I mean.'

Tom swallowed hard. 'You look wonderful. I mean... you look very professional.' He could feel his ears turning pink. 'It's good to see you, Evelyn.'

Evelyn held his arm to take his pulse. 'You know, it was probably because of you I became a nurse.'

'Because of me?'

She wrote some figures down on his chart and nodded, then looked him in the eye. 'Don't you remember, you were always getting in scrapes, falling over, covered in bruises half the time. It was a lot more fun bandaging you than my dolls!'

Her words forced memories into Tom's mind. He and Evelyn playing out with the other kids in the street. Out in all weathers, often with a bottle of water and a jam sandwich each to keep them going. He remembered falling from a tree. It was an oak and he was desperate to get more conkers than the other lads. They were jeering, betting him to go higher all the time. Idiot that he was, he took their challenge and got a big cluster of the smoothest, shiniest conkers he'd ever seen. He was halfway down when he slipped. A pile of leaves saved him from anything worse than a painful elbow.

Now, Evelyn found a pillow and helped him hold his head forward so she could slip it in place. She spent a few seconds smoothing it, unnecessarily, then stepped back.

'There, now you look as gorgeous as ever,' she said, smiling at him, and his heart gave a little jump. It was as if the years that had passed since those days meant nothing. Now, though, it wasn't childish friendship he felt as he looked at her but a strong emotional pull.

Patting his hand, Evelyn pulled a metal trolley towards her and began checking she had everything she needed.

'Well, let's get started then,' she said, a warm smile on her face. 'I'll need all your details to pass on to the doctor, but I'm sure he'll want you to go for an X-ray. Then the doc will have a look at it and decide what to do. I can't see that you've broken the skin anywhere so that's a good sign.'

Jane looked from one to the other, hiding a smile as she observed their obvious attraction. Tom's face, racked with pain only minutes earlier, was transformed. His eyes glittered as he looked at the nurse and his breathing had returned to normal.

'How do you two know each other?' Jane asked.

'We used to be neighbours,' the nurse said. 'I'm Nurse Gordon. I'm sorry, I should have introduced myself sooner. But as we know each other you can call me Evelyn.'

'I've never forgotten you for a minute,' Tom said, his ears going pink.

The curtain opened and another nurse almost ran in. She looked around, confused, then turned on her heel.

'Sorry, wrong cubicle,' she shouted over her shoulder.

The interruption made Evelyn jump. 'I'd better go and see what's happened to the doctor. He should be here by now, but you can never tell in the emergency department!'

She was gone five minutes, during which time Jane questioned Tom about his time with Evelyn. Now that she'd gone, his face showed his pain once again.

'We were young...' he started.

'You still are!' Jane said with a laugh.

He shifted his weight on the bed and Jane reached up and straightened the pillow for him. 'Is that okay?'

He shook his head. 'Not really. But not moving helps.'

Their conversation was interrupted by the sound of an ambulance pulling up outside and heavy doors opening.

'You asked me about Evelyn,' Tom said when the noise abated. 'We've known each other since we were about ten, I suppose. As we went to secondary school, we got in with different friends. Sometimes we'd see each other, and sometimes it would be weeks.'

Jane remembered her time at secondary school. It was an all-girls school in Canning Town. She didn't remember much about the academic subjects, but she remembered being taught to make cakes, sandwiches and how to wash and iron a man's shirt. The domestic science teacher was very strict about that. It wasn't to be her own school shirt, which was almost identical to a man's – it had to be a man's shirt. At the time, she thought nothing of the way the instruction was all about preparing her for her future role as a housewife. Since working in the library, though, she'd been exposed to different ideas, especially since she'd been working for Cordelia. She shook her head, thinking about how the school was simply preparing her to be a wife.

One of her friends had wanted to go to university, but the head teacher talked her out of it.

'Girls like you don't do that. You'd feel out of place. How about trying to be a primary teacher or a nurse? They're good jobs for a girl with your background.'

Her friend told Jane she had cried all that night. Jane struggled to remember her, but thought she'd married young and had three children in quick succession.

Evelyn's arrival into the room with a doctor roused her from her memories. The doctor was tall and so thin it was a wonder he could walk upright. His hair, prematurely white, stuck up at all angles and he kept running his fingers through it.

'So, young man,' he said, looking down at Tom. 'Nurse Gordon here thinks you've broken your ankle and she's not often wrong. Anything else hurt? Did you lose consciousness at all?'

As he spoke, he was carefully touching Tom's lower leg, ankle and foot, making him grunt with pain.

'Sorry about that, old man,' the doctor said. 'Off to X-ray with you.'

He spun round so fast as he left that his white coat swirled around him.

'I'll take you, Tom,' Evelyn said. She put her hand on his shoulder and gave it a reassuring squeeze. 'We're short of porters today so it'll save time. Sooner you're seen, the sooner you can get on with your life.'

'Will he be able to walk?' Jane asked.

Evelyn tapped the top of Tom's head. 'Yes. Laddo here will be plastered and given crutches. They take a little while to get used to, but he'll be able to get about.'

'Don't worry, Jane,' Tom said. 'It sounds as if I can still be Father Christmas. In a wheelchair if needs be.' He stopped and Jane could see him thinking ahead. 'I'll make a poster for Guy Fawkes Night. That'll have to do, I'm afraid. No more ladders for me for a while.'

Jane smiled at Evelyn. 'He's a wonder, you know. He volunteers in the library in Silvertown where I work. I don't know what we'd do without him.'

Outside the curtains, they heard more footsteps running and a phone ringing.

As Evelyn prepared to take Tom to X-ray, fetching a wheelchair and helping him into it, she said, 'You always were a bit of a wonder boy,' her warm eyes crinkling. 'It's been too long, Tom. Maybe this accident has brought us back together for a reason.'

As Evelyn leaned down to adjust his leg, Tom found himself staring into her eyes. He'd never forgotten them – a bright hazel flecked with green. They stirred hazy memories of laughter under the old oak tree in her garden, joking and teasing each other.

The nervous flutter in his chest reminded him of that same feeling when Evelyn had leaned towards him and pecked his cheek before running away, laughing. A flood of memories thrust themselves into his mind. Passing notes across the classroom, glances that lingered a beat too long.

That final summer before she and her family moved away, they'd lazed in the grass gazing at the clouds, arms so close he could feel the heat from hers. It was her last day and she had escaped from the chaotic packing at home, almost in tears at leaving all she knew and loved.

Finding courage he was unaware of, Tom had closed the slither of space between them. The kiss was a clumsy affair, noses bumping, teeth clacking, but it was his first real kiss, and nothing had ever felt so amazing, so perfect, so unforgettable. As they pulled away from each other, they collapsed in embarrassed laughter. Now, as he looked into Evelyn's eyes again, he felt the years slip away. They were older, and both had had many experiences before and during the war, but he felt the same magnetic pull between them. He sensed that she felt it too.

'We should never have drifted apart from each other,' he said, putting his hand over hers.

They were interrupted by the doctor pushing his head through the curtains again.

'Still here?' he asked, his voice harsh and impatient. 'I thought this man's X-ray would be done by now.'

The moment was lost but Tom took his time removing his hand before saying, 'I suppose we'd better find that X-ray department then.'

Jane felt like a third wheel on a bicycle made for two, as the attraction between the pair became more obvious.

'Tom. If you don't need me, I'll be off,' Jane said. 'Will you be able to get home okay?'

Evelyn put her hands on the wheelchair and swivelled it round to face the X-ray department. 'I'll see he's safe and sound.'

22

That evening, Mavis checked her reflection in the mirror nervously as she waited for her son Ken to arrive. He was late, but that was probably the trains. They were all over the place.

The smell of lamb stew filled the small kitchen and Mavis checked that everything was tidy. In the past, Ken had called her a slut more than once when even the smallest thing was out of place. Even as a boy he'd been difficult. He'd often had a clout round the head from the local bobby for getting into mischief. And he'd been no better at home, often being rude and taking money from her purse.

Then she heard his footsteps coming to the door and her stomach plunged. Which Ken would he be? The one she'd lived with for several years or the one in his recent letters? One of the most loaned books at the library was *Dr Jekyll and Mr Hyde*, about a man who changed personalities from a good one to an evil one, and she shivered as she thought of that, waiting for his knock on the door.

When he did, she clutched her hands together, counted to five, then answered it with a smile she hoped looked sincere.

'Hello, love,' she said, touching his sleeve, 'come on in out of the cold.'

He towered over her as he stood in the doorway, his army great-coat buttoned right up to the neck. Had he always been this tall? She looked for a trace of the lovely boy he had been, but this was no boy. This was a grown man. His jaw was square now, the dimple he'd inherited from his father still evident, his eyes tired.

'Hello, Mum,' he said. There wasn't a smile with his words, but neither was there a scowl. Mavis wondered if she could hope all was well.

'I've got some lamb stew cooking. Your favourite. Come in and take your coat off. I'll get you a beer.'

He took off his coat and hung it up on the peg in the kitchen. He hadn't done that since he was a little lad. He usually just threw it anywhere.

'That sounds good, Mum. Army cooking is rubbish. Absolute rubbish.'

His words made her heart squeeze. Was he going to go on one of his rants? He could rant about anything, from the weather to the state of the roads to beer. She decided not to rise to the bait.

'Well, warm yourself up and 'ave some good cooking for a couple of days.'

To her surprise, he walked over to the stove and lifted the lid, picked up the spoon she kept nearby and tried the stew.

'That's smashing, Mum. My girlfriend is a good cook. But not as good as you.'

Mavis almost dropped the tea towel she was holding. She looked at his face for a trace of sarcasm but saw none.

'I hope you don't tell 'er that,' she said. 'Never compare your girlfriend's cooking with your mum's if you want to avoid a row.'

She longed to put her arms round him, to hug him as she had once done so often. But she didn't dare risk the rejection.

He laid the spoon down again and opened the beer, taking a long swig. He wiped his mouth on his sleeve. 'Just the ticket. Her name's Flora. My girlfriend.'

He'd mentioned having a girlfriend in his letters, but this sounded much more serious than any relationship before. He'd had several girlfriends, used them and dumped them, from what she heard around Silvertown. She'd sometimes been embarrassed when people realised she was his mother.

'Well, sit yourself down, lad, and tell me all about 'er.' She bustled about getting out the crockery and cutlery. 'And about your life up there in Scotland. It must be so cold.'

He nodded. 'It's cold, sure enough. Cold enough to make your fingers drop off.'

'You're sounding a bit Scottish already!' Mavis said with a smile. 'Did you know?'

'Aye,' he replied, then laughed at himself. 'It's hard not to pick it up when you hear it all day long. They still know I'm a proper Cockney, though.'

Mavis dished up the stew, adding a plate of bread and butter on the table.

Ken ate quickly, barely swallowing each mouthful before putting in the next. Mavis longed to tell him to slow down but didn't dare say anything. She couldn't risk fracturing the unexpected harmony of their conversation.

'So, is it serious between you and Flora? You can't 'ave known 'er very long.'

He folded a slice of bread and butter in half and took a bite. 'That's where you're wrong. I met her two days after I was posted to Inverness. She works in the NAAFI, serving in the shop. I go in there every day for something.'

They were interrupted by the front door opening and Mrs O'Connor, their next-door neighbour, walking in. She never knocked.

'Oh, you're home, Ken. I didn't know,' she said. 'I just popped in to borrow a twist of sugar, so I did.' She walked towards the table. 'How're you getting on up there in Scotland? It sounds like a beautiful place, so it does.'

Ken's eyes narrowed and a pulse on his forehead began to show. Behind her back, he'd always called Mrs O'Connor a nosy old bat. And that was when he was feeling polite.

Mavis gave the woman a forced smile and hurriedly put some sugar in a teacup. "Ere you go, sweetheart. Sorry if I can't chat now. We've got a lot to catch up on.'

She led the woman back to the door and closed it firmly behind her.

'Bloody busybody,' Ken said, his voice harsh enough to bring familiar fear back into Mavis's heart. 'Didn't know I was here! She must take me for a fool. She knows everything that goes on in this bloody street. Couldn't wait to stick her nose in.'

Mavis got up and went to the kettle that was gently steaming on the stove. 'Fancy a cuppa? And I've made some bread-and-butter pudding. That was always your favourite.'

Ken nodded, stood up and stretched his back. He walked around the small room, picking things up and putting them back down. Then he stopped at a small vase, white with a simple rose pattern round it.

'You've kept this, all these years,' he said, running his fingers round the rim.

'Of course. You gave it to me for a present when you was about – I'm not sure – ten I think it was. I've always treasured it. Mums always love what their children give them.'

'I remember buying that. I shouldn't tell you this, but I pinched the money out of your purse...'

She knew he'd done it but saw no point in saying so when he was reminiscing.

'It was a cold day and me and my mate Jimmy went all around the market twice trying to find something I could afford for your birthday. It was cold enough to stick your tongue to a lamp post. Jimmy wanted me to nick something, but I knew you wouldn't want me to do that.'

Mavis smiled. 'Especially when you'd "borrowed" the money to buy it in the first place!'

He put it back down and went to his kitbag where he took out a brown paper-wrapped parcel tied with string.

'This is for you from Flora. It's called Selkirk Bannock. I think the shop might've been a bit short of dried fruit when she made it.'

The brown paper crinkled as Mavis began to open the parcel and sweet aromas began to drift up. The cake inside was wrapped in smooth greaseproof paper as well. She slid it open and the smell made her mouth water, even though she'd just had a good helping of stew. Rich, spicy and fruity. The scent of cinnamon, raisins and nutmeg reminded her of cakes her granny used to make.

She stood up and kissed Ken on his head. The first time they had had physical contact for years, apart from when he'd hit her.

'It looks a treat,' she said with a smile. 'You've got yourself a lass who can cook then.'

While Ken went outside to use the lavvy, Mavis cut a tiny bit of the Bannock off and popped it in her mouth. It was delicious. She basked both in the flavour of the cake and the difference in Ken. It was like getting her son back after all this time, as if the nasty person he had been was a mirage. She knew she hadn't been a perfect mother. After all, she had him when she was only sixteen.

She shivered, remembering her father's outrage when he found out she was expecting.

'You? In the family way? You stupid slut. Who is it? Who's responsible? I'll go and wring his bloody neck!'

She thought the curses and name-calling would never end. Her mother, a sweet yet meek woman, didn't defend her. Instead, she just worried about what the neighbours would say.

In the end, her father gave her ten minutes to pack her things and then threw her out of the house.

She'd had to fend for the pair of them. Friends told her to have Ken adopted but she couldn't do it, even if he had been conceived in such a dreadful way. It wasn't his fault. But shortage of money and exhaustion meant that sometimes she was short-tempered and occasionally lashed out at him.

But that was rare. He'd had plenty of hugs too.

Other boys had much worse and never turned on their mum like he had when he got in with the wrong crowd.

She jumped when he strode back into the room and her heart sank when he walked straight to the photo on the windowsill. She'd bought it from a bric-a-brac stall on Rathbone market when he was a baby and it showed a handsome soldier in uniform. She had no idea who he was but had always told Ken the man was his father.

He'd never quite believed her.

He reached out and picked up the frame, shaking his head, the vein in his forehead pulsing again.

'It's not him, is it.' It was a statement, not a question. 'You've lied to me all my life.'

Mavis opened her mouth, but no words came out. He fumbled with the frame, breaking a fingernail as he twisted the catch on the back. With a guttural cry, he pulled his arm back and threw the frame across the room. The glass shattered and skittered across the lino.

Mavis flinched as he took the photo of the soldier in his hands.

'This uniform is too old. There is no way this is my father.' He tore the photo into two, then four, then eight, then into smaller and smaller pieces as if doing so would make the man disappear.

False memories of the story she'd told him floated like confetti through her mind, guilt adding to her fear.

He threw the last few pieces at her and Mavis flinched. One tiny piece stuck in her hair. Her pulse raced and she felt herself shrinking into the chair as her adrenaline tightened.

Ken stood there shaking his head and biting his lip. His fury was barely contained. 'What other lies have you told me?'

Outside, they could hear Mrs O'Connor talking to a neighbour, her Irish lilt easily identified. Then another woman joined them, and they greeted her cheerfully. The atmosphere out there, chatting about the price of lamb, was so different from that in this kitchen.

Mavis took a deep breath. 'There's one truth I've always told you, Ken. It's the most important one there is. The most important one in the world.'

His eyes narrowed and his top lip curled. 'What's that then?'

She held out her hand, inviting him to take it. 'I've always told you I love you. Maybe I 'aven't said it in words. I'm not so good at that.'

No one in her family when she was growing up talked about emotions. They'd have been called a sissy if they did.

'But I've shown you I love you every day of your life. I cuddled you as a baby. I stayed awake all night nursing you when you was poorly. I often went without food so you could eat. I stopped lads bullying you when you was little.' She watched him to see if her words were having an impact. It was difficult to tell.

'And since you've got older you've... well, you've been mean to me over and over again. But I've still loved you. I've still cooked your favourite meals, made sure there was a bottle of beer for you and a pack of fags if I could get them.' She sighed and shook her head. 'That's not saying love, but it's showing it with every action.'

Like a rag doll with the stuffing removed, Ken fell into the old armchair and buried his head in his hands. He said no words, but his shoulders shook and to her surprise Mavis realised he was sobbing. Great heaving sobs racked his body as if he was releasing a lifetime's worth of anguish.

Mavis watched him for a minute or two, unsure what to do. Then she quietly went over to him and gently placed a hand on his shoulder, half expecting him to knock it away. But when he didn't, she stroked his hair.

'It's okay, love,' she said. 'You're a good man. You can look forward to a brighter tomorrow.'

23

The train slowly chugged into Glenossary station, far in the north of Scotland. For miles Cordelia had been watching the harsh, rugged landscape out of the train window. It was both beautiful and haunting. Craggy mountains covered with heather were sometimes on both sides of the train and twice she spotted waterfalls, adding magic to the scene. Nature was in charge here in a way she was never aware of in the city.

Over the last hour, the train had stopped at tiny stations and at each one a few people had alighted, pulling their scarves and hats on more closely as they fought the unforgiving wind. Now there was just her and one other person in the carriage. The man had been asleep for most of the journey, waking up occasionally at a stop to check where he was before going back to sleep without a word.

But when they were slowing for Cordelia's station, her movements woke him.

'Goin' to Glenossary, are you, lass?' he asked, and she realised from his voice that he was older than he looked.

She nodded. 'Are you going there too?' She hoped he was. If

there was no one to meet her at the station, being alone in this weather terrified her.

'Och, no. I'm away at the next station. Killiemory. I've been away too long.'

She longed to ask him where he'd been, but the train finally stopped.

He opened the window, leaned out and twisted the handle, opening the door for her. 'Enjoy your stay, lassie,' he said with a smile.

The station house was small, both a home and a station office. The black paint on the door and windows was peeling and even in the poor light she could see one or two tiles on the roof were coming loose.

The stationmaster acknowledged Cordelia, gesturing she should hang on while he waved the train on. Then he pulled away the knitted scarf that had been covering his lower face and looked at her.

'Are ye Lady Cordelia? I'm guessin' ye must be. Nay other soul got off.' He chuckled at his poor joke. 'Nivver had the chance tae speak wi' someone holdin' a title afore. Aye, there's a first time for everyin'. Come along a me noo.'

They didn't have far to walk. The road behind the house was narrow and beginning to break up in places.

'This'll be for you, then,' he said. 'Bess is waiting for you in there.' He waved at the old, battered Model T Ford. There was a dent above the front wheel and the lights weren't quite aligned.

Slowly and with many creaks, one window wound down.

'Come on, Cordelia. Get in quick before we all freeze to death!'

Cordelia hid a grin as she thanked the stationmaster and headed towards the car. Her great-aunt could be a sweetie, but she could also be blunt, or even downright fierce.

She put her case and bag on the back seat and got into the front passenger seat.

'Hello, Aunt,' she said. 'Thank you for collecting me.' As she spoke, a few flakes of snow drifted down like confetti.

'You're late!' her aunt grumbled, grating the gears as she put the car in first. Before she'd gone a hundred yards, a stray sheep wandered onto the road. 'Away with you, you numpty animal,' she shouted, beeping her horn long and loud. Then, without waiting, she spun the wheel and drove round it. Cordelia's heart almost stopped when she saw the boggy, frozen land on each side of the road.

'How is Jasper?' she shouted over the sound of the old engine and the howling of the wind.

'He's much the same,' her aunt shouted back. 'Get out of the way, you stupid sheep!' she shouted again. 'Maybe I should run over one. We could have it for our dinner. They're not mine, though.'

Cordelia imagined a bloody carcass in the small car. She hoped her aunt was joking. But she looked at her and saw she was deadly serious. Her face was set, jaw firm, eyes fixed firmly on the road, knuckles white as she gripped the wheel tight. Cordelia realised she had a lot to learn about farming life so far north. It was very different from her father's land, which was lush and flat. Easy to farm by comparison.

It was simpler to sit in silence for the rest of the journey, clutching the edges of her seat to stop her being thrown around. Her aunt didn't slow down for corners or any other animals. Cordelia saw her squash one rabbit and looked away, feeling squeamish.

Finally, they drove up a muddy track and stopped outside the farmhouse with a jolt. The house had weathered many long, cold winters. Built from rough-hewn stone, its walls were thick and sturdy, grey from many decades of exposure to the elements. The wooden front door was scratched at the bottom where generations of dogs and cats had wanted to be let in.

Cordelia grabbed her belongings and followed her aunt. It had been so long since she'd been there that she'd forgotten how welcoming the kitchen was, generously proportioned with stone tiles. A huge wooden table stood in the middle, scratches and scars showing its decades of use. The deep butler sink and wooden draining board were spotlessly clean. The tartan curtains gently moved in the windows, testament to the draughts from the poorly fitting frames. But a large fire burned in the grate and a ginger cat sat on a Bute rug close to the fireguard. Next to it was an old wooden rocking chair covered with a multicoloured crocheted blanket.

'You'll be wanting the toilet and a cup of tea, I dare say,' Bess said, taking off her outer clothes. 'I'll put the kettle on while you do your business. Then we'll go and see your brother.'

Cordelia went upstairs to the bathroom, resisting the urge to look in the bedrooms to see Jasper in case he was asleep and she disturbed him. She hurried to be as quick as possible in the chilly bathroom, hearing the wind whipping round the house like a banshee and the bare branches of a nearby tree scraping on the bricks. A little distance off, a barn door banged.

She quickly unpacked her few things, glad she'd brought three layers of warm underwear with her. The tiny fire in the bedroom did little to heat the room and she closed the curtains to conserve what heat there was. To her surprise, there was a battered teddy bear on the pillow of the single bed. She smiled as she remembered it from visits to her aunt when she was young. She struggled to remember what she'd called it – Robin? Robert? Richard? Then it came to her, a good Scottish name, Donald, which she'd abbreviated to Donnie. She'd always wanted to take it home, but Bess had always said, 'No, I'll keep it until next time you visit.' And she'd kept it all these years. She might be a cussed old thing occasionally, but she really had a heart of gold.

Tiptoeing downstairs, Cordelia joined her aunt in the kitchen, putting her arm round her shoulders and kissing her on the cheek. Her aunt was as stiff as a plank. Words and demonstrations of affection were not part of her behaviour. Remembering the teddy was one way she showed her feelings.

'Can we go to see Jasper before we have something to eat?' Cordelia asked.

Her aunt had seemed in no hurry. 'I've been in there a couple of times during the night and then this morning. He's much the same,' she said as she picked up her teacup. 'But follow me. Bring your tea if you like.'

Cordelia followed her up the old creaky wooden stairs. Her mouth was dry with fear for her brother. She was glad her aunt went ahead, knocking lightly on the door before opening it.

The sight that met her eyes horrified Cordelia.

Jasper lay frighteningly still amid the damp, rumpled sheets, his skin ashen and his forehead beaded with sweat. His dark hair, longer than it ever was in London, clung damply to his forehead as he struggled for each gasping breath. The room reeked of prolonged sickness, stale sweat, and poultices.

'I'll open the window a bit again,' her aunt said. 'It's important to keep him cool to get his temperature down.'

An icy draught blew through the open window and Cordelia's cheeks stung from the freezing air. A few flakes of snow sneaked their way past the billowing curtains and landed on the wooden floor.

'There's a wee blanket there if you're cold,' her aunt said, pointing to a large knitted square.

Cordelia was almost too scared to approach Jasper, unsettled by her once-vibrant brother's sad state. When they were children, he was always so much healthier than her, so much tougher. 'You're just a silly girl,' he'd say when he climbed trees faster than her. Now he lay here in this lonely bed, fighting for his life.

Aunt Bess looked down at him, sadness in her eyes. 'When I was a wee lass, we thought you had to sweat out a fever,' she said to Cordelia. 'We'd put the patient next to the fire and cover them in blankets. No wonder most of them died.' She shook her head at the memory and took a couple of steps towards the bed where she put her hand on Jasper's forehead. 'No worse,' she said. 'That's a blessing. But we need to keep him cool to get his fever down.'

Cordelia nervously approached the bed and held her brother's hand. There was no response, not even a little twitch, and despite his fever, his hand felt cool and lifeless.

'What can I do?' she asked. She'd never felt so helpless in her life. All her expensive education came to nothing in a situation like this.

Her aunt went over to the small table by the bed. On it was a bowl of water and a flannel.

'You can cool him down with some cold water. Wait here while I get some fresh. It'll be colder.'

As soon as she left, Cordelia began to speak to her brother. 'Come on, Jasper, you can begin to get better now. It's me, Cordelia, come all the way from London to see you.' She brushed his damp curls off his forehead, alarmed at the heat emanating from it. 'Remember how we enjoyed coming here to stay with Aunt Bess when we were children? You pushed me into the loch more than once, beastly brother that you were.' She leaned forward and kissed his cheek, then spoke directly into his ear. 'Come on, brother, you're strong. You can fight this illness and be well again. Aunt Bess needs you; the farm needs you. I need you.'

She got no further as her aunt nudged the door open with her bottom and entered with the bowl of water.

'Right,' she said in her no-nonsense way. 'It's simple. Just soak the cloth in the cold water. Wring it out, then put it on his forehead for a minute. Then wipe his face and neck. When you've done that, start all over again.'

Cordelia reached for the cloth. 'What about his chest? Should I do that too?'

'There's a mustard poultice on it,' her aunt said. 'Stinks something awful. It's an old wives' remedy, but worth a try. But you could wipe round it. I plan to change it this evening.'

Aunt Bess nodded towards a jug and glass beside the bed. In the jug was a brown-tinged liquid.

'That's willow bark tea. It tastes horrible, but he's sweating so much we must keep his fluid levels up. My mother swore by it.'

Cordelia poured some into the glass. 'How much should I give him? How often?'

Outside, they could hear cows mooing and the sound of cow bells. Cordelia was reminded of a holiday in Switzerland before the world went mad.

'It's milking time,' Bess said. 'Can I leave you in charge here? My girls don't like to be kept waiting.' She opened the window a little more and Cordelia shivered. 'Try to get him to drink every twenty or thirty minutes. And that other bowl, under the table, that's a weak mixture of whisky and water. Another old wives' tale but they say if you rub it on their backs, it brings their temperature down.' She snorted. 'Of course, I didn't use the good whisky. We'll share a dram of that this evening.'

When Bess had gone, Cordelia felt overwhelmed by the responsibility of looking after her brother. What if he got worse while her aunt was outside? She had no idea what to do. If only Robert was here to advise her. She trembled just thinking about it. Then, getting herself under control, she dipped the flannel in the icy water, noticing the droplets roll down the sides of the ceramic bowl.

She wrung out the excess liquid then gently pressed the cool cloth on Jasper's burning skin. She expected a response, if only a groan of complaint or a movement as he tried to get away from the cold. But there was nothing.

She watched his face as she tenderly wiped away the sweat, hoping he might come back to consciousness, but his eyes remained closed.

She continued with this pattern of wiping his face, getting him to drink and talking gently to him, and gradually she lost all track of time. Some time later, she became aware of a delicious smell of cooking drifting through the open door. It smelled like roast lamb, something she hadn't had for longer than she cared to remember.

Finally, her aunt appeared. 'Come on, Cordelia,' she said. 'We can't help him if we don't look after ourselves. Come and have something to eat.'

Cordelia looked at Jasper's pallid face and sent up a prayer for his return to consciousness. Then reluctantly she followed her aunt back to the kitchen. The delicious smell of roast lamb was stronger there.

'Our tea'll be late tonight, what with looking after Jasper.'

Aunt Bess poured boiling water in the blue and white striped teapot Cordelia remembered from her childhood. Then she opened her big larder door and took out a round tin. Cordelia's mouth automatically watered at the sight of it, recognising it immediately. The battered lid was bright yellow and there were daffodils painted around the side. When she and Jasper used to stay with her aunt, it seemed at least once a day the tin would come out and they would be offered a generous slice of a delicious home-made cake. Most often it was a Victoria sponge with a strawberry jam filling. But sometimes it was a carrot cake when there'd been a recent carrot harvest on the farm.

Today was a Victoria sponge. It was coated with icing sugar and smelled of vanilla and butter.

'Just a wee slice, mind,' Bess said, handing her a knife. 'Don't go spoiling your appetite for your dinner.'

Cordelia sat at the table, feeling guilty that she was here in this warm, homely kitchen when Jasper was in that cold bedroom fighting for his life.

'Do you think Jasper will make it?' she asked.

'Dinna fash yersel.' Her aunt, who'd grown up in England, occasionally slipped into Scottish expression. 'Dinna meet worry half-way, lassie.'

Cordelia wished she could let go of worry that easily and she suspected her aunt was worried too. Even up here, where it was hard to remember there was a war on, they used blackout curtains. But the light in the kitchen was low so Cordelia pushed aside a curtain and looked outside.

The world was white. It was still snowing.

Her heart sank. If they needed to get a doctor, would they even be able to get to the nearest village three miles away? Were they stuck on the farm until the snow melted?

'Aunt,' she said, wiping cake crumbs from her lips. 'Do you have any land girls?'

Her aunt was busy preparing parsnips. 'We do, but they've got a week off. First one for ages. They work hard, those girls. I was a bampot to give them so long off. I should have listened to the weather forecast on the wireless there.' She chopped the parsnips and put them in the oven with the lamb. 'Now I'll have to do everything myself. Thank the heavens it's not harvest time.'

She put another cup of tea in front of Cordelia and nodded towards the stairs. 'Away with you now. Take that and go see to your brother. I'll call you when the lamb is ready. I've got to feed the animals first.'

24

The cold November wind nipped at Tom's cheeks as he balanced unsteadily on the slick library steps. Behind him, he could hear the paperboy calling out the latest news: '*Ark Royal* torpedoed! Come and get it, *Ark Royal* torpedoed!'

Despite the chill, he felt warmed at the sight of the old library in front of him. It had seen better days and war damage had left it looking like it was – the battered but beloved heart of the community.

Grunting with the effort, he nudged the door open with his crutch, the old wood groaning in protest, and he was greeted by the welcome smell of old paper and floor wax. Limping across the threshold, he looked affectionately at the circulation desk's wood, smoothed by generations of hands.

He knew it was too soon to go back to work, even voluntary work, but he missed the library girls and the readers so much. Being at home all day was boring when he couldn't walk very well.

Jane and Mavis rushed to him as soon as he walked in.

'Tom, what are you doing 'ere, you daft 'aporth?' Mavis said, giving him a hug and nearly unbalancing him. 'You can't be ready to come back yet.'

Tom smiled, glad to be into the warmth of the old library and to be in the company of these two women who, along with their boss, had become his friends.

'Have you come to get a book?' Jane asked. 'I could fetch it for you.'

The door opened again and a mother pushing a big, battered Silver Cross pram came in. A little boy walked beside her, holding on.

'Hello, Mrs Baker,' Tom said. 'Nice to see you and little Frankie. You know where the children's books are.'

Jimmy reached into the wooden box at the bottom of the pram and handed Tom two books wrapped in newspaper. They were slightly damp.

'I've finished these. They were smashing. I'm going to grow up and visit lots of countries.' He imitated a plane, arms swinging round, up and down, round and round.

'Come on, Jimmy,' his mother said. 'Let's get you some more books before the little one needs another feed.'

Tom turned to Mavis and Jane. 'I'm so bored at home, I thought maybe I could come here and work on the front desk. There's loads I can do here as well as the usual taking in books and stamping outgoing ones.'

Mavis clapped her hands. 'You have no idea 'ow much we need you, Tom. Cordelia is still visiting 'er brother in Scotland and we're not sure when she'll be back. 'E's very ill.'

Tom paled. 'Is his life in danger?'

Mavis thought about Cordelia's voice on the phone the previous afternoon. She'd called every day, even though the line was terrible, and she sounded so tired and worried it was amazing she could talk at all.

'Last time she said his fever was down. For the first time they're feeling 'opeful.'

'That's a relief. She always loved her brother.' He rubbed his painful leg. 'Well, if you don't object, I'll get started, ladies.' He hobbled behind the desk, taking off his coat, scarf and gloves. 'Tell you what, I'd really like a cuppa. I can have it here while I work.'

Jane went off to make the tea while Mavis took the returns trolley and headed off to put books back in their rightful place.

Sitting at the familiar desk almost felt like coming home. He loved being here with these friendly women and he loved feeling that he was helping the impoverished community. The children had suffered so much since the war started, not least their education. The library was one place where they could help to catch up, dream their dreams and reach their potential. That's why he and Jane worked hard to make the children's section as welcoming and fun as possible.

He'd barely caught his breath when one of the library's regular customers came to the desk.

'Just this today, please, young man.'

Tom knew Mr Carpenter well and sometimes helped him find just the right book. He was keen on thrillers and often said he'd like to write one himself.

Unthinkingly, Tom opened the front page of the book ready to stamp the date sheet. But it wasn't there. No sheet.

Puzzled, Tom looked at the front cover.

'I'm so sorry, Mr Carpenter, but this is a dictionary. It's not for loan.'

Mr Carpenter looked offended. 'What do you mean, it's not for loan? I borrow books here all the time. It's a book, isn't it, or have I lost my marbles?' His voice gradually rose as he spoke.

Out of the corner of his eye, Tom saw Mavis stop what she was doing and begin to watch the conversation.

'I'm really sorry, Mr Carpenter, but this is a reference book. It needs to be kept in the library so anyone can use it any time we are open.'

The man's shoulders slumped in disappointment. He pushed his glasses further up his nose, his bushy grey eyebrows knitted together in confusion. He picked up the dictionary and turned it over as if double-checking the cover. He tugged at the sleeve of his jacket and cleared his throat.

'But it's a book,' he repeated. 'It's a book and this is a library. I've borrowed dozens of books from here.'

Tom breathed deeply to keep calm. 'As I've explained—'

But Mr Carpenter interrupted him. 'Okay, then, if I can't borrow the whole book, how about lending me J to Z? When I'm done with them, I'll come in with the pages and some glue and stick them back in. Is that a deal?'

The corners of Tom's mouth twitched, and he faked a cough to stop himself grinning.

By now, Mavis was doubled up with laughter, her hands over her mouth to suppress the sound.

The man took a lot of convincing, but they finally got him to leave when they suggested he might find a cheap dictionary on the market.

As the rain tapped against the windows, Jane handed Tom his steaming cup of tea. He thanked her and she patted his arm affectionately.

'My goodness, Tom,' she said. 'That may just be the most ridiculous thing I've ever heard in this library. How on earth did you keep a straight face?'

Mavis had joined them and she absent-mindedly thumbed through the pile of books returned. 'That's nothing. Yesterday a young lad came in asking for a book on how to propose to his girlfriend.'

Jane's mouth dropped open. 'You're kidding. He really wanted a proposal book?'

'I couldn't believe it neither. I 'ad to check it wasn't April Fool's Day.'

'Well, did you help the lad then?' Tom asked. 'Is some girl in for a lovely surprise? If she wants him, of course.'

Mavis raised an eyebrow. 'I told 'im we didn't have any books on proposing, so 'e asked my advice. I must look like that agony aunt, Marjory Proops who writes for the *Mirror*. I took 'im to the periodicals room and we thrashed out how 'e'd do it.' She paused, remembering how he stumbled over his words, going red and doing anything but look her in the eye. 'Poor lad. I wonder if 'e'll come back to tell me 'ow 'e got on. Perhaps I'll get invited to the wedding.'

Three more people came into the library and the two women left Tom to deal with them. Mavis went over to a rarely used corner of the library. She knew her favourite reader was there. Mrs Dace. As usual, she was sitting knitting with a book propped up in front of her. She never appeared to look at her knitting, but somehow she knew when she'd dropped a stitch. Then her swear words could be heard by half the library.

'Now, Mrs Dace,' Mavis whispered. 'You know you're not supposed to talk in the library, much less swear loud enough for the king to 'ear from the palace!'

Looking down, Mrs Dace picked up her dropped stitch before she answered. 'But it always happens at an interesting bit of the story. How'm I supposed to work out who done it if I have to stop reading to pick up stitches, that's what I want to know?'

Mavis had noticed that she always seemed to be knitting the same thing. A black scarf. Surely they couldn't always be the same one. She must be knitting endless black scarves. Mavis decided not to ask where she got so much wool from. With so much black marketeering, it sometimes paid not to ask questions.

'Well, try to keep it down in future,' she said, patting the woman on the shoulder. Walking away, she knew she might as well have talked to the wall. She went to the front desk where Tom was entering some figures in a notebook.

'There might be a war raging out there,' she said, nodding to the doorway, 'but life goes on much the same in 'ere, thank goodness.'

But the day wasn't over yet. Not by a long way.

25

'I'm telling you, you're a silly bampot if you try to get to the village in this weather!' Aunt Bess cried, fear in her eyes.

It wasn't quite daylight and Cordelia shivered in the predawn chill as she hurried to her aunt's old car cursing that the phone line was down. Dawn was still half an hour away, the farmhouse quiet except for the soft sounds of the cows and chickens in the barn. The snow had eased off, but still fell, gently dusting everything like icing sugar on one of Aunt Bess's Victoria sponges.

Jasper had got worse during the night. It had been harrowing just to see him struggle to stay alive, to get air into his diseased lungs. All night she had administered to him, the room freezing, apart from an hour or so when her aunt relieved her so she could warm up and get something to eat.

But she could wait no longer. She had to fetch the doctor. Immediately. Jasper's life depended on it.

Bess tried to talk her out of it. 'It's too dangerous. You'll end up dead too.'

Cordelia refused to wait. She put on so many layers of clothes she could hardly move her arms, then ventured towards her aunt's car. She pumped the accelerator then gripped the metal starter handle. Pain from the cold metal stabbed her palms. She turned the handle again and again, wishing her aunt had a newer car. It was no good. The car refused to start.

As the icy wind whipped round her, swaying trees as if they were as insubstantial as thread, she considered her options. Walking was out. Three miles on icy, snow-covered country tracks would take forever, even if she could see where she was going.

She had to find a way.

Then she heard the old plough horse, Angus, neighing in the barn. It gave her an idea. He had to be fit and strong for his job.

She went back into the house. 'I'm going to take the plough horse. Will you help me attach the cart to him? I don't know how to do it.'

She knew her aunt was against her going for the doctor so was surprised when she put on her coat and fetched the harness and leads. They managed to coax him to stand while they prepared him. His patient brown eyes watched them as they put a blanket over him before attaching the harness. The wooden cart creaked under her weight as Angus took the strain.

'Good boy,' Cordelia said, patting his head. 'You're helping Jasper.' The horse snorted as if he understood her words.

'Wait!' Aunt Bess called as Cordelia climbed onto the cart.

Bess returned a minute later with a rough grey army blanket.

'It kept the men in the trenches warm in the Great War,' she said as she reached up and put it round Cordelia's shoulders.

Cordelia flicked the reins and Angus began the long, cold journey to the village, his breath forming billowing clouds in the icy air. Cordelia pulled the scratchy blanket around herself and tightened her fingers around the worn leather reins, praying she would be in time to save her brother's life.

The snow had eased to an occasional flurry, often falling from trees they passed. Cordelia glanced back to check the farmhouse lights to feel confident she was on the right track. They'd agreed to break the blackout rules just this once.

Angus plodded along at his own speed, steadily, his shaggy hooves crunching the frozen path. No matter how much Cordelia flicked the reins, his pace never changed. It was painstakingly slow.

They were halfway there when it happened.

The wooden wheels skidded off the buried road. The cart lurched and stopped, resting at an angle. Her heart raced. She couldn't afford to waste time when Jasper's life was at stake. Bracing herself against the cold, Cordelia turned around to see if there were any farm implements that could help her get the cart out of the furrow. The cry of a hawk flying overhead added to her jumpiness, sending a shiver of fear down her spine.

She found a wooden sort of trowel in the back and carried it down to the road, walking on the frozen snow. The cold instantly forced its way through her shoes and socks, making her feet tingle. Fearful of falling over, she clutched the side of the cart with every step. She could barely feel her fingers, but grasped the unfamiliar tool and began to dig around the half-buried axle. It seemed to take a lifetime to toss aside the shovelfuls of snow until she was confident Angus could pull the cart free.

With hands soaked from the icy slush, she reached up and pulled herself back into the cart and, talking to Angus the whole time, she flexed her frozen fingers and flicked the reins, almost scared to breathe. The cart jolted twice, almost throwing her back onto the frozen ground. But then the ice cracked, and they moved forward. The wheels skidded on the frozen ground, but somehow kept moving ahead.

Cordelia talked constantly to Angus, her words really more to reassure herself she would get to the doctor in time to help Jasper.

She promised the horse sugar cubes when they arrived, and he shook his head as if he understood.

The journey seemed to take an eternity. But finally, just as the pale winter sun began appearing above the mountains, the huddled buildings of the village appeared. Cordelia could have wept with relief. Her aunt had told her where Dr Smithers lived and she quickly noticed the large house on the outskirts of the village, surrounded by a garden with a wooden fence.

She pulled on the reins and stepped down from the cart, then hitched the horse to the fence and ran to the front door.

Thankfully, a young maid opened the door quickly. 'Is it the doctor you'll be wanting?' she asked without ado. 'Come inside while I fetch him.'

Cordelia guessed the house must be used to being disturbed in this way.

Ten minutes later, she was in the doctor's car heading back to the farm.

26

The farmhouse door flew open before Cordelia and Dr Smithers had even got out of the car.

'Thank goodness you're here!' Aunt Bess said, ushering them into the kitchen. 'He's upstairs, doctor. Thank you for coming.'

The two women followed the doctor to the sick room. From outside, they could hear Jasper's rasping cough and wheezes.

'Have I taken too long?' Cordelia asked herself. 'Is it too late to save him?'

Jasper was sitting upright in bed, resting on several pillows. 'He came round and said it was easier to breathe like that,' Bess said. 'I hope it was the right thing to do.'

Dr Smithers took off his coat and patted her on the arm. 'Anything that helps his breathing is the right thing to do, Bess.'

Jasper's lips had a bluish tinge and he struggled to get each breath, air rattling in his fluid-filled lungs. But Cordelia was encouraged that he was conscious, and he even managed a small smile when he saw her.

Dr Smithers took out his stethoscope and listened to Jasper's chest and back. His forehead creased in a deep frown.

'Jasper,' he said. 'Can you understand what I'm saying?'

To everyone's relief, Jasper managed a small nod.

Cordelia tried to remember everything she had learned on her first aid course and from stories Robert had told her about treating patients in his hospital. 'Can you give him morphine or penicillin?' she asked.

Dr Smithers shook his head. 'I wish I could. Their use is very restricted, mostly for the military. I don't have any.' He opened his bag again. 'But there are plenty of alternatives.' He took a paper packet out of his bag. 'Can you get me a glass of water and a spoon, please?'

While Cordelia ran downstairs, Dr Smithers turned to Jasper. 'Jasper, lad. I'm going to give you some medicine. It's sulfa and it will help your breathing. Do you think you'll be able to drink it?'

Bess spoke up. 'He has been drinking. I've been giving him willow bark tea. But it has to be given in very small amounts. He can't manage much in one go.'

Cordelia ran back in the room with the glass and spoon and Dr Smithers shook the white powder into it, then stirred it vigorously. 'While that's dissolving, I'm going to be patting your back and chest,' he said, and then turned to the two women. 'It looks brutal, but it will loosen the congestion.'

He sat Jasper up and using his cupped fingers tapped rhythmically on every area of his chest. Cordelia thought his hands were being used like a mallet. She guessed he was listening to the different sounds where his lungs were congested or clear.

Shaking his head, the doctor gently pushed Jasper forward and repeated the action on his back. 'The good news is there are some clear areas,' he said.

As he spoke, Jasper began coughing.

'That's a good sign. We've dislodged some of the mucus,' the doctor went on. 'Now to do some more. I'm going to show you two ladies a technique. It takes quite a long time but is easy to teach.' He turned to face Jasper. 'You needn't worry, it's not painful. But first, drink this sulfa.'

Cordelia took over from him, and helped Jasper to drink the cloudy white liquid. As she did, the doctor stretched his back.

'Any chance of a cup of tea and a slice of your delicious cake, Bess?' he asked with a smile. 'I didn't have any breakfast before your charming niece pulled me away from my warm home!'

When Bess went downstairs to fetch him a drink and a slice of cake, Dr Smithers spoke to Cordelia. 'I expect you've been using steam to help his breath?'

'We have, and cough mixture that Aunt Bess made up. I've no idea what was in it but it smelled dreadful.'

'Tasted awful too,' came a croaky whisper from the bed.

Cordelia's heart leapt. Jasper must be at least a little better to speak, to take part in the conversation.

'You know what us doctors say, young man, the worse it tastes, the better it is for you!' He rubbed his hands together and went to look out of the window. 'You've done the right thing keeping the room cold, and it certainly is cold. But I think the snow has stopped.'

Cordelia joined him at the window. The sun was rising higher over the mountains and the sky was summer blue. 'If only it got warm enough to melt the snow,' she said wistfully.

Dr Smithers patted her shoulder. 'This is Scotland, lass. When it comes to weather, always expect the worst.'

Bess came back in with a tray laden with a teapot, and everything they needed.

'While the tea cools, I'm going to show you two this method for getting all that nasty stuff off Jasper's lungs. It's quite time-consuming and you need to do it three or four times a day.'

Walking round the bed, he began moving pillows this way and

that. When he was satisfied, he laid Jasper down on his right side, with his right arm raised.

'This looks strange,' he said. 'But we're going to use gravity to shift that mucus. I'll show you each of the positions and you leave this poor laddie in each one for five to fifteen minutes. Jasper, you just breathe normally while this is going on. If it works, you'll be coughing up that mucus in no time.'

When he'd finished teaching her and her aunt how to help Jasper, the doctor drove Cordelia back to his home so she could fetch Angus.

She hardly dared ask the question she mostly wanted to ask, but fortunately, Dr Smithers knew what was on her mind.

'I expect you'll be wanting to know if I think he's going to recover,' he said, swerving to miss a pothole in the road.

She looked at him as if he were a mind reader.

'My opinion, lassie, is that there's a good chance he'll recover. You and your aunt have done all the right things for him and now you know other ways to help him.'

Another car screeched round a corner, almost hitting them. The driver didn't even seem to notice what had happened. In London, the other driver would probably have got a good mouthful of abuse. Dr Smithers just muttered, 'Reckless,' under his breath and carried on.

'I'm hoping the laddie will have a lower temperature by the morning. If he's still as bad, though, come and get me. If we're lucky, the telephones will be working by then.'

As Cordelia drove back on the cart with good, reliable Angus, she thought about how lucky they were. She was grateful the village doctor was so helpful. Robert had told her the occasional story about colleagues who shouldn't really be doctors. They were more concerned with their own status than with the welfare of their patients. She sighed, remembering that in every profession there would be good and bad workers. When she was doing her library training, she had a placement in a large city library. Most of the librarians were good at their jobs, helping readers in any way they possibly could. But one, Jessie, was a skiver. She'd come in late, find excuses to leave early and dodge even the simplest task if she could help it, like restacking the books.

Back at the house, Cordelia uncoupled the cart and led Angus back to the barn, making sure he had his sugary treats and a wrinkled apple. Aunt Bess was in the other barn, milking the 'girls', as she called them.

'Come round, Cordelia,' she called out. 'I've almost finished.'

Cordelia gave Angus a last fond pat and joined her aunt. 'How is Jasper?' she asked.

Bess patted the cow she had been milking and stood up, pulling the pail of milk away. She'd seen too many kicked over in her time.

'Well, that moving him around the bed did good. He coughed up a lot of stuff. Your turn next. I'm guessing we'll know before morning if he's going to live or die.'

27

Peals of youthful laughter scattered the early-morning gloom of the old farmhouse. Cordelia was halfway down the stairs, carrying a tray with Jasper's cup when she heard it. She stopped dead, confusion filling her mind. The house had been utterly quiet since her brother became ill, apart from the occasional wireless programme Bess put on. She and her aunt had tiptoed around, spoken in hushed voices, and done everything they could to avoid disturbing Jasper. Yet here was a new sound – happy girlish laughter. No burglar would make such a noise, she thought, trying to make sense of what she heard.

Tentatively she stepped into the kitchen, and there stood two girls, cheeks glowing from the cold. They didn't notice her at first as they chatted and took off their coats. Then they looked as startled to see her as she was to see them.

'Oh,' she said, at a loss for what to say. For a minute, she couldn't think who these two girls were or why they had let themselves in the farmhouse without knocking.

'Don't look so frightened,' the plump one with blonde curls

said. 'I'm Maggie and this is my mate Gloria. We're the land girls. We had a few days off, like.'

As she spoke, she hung up her coat and scarf. Gloria did the same.

Cordelia's shoulders relaxed a little when she absorbed this information. Help at last. She and her aunt had struggled to keep the farm going and nurse Jasper for quite a few days, not to mention the cold. She hastily put down the tray and hugged each girl in return.

'You have absolutely no idea how pleased I am to see you. Aunt Bess will be too. It's been awful—'

Maggie interrupted her. 'I don't mean to be rude nor nothing, but who are you?'

Cordelia felt her cheeks turn pink. 'I'm so sorry, but I haven't had much sleep. I should have introduced myself. I'm Cordelia, Jasper's sister.'

'The one what lives in London?' Ann asked. 'He's talked about you a lot. Work in a bookshop or something, don't you?'

Walking over to the stove, Cordelia put the kettle on. 'A library. In the East End of London. I should be there now, but Jasper—'

Ann put her hand to her mouth. 'Jasper! I forgot! He was a bit poorly when we left. Has he got worse then?'

Bess came in before Cordelia could answer. She brought a rush of cold air with her. When she saw the girls, she smiled, the first smile Cordelia had seen since she arrived.

But her aunt didn't speak to the girls. Instead, she looked at Cordelia.

'How is he?'

Maggie looked from one to the other. 'Has he been really ill then? Is that why you've come all this way?'

Cordelia nodded. 'That's right. Jasper has got pneumonia.'

'But how is he?' her aunt asked again, sharpness in her voice. 'Is he...'

'His fever has broken, Aunt. His breathing is much easier. I think he's over the worst.'

Her aunt collapsed into a chair as if someone had taken all the stuffing out of her. She put her head in her hands and let out a sob. 'Thank goodness, thank goodness. I shouldn't have let him go out in this weather.'

Ann folded her arms. 'Well, you let us, and we're girls. Ain't we as important as him then?'

The kettle began to whistle. Cordelia was relieved it distracted everyone. 'Let's have a cuppa. You two must be frozen. Have you had breakfast?'

'Excuse me, girls,' Bess said. 'I must check on Jasper myself. Cordelia will see to you.'

Over eggs, bacon, toast and huge mugs of tea, the girls told Cordelia all about their break. They'd both gone to Maggie's home. Her parents were delighted to see her and cooked all her favourite meals. Ann's family was too far away and from what Cordelia made out, they weren't very welcoming.

Jasper forgotten for a while, they chatted about seeing all Maggie's friends, going to a dance – 'my feet ached all next day!' – and a film they'd seen. 'It was *Dumbo*,' Ann said, smiling at the memory. 'About a flying elephant. I think it was for kids, but we loved it.'

Although they were young, Cordelia was impressed by their sensible attitudes to life. Aunt Bess had told her that they had never lived on a farm before, much less worked on one. But they'd soon learned their way around dealing with the animals and anything else she'd asked of them.

Maybe they could help look after Jasper as well.

When the girls had finished eating, they changed into their

farm clothes and headed off to work. Cordelia checked on Jasper again, then insisted her aunt sit down by the fire with her for a while.

'I never did ask you, Aunt, how Jasper was when he first arrived.'

Her aunt put some more wood on the fire and prodded it into life. 'I think you could guess. He resented being here, sulked like a silly schoolboy. I could have given him a slap a couple of times.'

Cordelia could relate to that. She remembered all the times she'd tried to get him to gamble less or give up drinking or enlist or just simply grow up. He'd reacted as if she was a spoilsport, ruining his fun.

'What turned him round?'

Aunt Bess thought for a minute. 'I think it was the horse. He's always liked them, he told me, so I gave him that job first. Gradually he got used to the other animals. I've got to say, it's taken less time than I thought it would to make him a good worker. I'm proud of him now.'

Cordelia reached out and put her hand on her aunt's arm. 'And I'm impressed by you, Aunt. You've done a sterling job on him and not just on the farm but with his illness.'

'We both did that, Cordelia. I don't think I could have done it all myself. Not with Maggie and Ann away.'

The next day, they were eating breakfast when there was a sharp knock on the door. Dr Smithers opened it without waiting to be invited in.

'Come to see the invalid,' he said, unbuttoning his woollen coat. He stamped his boots on the well-worn welcome mat and clumps of snow fell on to it. 'How is he doing? Any change?'

Aunt Bess got up from her chair and shook his hand as if they'd just met for the first time.

'He's doing much better. But I'm so glad you're here. We were wondering if we could trust that he's really turned the tide.'

Dr Smithers stomped up the stairs, each one creaking under his weight.

'Smells fresher in here,' he muttered as he entered the room. Then he looked at Jasper. 'And you, young man, look a whole lot like you've decided to live after all.'

He did all the usual checks, listening to his chest, taking his temperature and pulse.

'What do you think, doc?' Jasper asked. His speech was improved now he could breathe more easily.

'You'll live!' the doctor said briskly. 'As long as you continue like this, you can go downstairs tomorrow and sit by the fire. No need to stay here in this sickroom getting bored. Wrap yourself up with a blanket. But that's all you're allowed to do. Don't go out in the cold or do any work. Not for at least a week and only then if you can move about without getting exhausted.'

Cordelia was delighted the doctor had confirmed her brother was on the mend.

'I haven't discussed it with Jasper yet,' she said to him, 'but I was thinking about going back to London in a couple of days. Do you think that's okay?'

Dr Smithers smiled at her. 'Well, I saw those two bonny lassies in the yard as I came in. They can help look after Jasper just as well as you. No offence meant.'

For the next two days, Cordelia spent every minute she wasn't helping on the farm in the kitchen with Jasper. She took over the cooking, even though she was nowhere near as good as her aunt. She and Jasper talked in a way they hadn't for years, reminiscing about their childhoods playing in the massive gardens, going to the village to get shopping, playing tricks on their mother that she never seemed to understand and how Mrs Taylor, their lovely cook, had spoilt them with forbidden biscuits at every opportunity.

After so many years of not getting on, she cherished the chance to rebuild the bond they once had.

Two days later, she was on the train back to London and her beloved library.

The royal visit was looming. Mavis and Jane had kept her informed of progress, but she couldn't help worrying.

Would everything be ready in time?

28

Mavis's heart skipped a beat when she opened the door and saw the telegram boy looking up at her. Cold air pushed its way through her clothes and the acrid smells from the factory assaulted her nose.

Telegram boys nearly always brought bad news – death or at least injury or a loved one missing in action or taken prisoner.

The lad couldn't have been more than twelve. Even on a cold day like this one, he only wore a shirt, threadbare jacket and short trousers hanging loose on his slight frame.

'S'all right, missus,' he said with a cheeky grin, displaying two missing teeth. 'Good news for once.' He handed over the brown envelope and got back on his bike.

'Hang on a mo,' Mavis called after him, almost collapsing with relief. She reached into her apron pocket and took out her purse. Then she handed him a thruppenny bit.

'Cor, thanks, missus,' he said, tucking it in his pocket. 'I'll get meself some gobstoppers.' He winked and got back on his bike, pedalling as the wind rippled through his clothes.

Mavis hurried back inside her little home, ripping open the envelope with shaking hands. At first, she looked at the words as if they were written in a foreign language. Time seemed to slow as she struggled to comprehend their meaning. Then the penny dropped. What she read brought a happy smile to her face.

```
FORTY EIGHT HOURS LEAVE.
ARRIVE 7.30 TRAIN TONIGHT JOE.
```

Forty-eight hours' leave! So precious.

Mavis immediately looked at the clock. It was six fifteen. He'd be here soon. She longed to go to meet him from the train but had no idea what station he would arrive from. Like all troops, he had never told her where he was stationed so she couldn't even make an educated guess.

She ran to her bedroom to put on her best dress, wishing it was summer. In this cold, she would need to wear several layers. As she changed, her mind went back to the six days she and Joe had spent together. It seemed like a lifetime ago. They'd met at a dance on the first evening of Joe's leave and they'd hardly been apart the whole time, except when she was at work. Even then, he had found excuses to come into the library at least twice a day. Once he handed her a small posy of flowers, making Jane jealous.

She'd been so happy to find a man she instinctively believed she could trust; she had let down the tough emotional guard she usually wore like a suit of armour and allowed herself to be vulnerable. He had never abused that, not even for one second. They'd gone for walks, seen two films, and gone to the Victoria and Albert Museum.

'The museum's not all open,' she had warned him. 'The ground floor is full of evacuees, and a lot of the offices are used for goodness knows what.'

He'd squeezed her hand. 'I don't care, love. I just want to be with you.'

They'd written regularly after he went back to his camp, at least twice a week. She tried to send him little gifts when she could, socks or a thick scarf. He said he'd never been a reader. She found that astonishing. Her childhood had been far from perfect in lots of ways. In fact, she suspected her mother had sent her off to the library to get a bit of peace and quiet. Even that young, she'd realised that books could transport you from everyday life to different places and different times.

As a child she'd loved walking to Canning Town library with its imposing frontage – seven windows on the first floor. How many times had she stood looking up at the much-loved building? She had clutched her precious frayed library card, imagining all the adventures she could read about if she chose the right book. Stepping inside seemed like entering a palace full of rare treats. The towering wooden bookshelves dwarfed her, but in the children's section she could reach all the books. As she reminisced, she tried to recollect the name of the kindly librarian who always remembered her. What was it? Miss Mortimer? Yes, that was it.

She'd heard someone say she was another of the 'spare women'. Mavis had no idea if this was true, and even if it was it didn't stop the thin, angular woman from having a ready smile and a kind word each time they met.

Little did Mavis know that one day she would be a librarian in nearby Silvertown.

Bringing her thoughts back to the moment, she realised it was unlikely she'd convert Joe into an avid reader. But she had a great belief that it was just a matter of finding the right books. She'd sent him two books she thought might interest him – *The Brigadier General* by Arthur Conan Doyle and a book of short stories by Edgar Wallace. He'd been reading the short stories and when he wrote about them she would smile. Perhaps she could convert him.

She'd started tidying the living room and when she'd finished she stood back, trying to see it through his eyes, though she knew he would probably only have eyes for her. Next, she hurried into the kitchen. She'd already eaten her tea, just some vegetable soup left over from the previous day and a fish paste sandwich. There was so little she could offer him when he arrived, and she wished she'd had warning he was coming. As she hurried around her thoughts went to Joyce. She had written to Joe about her intention to adopt little Joyce and made it clear that she would come first. In effect, if she and Joe were to continue with their relationship, in time there would be two of them, herself and Joyce. Remembering how much time and attention small children needed, she realised that the sort of special time she and Joe had just enjoyed might have to be more carefully arranged. So far, he'd been positive about her plans. He'd never had children but assured her he loved the idea of being involved in Joyce's life.

His knock on the door, when it came, made her jump, every nerve tingling. With wobbly legs, she walked to open it. Would they still feel the same about each other? After so long apart, would they be able to pick up where they'd left off?

Although the war had only been going on a couple of years, she knew several couples whose marriages were fracturing. The women had become accustomed to making their own decisions, to managing their own money, to looking after themselves and their children without having to consider a husband who may or may not be kind. And war often changed the men. Some came back with terrible injuries to their body or mind, or both. In her role as unofficial 'aunty' in her area, Mavis had been visited by several women for advice on how to cope with their husbands who were changed beyond recognition. Or who had changed themselves.

Sally, who lived several doors away, was one. Her husband had made all the financial decisions in their household. He'd just given her weekly 'wages' for housekeeping, taking care of bills himself.

Sally had been happy with that; it was how her parents had operated. But while he was away at war, she found she could cope with money on her own, albeit with occasional advice from Mavis. Then, when Bob came home on leave, he resented her new-found independence. There'd been rows almost every day until his leave was up.

So it was with a mixture of excitement and fear that Mavis opened the door.

But she needn't have worried.

Joe's wide smile told her all she needed to know. He stepped forward, dropped his kitbag without a second thought and rushed forward to sweep her into his arms, crushing her to his chest. Their long-awaited kiss was one of fiery intensity, breathlessly making up for lost time. Joe tenderly cradled her face in his hands, as though she were the most precious jewel in the world. He looked at her hungrily, his eyes telling her his feelings hadn't changed.

'Come in, you daft 'alfpeth,' Mavis said, holding his hand tight. 'Come in the warm so I can kiss you properly.'

Hand in hand, they hurried inside, shutting out the cold night air. No sooner had the door closed behind them than their lips met again with yet more passion. All the longing of months apart melted away in that embrace.

Finally pulling apart, Joe brushed a stray hair from Mavis's face. 'You have no idea how much I missed you, sweetheart,' he said. 'More than you'll ever know. Sometimes it was the thought of coming home to you that kept me going.'

Mavis led him to the cosy settee by the fireplace. She busied herself putting on the kettle and stoking up the fire. While she did so, Joe took off his greatcoat and settled into the settee, exhaustion showing in his face.

'Do you want anything to eat?' Mavis called from the kitchen. 'I can make you a sandwich.'

He shook his head. 'I had something at the station.' He paused. 'A cup of tea and you beside me is all I want.'

She soon put two cups of tea in front of them and studied his face properly for the first time. New creases lined his forehead and the familiar sparkle in his eyes was dimmer than before. But she could still read the love in his eyes.

'Tell me what's been 'appening to you,' she said.

He took a sip of his tea. 'D'you know, love, I'd rather just sit here quiet like, feeling you next to me, if that's okay.'

They could hear music on the wireless from the people who lived in the upstairs rooms, but it hardly registered as they got to know each other again. Outside, the city bustled on oblivious of their emotions. But cocooned together in front of the glowing fire, they found again the love they had shared before he'd been sent away.

* * *

'I look a total mess!' Mavis said, looking in the mirror next morning. She was struggling to get her hair to behave before heading off to the library.

Joe grinned at her from the bed. 'Well, if you will stay awake all night...'

She turned and pretended to swipe him. 'All your fault, you cheeky beggar!' She grinned and leaned over to kiss him, making herself later than ever. 'See you later at the library when you've finished whatever it is you're doing. I'll do my best to get the day off.'

She hummed a cheerful tune as she finished getting dressed. 'Pity you have to put clothes on,' Joe said with a grin. 'Bert at the library could have been in for a treat.'

Mavis punched his arm. 'You have a dirty mind, soldier!' The banter between them felt so natural, as if they saw each other every day. After their long time apart, it was a relief to find their feelings for each other hadn't changed.

It was a crisp winter morning as Mavis walked briskly towards the library, her breath trailing behind her, the chill in the air belied by the cloudless blue sky worthy of midsummer.

She couldn't contain her elation after the blissful night she and Joe had spent together. Humming softly, she replayed in her mind each tender moment – cuddling by the fire, passionate kisses and so much more. She was longing to tell Jane her news – well, not the intimate moments. She knew both Jane and Cordelia would be pleased about the progress of their relationship.

As she walked past his shop, Mr Green, the grocer, called out, 'You're looking perky today, Mavis! 'Ad a good night, did ya?' She grinned and blew him a jokey kiss, glad he couldn't read her mind.

She passed children playing hopscotch when they should be hurrying to school and wondered if they had a school to go to. So many had been bombed. And because many children were evacuated, some school buildings had been given over for other uses. She shook her head, thinking of everything the children were missing, and was grateful the library could help in some ways.

As she opened the library door, slipping happily into the warmth, she couldn't wait to tell her colleagues her news.

The library was unusually quiet when she closed the rear door. The familiar smells drifted towards her, old books, pipe smoke, furniture polish. Entering the library was as comfortable as going into her own home.

Normally Cordelia, Jane and sometimes Tom would be getting everything ready to open up for the day, but not this time. She frowned and looked around, not yet alarmed. Sometimes circumstances made people late. While the Blitz was over, there was still occasional bombing, and it wasn't unusual for unexploded bombs to be found. When that happened, everything around it ground to a halt. She shrugged and took off her coat, noticing that Cordelia's office door was open and her light was on.

'Morning, boss!' she said, poking her head around the door.

Cordelia looked up from a letter she was reading. It was one of four she had received all at the same time from her Robert, bundled together. She'd been worried something terrible had happened to him when she didn't receive his letters as usual. Her relief as she scanned the first one distracted her from noticing Mavis's excitement.

'Boss, I...' Mavis started and something in her voice made Cordelia look at her properly. Mavis almost glowed with a radiant joy that Cordelia had never seen from her before. Seeing her flushed cheeks and sparkling eyes, it was obvious something special had happened.

'You look like the cat that's got the cream,' she said. 'Come on, spill the beans. Did you win the pools?' As she spoke, she put the letters back in their envelopes and locked them in her desk drawer.

Mavis stepped into the office, looking years younger than normal. 'It's Joe. He's got forty-eight hours' leave. Can I take today and tomorrow off so I can spend time with 'im? I'm owed plenty of 'oliday.'

Cordelia's face dropped and so did Mavis's heart when she saw that.

'What's wrong? Has someone died?' Mavis asked.

'No, not died. But Jane can't come in today. Helen is poorly. And Tom can't come until this afternoon. If you take the day off, I'll be here on my own. It's IIP day and children's session.'

Mavis's shoulders drooped. She and Joe only had forty-eight hours, less now after their night spent together.

'And the kiddies' craft session is due to start at ten thirty,' Cordelia continued. 'I was anticipating you taking it on as Jane can't do it. It's too late to cancel now. I'm sorry but I need you for this morning. You can have the afternoon and tomorrow off.'

There was a hammering on the door, and they looked at the clock, realising they should have opened up five minutes earlier.

'Rats!' Mavis said. 'Bert'll be hopping mad and cold as hell.'

She hurried to open the door and Bert pushed past her with a grunt. Behind him was Floppy Flossie. She used to regularly pretend to collapse in the library, and elsewhere. But since they gave her some attention, she'd more or less stopped doing that.

Today was an exception.

She took one look at Mavis, let out a loud groan and collapsed on the floor, crying, 'Me stomach, me stomach!'

Mavis had learned to bite her tongue with Flossie, even when she was busy, but this morning her acting was too much too cope with. Mavis was already fed up with having to work. The last thing she needed was Flossie messing her about as well.

'Up!' she shouted. 'Get up! There's nothing wrong with you, dippy madam.'

Flossie just wailed louder.

Two other people came in and looked at the scene, open-mouthed. 'Should we call an ambulance?' one asked.

'Police, more like,' Mavis muttered. Then she walked away, leaving Flossie where she was. 'Come with me, please,' she said to the newcomers. 'How can I help you?'

They looked stunned, glancing from her to Flossie and back, unsure what to do. Flossie looked at them, silently pleading with them to give her attention.

Outside, a police car rushed by, its siren wailing. Mavis felt like going out and flagging it down.

'Flossie will be fine,' she said to the two people waiting, her voice impatient. 'Let me 'elp you, then I'll see to 'er. I'm used to 'er and 'er ways.'

Cordelia had come out of her office and witnessed the conversation, alarmed at Mavis's handling of Flossie and her funny ways.

Letting Mavis deal with the newcomers, Cordelia went over to Flossie.

'Are you okay?' she asked, helping her up. 'Why don't you come and sit over here? I'll find a book I think you'd like.'

Flossie loved nothing better than attention from the women in charge of the library.

'It's my stomach,' she pleaded.

Cordelia nodded, trying not to think of the pile of work on her desk or the letters from Robert she hadn't read yet. 'I just know that sitting with a good book will take your mind off it. It always works for me.'

She made sure Flossie was in a quiet area and fetched an Agatha Christie book.

'There, I think you'll like that one. You can borrow it if you like. But I must get on with some work now.'

As she walked back towards Mavis, her steps seemed weighted down and her stomach clenched. She rarely had to speak sternly to her or Jane, but she couldn't let her harsh words and unkind behaviour towards Flossie go unremarked.

She waited until Mavis had finished stamping someone's book, then called her aside. She fixed her with a stern look.

'I know you're disappointed at having to work today, but you were very blunt with Flossie. You don't need me to tell you it's not professional.'

Mavis's cheeks flushed and her jaw clenched. She was normally so strong and in control of her emotions but now she struggled to hold back tears.

'I know but...'

Cordelia put a hand on her arm. 'There can't be any buts, Mavis, you know that. If things get on top of you, make an excuse and get one of us to take over.'

She'd no sooner spoken than the library door was flung open with a bang. They both turned to see who had made such a noisy entrance and there he was. Joe.

And he had the biggest smile on his face either of them had ever seen. He almost skipped towards Mavis, not noticing her slumped shoulders and downturned mouth.

'Ready to go?' he asked, bouncing up and down on his toes.

Cordelia's heart went out to the pair of them. If there was any way to let Mavis go, she would have done so.

'I'm really sorry, Joe, but I need Mavis here until lunchtime.'

'And I've got to do the children's craft session soon,' Mavis chipped in, struggling to keep tears from falling.

Joe stopped moving. He bit his lip for a few seconds, looking down at his feet, then he looked up.

'If the mountain won't come to Mohammed...' he said, 'then Joe will help with the craft session. I'm pretty handy.' He looked at Mavis as he said the words that left neither of the women in doubt as to the meaning.

Mavis looked at him as if she couldn't believe what she was hearing. 'You'd help...?'

'Yeah, sweetheart, anything for you.' He looked at Cordelia. 'You don't mind, do you? I don't need paying or nothing.'

Cordelia tried to think of a reason why he shouldn't but there simply wasn't one. 'That would be great. Today's task is making peg dolls.'

They were interrupted by more customers coming in. While Cordelia attended to them, Mavis took Joe aside to explain what to do and the craft area which was where the children's books were.

As she walked ahead of him, he playfully pinched her bottom.

She gave a most un-Mavis-like giggle. 'Stop that now, you dirty soldier,' she whispered, pretending to swipe him yet again.

As he began to get everything ready, she thought how lucky she was that he was happy about little Joyce. She'd always believed that children came first.

That had even been true in the early days when Ken was a newborn baby. She could have had him adopted; her dad tried to make her.

'You ain't bringing no bastard kid into this 'ouse!' he'd said when he saw his grandson for the first time. He shouted so loud all the neighbours must have heard him. 'What'll the neighbours think? We've got our reputation to think of, my girl!'

Mavis stood in front of him, trembling. She'd expected this reaction but still hoped he would be more understanding. Before she could say a word, he continued angrily, his face red and his eyes narrowing.

'You bin putting it about, ain't ya! I bet you don't even know what lad this one belongs to. You're a slut, that's what you are!'

She longed to tell him she had guarded her virginity as carefully as her mother urged her to. Could she tell him this baby was the result of her being cruelly raped in an alleyway when she was on her way home from work one day? Looking at him, she quickly realised he'd never believe her. He'd already made up his mind.

She glanced down at the innocent baby in her arms. He may have been conceived in violence but there was no way she was going to give him up. As the months of her pregnancy went on, she had found herself talking to him and when he began to move, she knew for certain she would never let him go.

She waited for her father to catch his breath then said, 'I'm keeping my baby, I don't care what you or the neighbours say.'

He sneered. 'Not under my roof, you ain't.' His voice was cold and unforgiving. 'Neither of you are welcome here, not now, not never.'

She wondered if he'd been right when she first noticed her baby had eyes that reminded her of the attacker who got her in the family way. But she told herself that wasn't the fault of the tiny scrap clinging on to life as the last ravages of Spanish flu spread across the world. The newspapers were saying over fifteen thousand had died of it in London alone. Mavis had lost a school friend and two aunts to the terrible disease. But she'd brought a new person into the world and she would keep him.

No, instead she'd moved to a part of the East End where nobody knew her. Nobody would know she wasn't a young widow. She'd often had to say she looked young for her age when people commented on her looks. It had been hard, living in one room with the baby. She remembered that room with a shudder. It was small with a single flickering gas lamp in the corner. Her narrow bed was pushed against a wall with peeling wallpaper that had once been pretty with flowers and leaves across it. Ken slept in a drawer taken out of the old wooden chest, a pillow for a mattress. Two vegetable crates she'd got from the market served as her pantry. The reek of boiled cabbage from the people living below her never went away.

'Mavis, did you hear what I said?' Joe's question shook the memories from her mind and brought her back to the present.

'Sorry, what did you say, love?'

'I asked you how long the session is supposed to last and how many kids to expect.'

When she'd given him all the information he needed, he picked up her hand and squeezed it. 'I've got something special to ask you when we've finished here,' he said with a secret smile.

Mavis's eyes widened. What could he possibly want to ask her?

29

Although she didn't set out to do so, Mavis found herself watching how Joe responded to the children during the craft session. Belatedly she realised it was an opportunity to discover if he would make a suitable father for Joyce. She'd never really found a man she felt she could trust in her entire life. But Joe had that something special she found hard to explain to herself. Perhaps it was the way he always spoke about people respectfully or the way he always kept his word. Then it came to her. He had something she'd rarely found in other men – integrity.

Working together, they laid out the craft materials. Mavis was relieved to find Jane had everything prepared – templates for cutting out the dresses, scraps of string for belts and a selection of wool and fabric scraps, paintbrushes and pencils to draw faces.

As always, the children bounded in in a flurry of chilly air and red-nosed enthusiasm, their laugher cutting through the hush of the library.

'You can keep your coats on for a while if you like,' Mavis told them. 'And helping me today is Joe. 'E's a brave soldier and 'e's very good at crafts.' She had no idea if he was. 'Say hello to Joe, children.'

They all chimed, 'Hello,' but their attention was already on the pile of materials in front of them.

'What're we making today, missus?' little Rosie Simpson asked.

'We're making peg dolls.' She held up two that Jane had provided. They wore different dresses and had different-coloured hair.

Soon the library was abuzz with chatter as their busy little hands worked on transforming the scraps of material and wool into toys. Scissors snipped at fabric and wool. Flour and water were mixed for glue. Wooden clothes pegs, once used for hanging out laundry, were gradually transformed into a variety of characters. Two children, aware of the upcoming royal visit, cut brightly coloured paper out of magazines and made tiny crowns. Others made dresses, mostly with shawls around their 'shoulders'.

Mavis and Joe wove in and out of the tables, providing guidance when asked but allowing the children's imagination free rein. As Mavis slyly watched Joe, she saw he was a natural – kind and patient yet with a gentle air of authority the children responded to.

They were as easy with him as he was with them, giving them helpful suggestions: 'Not too much water or that glue won't work.' 'Watch your fingers with those scissors.' 'You've got a good eye for what colours go together.'

Two girls, Maisie and Nicola, began arguing over who was to have a bright red shiny piece of fabric and Joe bent down to talk to them.

'Now, girls,' he said, his voice low but firm. 'We like everyone to share. This is enough fabric for two dresses. I'm going to cut it in half.' He looked at each of them in turn and ruffled their hair. 'Share, not argue, that's what we do here.'

When they were all finished, Mavis looked at their finished

dolls, noting how each one reflected the personality of the maker. Colourful or muted, carefully constructed or flung together, finished or unfinished.

One of the girls clutched her doll, running her fingers across the tattered dress she'd carefully wrapped round the peg. She'd chosen material the same colour as her dress, and the wool hair was fair like her own.

'Look, Mrs Kent,' Amy said. 'Her hair's black and curly like mine!'

'Ahoy, me hearties!' Henry shouted, waving his peg sailor through the air. His father was a docker and he'd become obsessed with the river and pirates he'd read about in books.

'Hey, kids,' Joe said as the children were getting ready to leave. 'Let's wrap your dolls up to keep them safe.'

He used old magazine pages to wrap each one and passed it to the child who'd made it with words of encouragement.

When they'd tidied up, Mavis and Joe looked at the clock. 'Another hour and a half until I'm free,' she said.

He nodded. 'I'll get a newspaper and get a cuppa in the café while I read the sports pages. See you there when you're ready.'

The previous evening, Joe had made several comments that led Mavis to suspect he was going to propose. Her first response was excitement. They hadn't seen each other much, but she already felt she'd like to spend the rest of her life with him.

But as she walked to the returns trolley, she suddenly remembered her secret. One that might make him feel very different about her. She might lose him forever.

30

As Mavis walked around the reading room, each footstep echoed mockingly. She thought back to conversations with Joe, the man she loved.

One night when they were in the pub, he'd told her about a man in his barracks, a smoothy called Jim who'd boasted about how he'd got away with two-timing his girlfriend with a succession of lies.

'If there's one thing I can't stand, it's a liar.' His brows had wrinkled in disgust.

Putting books back in the stacks without being aware of it, Mavis winced, Joe's remembered words twisting like a dagger in her heart. She was a liar. She'd never said much about her imaginary husband, saying she didn't want to bring up old memories. But each time she did so, the layers of deceit grew deeper.

Shame coursed through her body, making her hands tremble. She thought of Joe's open, trusting face as he'd confided in her, believing there was something honest and true between them. He would feel so betrayed when she told him the truth. She imagined the contempt in his eyes when he discovered her deception.

Leaning against a table for support, she shut her eyes tight to stop those tears flowing. She had convinced herself the lies were insignificant, that they didn't matter when it was all so long ago.

But she couldn't do it. She couldn't break his heart like this. He didn't deserve that fate.

* * *

'Ello, Mavis. Shepherd's pie is it for you today?' Rita the waitress greeted her as if it was just any other day. Not one where Mavis's new relationship would split into a million pieces.

She shook her head and looked around for Joe. He was seated at a corner table, engrossed in the newspaper.

She took a step towards him, her stomach twisting and heart beating fast.

Sensing her approach, he looked up and smiled. 'Hello, luv,' he began, but paused when he saw her expression. 'What is it? Is something wrong?'

She remained where she was. 'Joe, I... I can't see you any more,' she blurted out.

The waitress, who had been walking past, stopped in horror, watching the scene unfold.

Confusion creased Joe's forehead. 'What? What do you mean?' He started to stand but she backed away, avoiding his eyes.

'I'm sorry, Joe. This is the end.'

Joe reeled as if physically struck, unprepared for the strength of her farewell.

Without waiting for a response, she whirled around and rushed for the door, Joe's concerned cries fading behind her.

Outside, the bitter wind stung her wet cheeks. She hurried along the pavement, barely able to breathe.

'Mavis! Stop! Stop!' She could hear Joe's heavy footsteps behind her before she felt his hand gently grasp her arm. She turned but could not look him in the eye.

'Mavis, tell me. What's the matter? Have I done something wrong?' He looked at her pleadingly. As he spoke, the rain fell heavier, fat drops splattering on the busy pavement. He pulled her into the doorway of an empty shop. 'Talk to me, Mavis,' he pleaded.

She looked down, biting her lips. 'I can't... you won't...' She struggled to get away from him, but he held on tight.

'I won't what?'

She shrank against the door frame, shaking her head. 'You don't know everything...'

He let go of her arm so suddenly she almost stumbled.

'What? What don't I know?' He raked his fingers through his hair. His face, full of concern until that moment, now showed suspicion. 'Tell me.'

Around them, people were rushing here and there, umbrellas or newspapers over their heads, unaware of the drama playing out in that doorway.

Breathing was so hard that Mavis thought she might faint. 'I have to tell you...'

He looked at her without speaking. His silence was worse than words.

'Joe, please... please don't hate me. I've never told you something. I'm not... not a widow.'

His forehead creased again. 'You're... You're not a widow? What do you mean, you're not a widow? You've got a son, haven't you?' He paused, struggling to make sense of what she had said. 'Or is that something you made up too?'

She clutched his arms. He didn't break away but neither did he respond. 'Joe, I do have a son. It's just... I've never been married.'

It seemed like time stood still as he looked at her. It was as if he were looking at a stranger.

'So you lied to me.' It was a statement, not a question.

She clutched his arms. 'Joe, let me explain.'

But Joe shook his head, the hurt in his eyes piercing her more deeply than the force of the rain. Without a word, he turned and walked away, deaf to her desperate cries.

Mavis slid down the wooden door behind her, her bottom on the damp floor, knees up to her chin. Sobs racked her body as she buried her head in her hands. She felt as though she was breaking into a thousand pieces with no way to put herself back together. The freezing chill from the pavement seeped through her dress, but she barely noticed. Around her, the downpour pounded relentlessly.

She berated herself over and over again. She should have told Joe the truth sooner. He was a kind man. If she'd been able to explain, he surely would have understood. He must know how difficult life was for mothers who were unmarried. How they were scorned by everyone. Called all sorts of horrible names. How they struggled just to survive.

Then she heard footsteps coming and looked up, holding her breath. Was Joe coming back? But the steps continued and faded away, leaving only the hammering rain. The crushing weight of regret and grief made it hard for her to even stand up, but when a man passing by asked her if she was ill, she realised she had to move. Without conscious thought, she walked away from the library. She couldn't face going back to Cordelia, her kindness would be too much for her. She didn't deserve it.

The chilly rain continued to soak through her clothes, plastering her hair to her head. She looked up and saw she was outside the Empire picture house. It would be dry and warm, and dark. She would be invisible.

The film, *The Shop Around the Corner*, was just about to start.

Mavis walked to the pay booth. 'One, please,' she said, getting the money out of her purse.

The girl taking ticket money looked at her, aghast. 'Cor, luva-duck, you're like a drowned rat. 'Ope you dry out inside.'

The film was just starting, not that Mavis took any notice. Wiping her face and hair on her hankie, she found a seat as far away from others as she could. Struggling to calm her emotions, she tried to concentrate on the figures on the screen, Margaret Sullivan and James Stewart. Normally she would look at him on screen like a lovesick teenager, but she was so distracted she didn't notice the main characters' budding romance or the luxury items in the shop where they worked.

Joe's face kept flashing into her mind – his look of disbelief then betrayal. He would never forgive her; he hated liars above all else.

She pressed her sodden hankie to her mouth to muffle her sobs. People in the audience laughed at the couple on the screen but Mavis was trapped in her own misery.

When the film ended, she followed others out, almost bumping into a young woman in a crisp ATS uniform.

'Mavis? It is Mavis, isn't it? From the library?' It was Doreen, who had been one of the quilters and the lady who Cordelia had helped. She looked rosy-cheeked, upright and somehow as if she had new life in her.

Taking a deep breath and straightening her back, Mavis managed a feeble smile.

'Oh, you've joined up then. Good for you. Where will you be based?'

Doreen shrugged. 'I don't know yet. I'm halfway through my training. Please tell Cordelia we bumped into each other and give her my thanks. I'll pop into the library next time I'm on leave.' She paused and grimaced. 'As long as you-know-who doesn't know I'm around then.'

The conversation took Mavis's mind off her troubles for a few minutes. It was common knowledge in Silvertown that Doreen's husband was a bad 'un. Initially surprised, Mavis thought joining up was a clever way to get away from him. Perhaps the only way if she had no money or relatives elsewhere to help out.

But the distraction didn't last long.

To Mavis's surprise, Doreen hugged her then strode on her way, kitbag over her shoulder.

Mavis watched her walk away towards her new, exciting life and felt envious. It was true Mavis still had her job and soon would have Joyce, but she had ruined the chance of having the only man in her life she had ever wanted.

Mavis plodded towards home, her feet dragging, feeling a hundred years old. Hardly aware of what she was doing, she let herself into her house and lit the fire. Then she put on the kettle and collapsed onto a chair, head in her hands. What a fool she'd been not telling Joe sooner. But when? She recalled all their time together like a film and couldn't remember an occasion when it would have been a good time to raise the subject. But she was just kidding herself. If she'd wanted to, she could have done so, or even told him in one of her letters.

The kettle whistled and she looked up just as there was a knock on her door.

That'll be Mrs O'Connor wanting a twist of tea or sugar, she thought. The last thing she wanted was her neighbour coming in for a long chat.

But it wasn't her neighbour.

It was Joe. In his army uniform.

Her eyes widening, Mavis instinctively took a step towards him, then stopped. What if he'd come to reinforce his wish never to see her again?

'Aren't you going to invite me in then?' he said with a smile. 'It's freezing enough out here to stick me boots to your doorstep.'

She opened her arms wide and pulled him towards her. He kicked the door closed behind him.

They kissed for what seemed like an eternity then he pulled away. 'I'm an idiot. A stupid blooming idiot. I shouldn't have gone at you like I did...'

'It's okay...' she began.

'No, it's not. I should have understood how difficult things were for you then when you had your lad. They would be now...'

Mavis shook her head and put a finger over his lips. 'None of that matters now you're back,' she whispered and hugged him even tighter. 'I thought I'd lost you.' She paused. She didn't want there to be any secrets between them. She'd spent her entire life covering up secrets. 'Joe, I 'aven't told you the whole story... it's not a pretty one.' She took a step back and looked into his eyes. 'I don't know if you want to 'ear it but I can promise you it is nothing I did wrong.'

Joe took her hands in his. 'I don't mind if you tell me another time, love. Let's just spend our time together now.'

He kissed her again and she breathed in his familiar scent, unable to believe he was truly there.

'I've got something to ask you,' he said, pushing her away a little.

'Do you need some tea? I can find something if you're 'ungry.'

He smiled. 'I'm only hungry for you.'

As he was speaking, he reached into a pocket of his greatcoat and took out a small box.

She watched him, open-mouthed, as he fell on one knee and gripped her hands.

'Do you think, Mavis Kent, that you could marry an idiot like me? I promise to love you forever and look after you and little Joyce. We'll be a proper family.'

Mavis's breath caught in her throat as he knelt before her. Her mind reeled as she stared down at the open box cradled in his palm. The modest ring glittered brightly.

'Marry you?' she whispered, her words barely audible over the frantic hammering of her heart. After the terrible anguish of nearly losing him, his proposal seemed unreal, a miracle she could barely take in.

But he was saying it again. He wanted to marry her, to be with her and Joyce. Joyce would have a father again, one who would love her as she deserved to be loved. And for the first time in her life, Mavis would have a good man by her side.

With trembling fingers, she reached out to touch his cheek, then the beautiful ring. 'Oh, yes, Joe,' she whispered. 'Of course I'll marry you!'

He took her hand and placed the ring on her third finger. 'I wish we could get married tomorrow, but I'm afraid I've been called back to camp.' He pulled her into his arms again. 'I'm so sorry but I've got to leave now.'

For the first time, she noticed his rucksack on the floor beside them.

'Now? But you've only just got 'ere.'

He kissed her hand and twisted the ring on her finger. 'I was so relieved to see you were home. I'd written a letter in case I missed you.' He took it out of his pocket and put it on her table. 'I really need to leave now, but you can walk with me to the station if you'd like to.'

Struggling to hold back tears of disappointment, Mavis put on her coat and scarf, and they set off towards the station in Canning Town. Soggy brown leaves swirled around their feet as a chill December wind nipped at their faces. Joe tightened his grip on

Mavis's hand, pulling her closer to him. As they walked, they talked about the future – the wedding, finding somewhere different to live, making a family with Joyce, all manner of small and significant things they would need to sort out.

All too soon, the station loomed ahead of them with its sturdy shape and two high chimneys. Billows of steam from idling engines mingled with the cold air.

'I'd rather you didn't wait, love,' he said. 'You know what trains are like. It could be hours and partings are hard enough without all that.'

'But...' Mavis wanted to spend every possible second with him.

He bent forward and kissed her cheek. 'No, love, please go home and get warm in front of the fire. Tell you what. You can begin a letter to me, then I'll have it soon after I get back. It'll cheer me up no end.'

Mavis was torn. She wanted to stay but knew he hated goodbyes, and they were always painful. She gave him one last hug and kissed him goodbye.

'Come home to me soon,' she softly said.

With a heavy heart, Mavis slowly turned and began the walk back home as Joe disappeared into the station. But her heartbreak was eased when she felt the ring on her finger. It reminded her he would return for good one day.

As she walked through the late dusk, she passed familiar buildings – houses, shops she used regularly and a pub she avoided because of its reputation. Deep in thought, she crossed the road without looking and was nearly run over by a horse and cart. The horse reared up, and it was impossible to tell who was the more terrified, the animal or herself.

'Whoa, boy,' the driver called, struggling to get the horse back under control. Then he turned his attention to Mavis. 'You tired of living, missus?' he shouted.

She called her apologies and ran the rest of the way across the road, the icy wind stinging her wet cheeks. She pictured Joe sitting on a train surrounded by other soldiers, smoking, sharing a joke, no doubt. She wished she had someone to tell her news to, but it would have to wait until she was at the library the next morning.

For now, she made herself concentrate on what she would write to Joe, and she quickened her pace. The sooner she got home, the sooner she could begin writing and feel connected to him again.

31

Saturday mornings were always busy at the library. Workers who couldn't get in Monday to Friday came to change their books, kiddies came for story time, then the local Home Guard man often popped in for a sneaky cuppa. Housewives sought a new romance to read at home and wanted to swap their *Woman's Own* magazine for a different one. Although it only cost thruppence, many women were too stretched to spend money on anything other than absolute necessities. Often, they enjoyed hushed conversations with other women about the recipes or stories in the magazine. They were always interested in photos of the royal family and reading about what they'd been doing. Their interest was heightened by the upcoming royal visit. They knew the likelihood of the king and queen even seeing them was remote but they still planned what to wear and what they would say if they were introduced. The royal visit was a ray of sunshine in the gloom of the ongoing war.

But this was a special Saturday. Not about the royal visit. Not yet.

A visitor the children who went to the library regularly were very excited about.

Father Christmas was coming!

As the clock behind the desk moved the big hand to meet the small one at the top, a merry jingle sounded from the hallway followed by a merry, 'Ho, ho, ho!'

The children, who had heard rumours about a visit from the great man, had been fidgeting and giggling in the children's area. Now, like balls fired from a cannon, they catapulted themselves towards the sound.

It was all well planned. A reporter and photographer from the local newspaper quietly followed Father Christmas in – Tom in a wheelchair, carefully disguised. Mavis and Jane were strategically stationed to keep everything in order, holding the children back so Father Christmas could make a proper entrance.

'Ho, ho, ho!' Tom repeated and the sound seemed to reverberate around the large room. 'And what have we here? Some smashing children who like books. And presents, I'll bet. I've come to the right place.'

He had a big sack over his shoulder, which he dropped it at his feet. The children looked at him, wide-eyed. This larger-than-life figure dressed all in red and white patted his massive stomach.

'I wonder,' he said as if speaking to thin air, 'if any children would like a present?'

Little Jimmy Smith jumped up and down, his hand held high. 'I would, Santa.'

Susan Glass, tiny for her age, nudged him. 'Don't be greedy.' She looked up at Santa. 'If you give us some presents, will you 'ave enough for Christmas night?'

'I can tell you're a very thoughtful girl,' Santa said. 'I'm very proud of you. But never fear. You'll all be going home with a present today. But first, I've got a very special Christmas story for you.'

Tom and the three librarians had wondered whether presents before or after the story would be best. Both had advantages and disadvantages. The young ones would be anxious to get their gifts while they listened to the story. But if they got them first, they'd probably be too distracted to listen.

'Let's go and sit down in the children's section while I tell you a story about Twinkle, a little elf.'

Faces dropped as the children realised they wouldn't get their gifts immediately.

Mavis and Jane gently nudged them to the children's area. They'd already warned all the readers who'd come in that there would be precious little peace and quiet for a while.

'I'd never have known that was Tom,' Mavis whispered as she and Jane took their places. 'Great beard!'

Tom sat down and leaned forward, catching each child's eye. 'So, do you want to know about Twinkle?' he asked.

Several children nodded and others said, 'Yes.'

Tom cupped his hand behind his ear. In best pantomime tradition, he called, 'I can't hear you. Do you want to hear about Twinkle? You'll have to shout louder than that!'

After repeating this twice more, the children were all eager for the story.

'There was this little elf called Twinkle,' Tom began. 'He was a lovely little chap but smaller than the other elves. Sometimes they poked fun at him because he wasn't as strong as them. But the head elf wanted to make him feel special.' He paused and looked around. 'Do you have any idea how he could do that?'

The children were rapt with pleasure in the story, hugging their knees and totally concentrating on catching every word. He got very varied answers. 'He could give him some money.' 'He could give him a ladder to stand on.' 'He could change his name to something strong, like Lion.'

But Father Christmas shook his head. 'Lovely ideas, children, but the head elf asked him to deliver a special gift – a golden ball –

to a poor little boy in Silvertown. Twinkle was thrilled to be trusted with such an important job. It was a cold and snowy night and he had to travel over rooftops, over the river, over the factories and the boats, past people going about their business. None of them noticed him. He looked in windows to find the right child. A little boy.'

'What's his name?' Jimmy asked.

Tom had to think on his feet. Luckily, he knew all these children so chose a name none of them had. 'Archibald,' he said.

'I've got an uncle called Archie,' Susan said. 'Was it him?'

Mavis and Jane were suppressing giggles, seeing Tom get more than he'd bargained for when he volunteered for this role.

'No, this was a very long time ago, so it couldn't be anyone any of us know. Now where was I? Oh, yes, Twinkle was looking in the windows and when he found Archibald, he was sad to find him shivering in a dark, cold bedroom. Using his elf magic, Twinkle lit a fire and hung up the boy's stocking with the golden ball inside.'

'Did he wait to see the boy find the ball?' someone asked.

Tom rubbed his painful leg before answering. 'He couldn't, there was far too much work to do in the toy workshop. But when he got back, the head elf called everyone together. "Twinkle here has done a very important job," he told them. "It proves that even the smallest elves can do very important work."'

He was met with a barrage of questions. 'Did the head elf tell the other elves off for being mean to Twinkle?' Jimmy asked.

'Will you have enough presents for everyone in the world?' another asked.

'Yes, the elves have been busy making toys all year.'

'Do you have to have an early night before you get on your sleigh?'

'I certainly do, and I hope you will on Christmas Eve. You need to be asleep when I reach your house.'

'What do reindeer like to eat?'

They almost caught Tom out with that one, but he remembered reading something in a nature book. 'They love mushrooms, and grass and leaves.'

A couple of the older children rolled their eyes. 'Don't be silly. He can't deliver all the presents in one night, can he?'

Tom pretended to look offended. 'Now, now, young man. Big as you are, you don't yet know everything in the world. I have magic on my side.'

'Your sack must get very heavy,' Jimmy commented.

Tom shook his head. 'It's magic. A magic sack, so it never gets too heavy.'

When they were finally running out of questions, Susan shyly held up her hands. 'Was Twinkle as small as me, Father Christmas?'

'Stand up and let me check,' Tom said. He made a great play of judging her size. 'Do you know, I think you are exactly the same size as Twinkle. And like Twinkle, you'll be able to do lots of brave things.'

He slowly pulled the sack towards him. The youngsters soon became silent and the buzz of anticipation in the room could almost be touched.

Cordelia had joined Jane and Mavis. 'My mother got some great gifts,' she whispered. 'I hope they'll like them.'

She remembered that precious day when the villagers had donated so much when they had so little themselves.

'Each child has an item of clothing and a toy,' she whispered again.

Jane nodded. 'Practical and fun then.'

Tom was making a big play of taking the wrapped gifts out of the bag. Each had a label on with the child's name.

'Where's Emily?' he asked.

A little girl, probably the youngest in the group, shyly came forward. She had fine hair and big blue eyes. She looked scared to go to the big man.

He called her towards him.

'I've got something very special for you, Emily,' he said and patted her shoulder. 'Here you are.'

Hesitantly she took the parcel from him and then hurried back to her seat, clutching it as if someone might snatch it from her.

It didn't take long to distribute the gifts and the library was soon full of the unfamiliar sounds of wrapping paper being opened and delighted gasps when the children inspected their gifts. There were dolls, games, a toy train, a sewing kit, a jigsaw puzzle and a football.

Some mothers had arrived and were watching the scene from the doorway, hushing babies and smiling at their children's pleasure. The three librarians knew that most of them would struggle to find money for Christmas presents. They were thrilled to give these youngsters an event to remember.

Tom clapped his hands. 'It's time for me to go now, children. I've got so much to do before Christmas Eve.'

There were many cries of, 'Aw! Don't go!'

Tom felt like a famous singer being asked for an encore. He held up his hands for quiet and sat down again. 'I think I can just find time for one more short story.'

When they'd settled, he told them a shortened version of 'The Fir Tree' by Hans Christian Andersen. He was gratified to note that they all listened intently, even the bigger boys. His booming voice spread through the room, bringing a sense of Christmas wonder even to the adults present.

When the story was finished, Cordelia stepped forward and held up her hands. 'Let's thank Father Christmas for coming all this way to see you today.'

She led a round of applause and singing of 'For He's a Jolly Good Fellow'.

Tom picked up his sack and waved to them all, calling, 'Happy Christmas one and all!' The photographer took another photo of him and then he was pushed towards a back room again.

Though war raged on across the world, here among the books and friends, light triumphed for a while longer. The faces of those happy children were balm to all the adults who saw them.

32

'Half an hour, everyone!' Mavis called out across the main library room. 'Library closes in 'alf an 'our but you can stay for the carol concert!'

A couple of people began to get their things ready to leave, but most stayed. It was impossible to know if they really wanted to attend the concert or simply preferred to stay in the warm. Many people struggled to afford coal to heat their homes.

The front desk area of the library was brightly decorated, with most of the work being done by the children who used the library. They'd had great fun working with Jane to make paper chains, using thickly mixed flour and water for glue, and cutting strips of paper from magazines too tatty to be loaned out again. The chains were strung from side to side and were colourful and jolly. Across the front of the desk were cut-out paper shapes – holly, robins and snowflakes. On the desk itself were three sets of candle holders with three in each. None were new and had been loaned by library users for the occasion. They were placed on plates for safety. And finally, Bert had found some mistletoe and small fir branches that lay on the side of the desk.

Cordelia left the paperwork she'd been working on with a sigh of relief.

'Right,' she said to Mavis, who was struggling to repair a paper chain that had fallen down. 'I'll get the urn on for the tea.'

They'd arranged that the church choir would perform at five o'clock. The sky outside the library's windows had taken on an inky hue, the last remnants of dust fading into the night. In the distance they heard the faint whistle from one of the factories announcing time for a change of shift.

A steady fall of thin snowflakes accentuated the darkness. No moon or stars pierced the cloud cover to illuminate the streets.

People outside pulled their coats around them closer as a bitter bite took hold of the air. The beginnings of frost could be seen on windowsills and bus stops. Gusts of wind blew down the smoke-stained streets, making stallholders decide to shut up shop early for the day. Their fingers quickly stiffened with cold as they packed up their wares and dismantled their carts.

Inside, the library was a haven of warmth, at least by comparison. Those patrons who had decided to wait for the carol concert moved to seats nearer the desk where the children would sing. Many had never spoken to each other before, but did so as they waited for the concert to start. Two offered to move the rest of the chairs and place them in rows for the expected audience.

There was an insistent knock on the back door and Mavis hurried to let the choir in. There were twelve children in all, shivering, with red noses and ears.

'Come in, come in out of the cold,' she said with a smile.

As arranged, she led them to a side room where they had laid on some flaky sausage rolls and tangy lemonade. The youngsters were high and giggly with excitement at giving a performance, although they'd already done one in the church.

While about half of the children looked well fed and clothed, the others looked poverty-thin with coats too light for the freezing temperatures outside. One only had plimsols on his feet and they were soaking wet.

As the children laid into the food and drink as if they hadn't eaten for a week, Cordelia stood watching them. She remembered they still had some of the clothes donated by the villagers near her family home. Most had been given to the WVS to distribute, but some had got missed somehow.

It was difficult to think of a way to offer them without offence, but she remembered that in poorer households, children rarely had new clothes. They'd be well used to hand-me-downs.

The children were still working their way through the food when she brought the clothes in.

'We've got some spare coats and things here and it's such a cold night out there. If you want one, see if you can find one to fit you and then you can have it.'

Some of the children almost knocked others over in their scrabble to grab something.

To her surprise, there were a few bits and pieces left when they'd finished.

'If any of you have brothers and sisters who would fit these clothes, why don't you take them?' Cordelia said. She knew some of the canny ones would sell anything they got, but she was philosophical about that. They probably needed the money.

'Makes me remember my time in the church choir,' Mavis said. 'Mum always made me wear two vests, a liberty bodice and two jumpers. She'd often knitted them from unpicked jumble sale ones. Horrible they were, but beggars can't be choosers.'

Cordelia turned to her in surprise. Mavis rarely talked about her childhood. 'So it brings back happy memories?'

Mavis nodded. 'Me and my mate Nellie used to walk to St

Mark's together. Freezing we were. Made us hurry to get there, not that the church was much warmer than outside.'

Cordelia compared her story with her own Christmases with her parents. They dressed in their finest to go to church and the vicar always treated her parents as if they were royalty. The conversation with Mavis made her remember the carols they sang, the same ones the little ones would sing in a minute.

More people had come into the library while she was with the children, mostly older women wearing shawls over their coats and felt hats. Some of the younger women were mothers of the choristers, several trying to keep other children entertained while they waited. The helpers had to hunt around for extra chairs, and one had the bright idea to give some of the children in the audience picture books to look at.

Among the audience was silver-haired Beatrice, a regular library user and member of the sewing group. As she waited for the choir, memories of her own childhood came flooding back. Like many others in the room, she had grown up in this very neighbourhood, the middle of five sisters.

'We'll never 'ave a football team if we carry on like this!' her dad would mutter, seeing each newborn.

'Just be glad she's got all 'er fingers and toes,' Beatrice's mother would reply, hugging her new baby tight.

Every Christmas they would all bundle up in layers of clothes and walk to church, excited to think about the songs they would sing. Beatrice closed her eyes, transported back to the musty smell of holly garlands at the end of each pew. She could imagine the wheezy notes of the organ played by ancient, arthritic Mr Stewart.

Walking home after the concert, her father would put the smallest girl on his shoulders and hold the hands of the others. Her mother was usually pushing the latest in a pram. She sighed, remembering. The memories were bittersweet now. She was the only one left and had never found a husband.

Cordelia came into the side room. 'We're ready for you all,' she said, smiling at the children. Behind her was the sound of the waiting audience – chairs squeaking, coughs, and chatter.

She went back into the room and held up her hand for silence.

'It's lovely to see so many of you here this evening. I'm sure you're going to enjoy listening to the wonderful choir from St Mark's church. Let's give them a big welcoming round of applause.'

The members of the choir marched in, trying not to look out for their mothers, and failing. Little Arthur fell over his shoelace and almost caused a pile-up of the children behind him.

It seemed like an age but they were finally in place, the choir mistress in front. There was no piano in the library so they would be singing unaccompanied.

Miss Wilkinson, a teacher well past retirement age, was in charge. She wore a grey suit that was probably fashionable twenty years earlier. She'd lost weight over the years, and it hung loose on her, but with her upright stance and natural dignity, she still cut an imposing figure.

She turned towards the audience. 'Good evening, everyone. The choir and I are delighted to see so many people here this evening. We'll be singing carols that will be familiar to you. I know the children are going to do us proud.'

She clapped her hands, turned to face the children, then lifted her right hand.

'Okay, children, it's "O Come All Ye Faithful". One, two, three!'

She sang only for a second before the little ones quickly joined in. Two little girls were taking it all very seriously, their mouths exaggerating every word. Arthur absent-mindedly scratched his backside.

As they sang, some of the audience joined in, but quietly so the young voices could still be heard.

Outside, a chill wind whistled down the street. Bomb debris still littered many corners of the battered area and papers blew along the pavements. A homeless dog rooted without much hope through the piles of crumbled brick, releasing an occasional mournful howl. Further off, machine noises from the factories and docks drifted on the wind.

But inside, the war and all worries were forgotten as the audience enjoyed seeing the sparkling eyes of the children, so proud of their performance.

Tommy and Arthur each had a brief solo during 'God Rest Ye Merry Gentlemen' and tried to outdo each other with volume and stance. The gentle rendering of 'Away in a Manger' almost brought tears to several of the audience and everyone joined in with 'We Wish You a Merry Christmas'.

When they got to the last carol, Miss Wilkinson was almost ready to breathe a sigh of relief that nothing had gone wrong. But she was too soon. Young Tommy, who liked nothing better than being the centre of attention, reached behind him and picked up a piece of mistletoe from the desk. Mischief written all over his face, he held it over the head of the girl next to him, Janet. Before she realised what was happening, he planted a noisy kiss on her cheek. She stopped singing and gave him a good thump on the arm.

He fell to the floor, acting as if he'd been shot. There was a second's silence then all the children started pointing at him and laughing.

Poor Miss Wilkinson looked on in alarm, her jaw dropping open, face scarlet.

'Get up now, Tommy! You're not hurt.'

She yanked him up by the arm and pulled him to the other end of the choir, well away from the girls.

'Now! Let us start our last carol again.' She glared at them all, waiting for them to stop giggling and pay attention. Then she clapped her hands again. 'Our last carol is "Hark! The Herald Angels Sing". Get ready, children. One. Two. Three.'

Tommy couldn't resist trying to distract Archie next to him, but Archie was having none of it. He hissed to Tommy to 'Pack it up, stupid', and somehow they got to the end.

'Now, choir, you may bow to your audience. Most of you have done an excellent job.'

They giggled again as they bowed to the applause of the audience. Cordelia thanked them all again and praised their performance. The audience burst into loud applause and the children took two more bows.

After a few closing words from Cordelia and thanking the audience for attending, the choir session ended. The children rushed to find their mothers and as people stood and got ready to face the cold, the room buzzed with activity.

At the door, Tommy's mother had a few words about his antics. 'You always show me up, you little bleeder!' Her words were accompanied by a slap round the head.

As the crowd slowly filtered out into the inky evening, at the doorway Cordelia shook everyone's hand as they left. When they'd gone, the four workers heaved sighs of relief as they rearranged the chairs ready for the morning.

'I don't know about you, but I think we all deserve a glass of something in the nearest pub,' Tom said, picking up his stick.

There was total agreement.

33

It was the day before the royal visit and already the librarians were nervous. They'd arrived early and inspected the list of tasks they needed to do before the big day.

But they couldn't get started immediately. It was opening time and Bert was up to his old tricks, banging on the door to be let in. Cordelia walked towards him, wishing they had been able to close for the day to prepare.

To her surprise, two well-built men were waiting on the doorstep too.

'We've come to check everything for the royal visit tomorrow,' one said, pushing past Cordelia.

'Blimey, you're bloomin' rude, ain't ya!' Bert said, loud enough to be heard. The men ignored him and walked to the desk.

Mavis looked up and frowned. 'Can I help you, gentlemen?' she asked, putting on the poshest voice she could.

'We are here to do a security check for the royal visit tomorrow,' the taller of the men said. His voice was pure cut glass.

'Well, we're open this morning later, ain't we?' Mavis said, her voice returning to normal. 'Don't you go disturbing our readers.'

'You can assume we will be discreet,' the man said.

But they weren't.

Starting in the main reading room, they searched every inch. Under tables, on bookshelves, even between books, turning chairs upside down, flicking through bigger books.

'They're trying to keep quiet,' Jane said. 'But it's not working, is it?'

Bert was muttering loudly, and Floppy Flossie had come in for some attention when she noticed the men. She walked directly towards them and collapsed on the floor, apparently crying in agony. But she still managed to flutter her eyelashes at them.

'Help me! Help me!' she cried, looking at the men beseechingly.

They stopped what they were doing, too stunned to move. But Cordelia had spotted Flossie coming in and was there immediately.

'Excuse me, gentlemen,' she said and gently pulled Flossie up by the arm. 'Come with me, Flossie, let's find you somewhere comfortable.'

As usual, giving her some attention did the trick and Cordelia sat her in a quiet corner with another crime book.

Back at the desk, the three librarians and Tom looked at the list of tasks to be done before the end of the day.

'Tom,' Cordelia said. 'You're the most artistic amongst us. Can you somehow make the book we're giving the royal couple look extra special?'

She remembered the Pathé news items she'd seen at the cinema. The gifts were never wrapped.

'No,' she corrected herself, 'not wrapped, but as it's a first edition about this area, maybe you could think of something you could attach. Can I leave it with you?'

He nodded. 'I've no idea what, but I'll think of something.'

Cordelia turned to Mavis and Jane. 'Can you fetch the books

and manuscripts we've chosen to leave on display? Put them in the office for safekeeping.'

She checked her list, muttering to herself as she mentally ticked them off. Some could be done that afternoon when they closed – hanging up more bunting, getting the chairs, checking all the lights worked, triple-checking all rooms were clean and tidy.

The next morning, they would hang up a garland of autumn foliage supplied by Mrs Montague-Smythe. Having been Cordelia's nemesis for a long period, Mrs Montague-Smythe now took every opportunity to help the library. She would be invited to the event in her role as local councillor.

The royal couple were due at ten thirty, so the three women and Tom would be coming in very early to finalise preparations.

Cordelia had hardly finished reviewing the list when Tom returned.

'Look, I've found this. I think it would be an ideal thing to give with the book.' He handed a very old postcard to her. It was a photo of a busy East End street from the late 1800s. The faded sepia image showed horse-drawn carriages, women in long skirts and men in top hats on a cobblestone road alongside Victoria Park, which was in full bloom.

'If they ever look at the book, they can use this as a bookmark,' Tom suggested. 'I'm sure one of the ladies could make us a tiny ribbon flower to put on it.'

'It's perfect, Tom. Just the ticket, thanks for finding that.'

As Cordelia spoke, Mavis came up and nudged her.

'Time to shut up shop ready for rehearsals,' she said.

Cordelia wished that Robert could be present to meet the king and queen. In his previous role doing free GP consultations for local people, it would have been legitimate for him to be present. She sighed, remembering the first time they met when he came into the library asking if they had a room he could use. There had been an immediate frisson between them that had grown and grown. With the terrible things that Hitler was doing to Jews and others, she was no longer sure she could believe in God. However, that didn't stop her praying each night for Robert to come back to her safe and sound.

An hour later, the library was full of chattering children, excited to be part of the royal visit even if this was only the rehearsal. In addition to the royals being shown around the library, the children were the centrepiece of the royal visit. Cordelia wished they could all wear matching outfits but knew that the parents of most children wouldn't be able to afford such an extravagance. Even if they could, they'd use their coupons for much more practical clothes. Instead, the children were given sashes in red, white and blue made by the nimble fingers of the ladies of the quilting circle.

The girls, cheeks rosy from excitement, had to conquer the art of the curtsey – a gentle bob like the dipping of a swallow in flight. The boys had to bow. Nudges, giggles and tripping each other up made their mastery of the task seem impossible at first and the librarians stifled giggles as they saw the many attempts.

The librarians loved hearing the children's laughter. They'd been through so much since the war started yet seemed able to keep their spirits high, at least when they were together.

'They're never going to get it right tomorrow, little blighters,' Mavis said with a grin. 'Let's 'ope their 'ighnesses 'ave a sense of 'umour!'

After countless attempts, the children got their curtsies and bows as good as they were likely to get. Singing the national anthem was next. This, at least, was more familiar. Every child had to sing it at school daily. That didn't stop all the nudging and giggling. But if anyone was good at sounding stern, it was Mavis.

'Right, you 'orrible lot!' They froze at the sound of her voice and looked at her, almost trembling. 'You gotta be serious now. We don't want the king and queen to think we've got 'orrible kids in the East End.'

'That's right,' Cordelia said. 'We know you are smashing kids. Let's show the king and queen just how good you can be!' She paused. 'And if you all do well tomorrow, I might just have a little surprise for you.'

'Cor, miss, what is it?' a little lad asked.

'Well, it wouldn't be a surprise if I told you, would it?' she replied with a grin. 'Now, let's get this singing right.'

Then it was time for little Enid to practise presenting a posy of flowers to Queen Elizabeth.

'I bet she's never had flowers like these before,' Jane whispered. That was certainly true. At first glance they looked like a normal bunch of flowers, albeit out of season. But they were far from it, as the queen would soon see.

They'd chosen Enid to have this honour because she was the smallest child in her class and had a lisp. Some of the bigger boys, and indeed girls, bullied her. She also had a very difficult home life with parents who drank too much for their own good – or hers. The librarians hoped that by giving her a special task to do she would gain in confidence. Jane had made her a new dress, Mavis had knitted a cardigan to go with it, while Cordelia had bought her some new shoes and socks. She wore these for the rehearsal, but they would be kept by Jane overnight. It wasn't impossible her parents would take them and sell them for the price of a pint.

'We'll get her here early tomorrow,' she whispered to Jane. 'She'll need a bit of a wash and brush up.'

The poor girl trembled like a solitary poppy in a strong wind as she took the few steps toward Cordelia, who was pretending to be Queen Elizabeth. Cordelia bent down to take the flowers, saying, 'You're a wonderful young girl.' Enid's eyes opened wide with surprise and Cordelia wondered if anyone had ever said anything

positive to her before. She decided to try to get her coming into the
library for Saturday story time and make sure she got plenty of
opportunity to receive more compliments.

'Come on then, girl,' Mavis said to Cordelia when the children
had gone. 'Let's 'ear your speech then!'

Cordelia spluttered. She'd joined a debating society at university, but this was different.

'I've worked out what to say, but I'm going to practise in front of
a mirror, not you lot!'

Inside she was terrified. Would she mess up the most important
event for herself and the library?

34

It seemed that everyone in Silvertown knew about the visit of the king and queen. The streets that usually echoed with the sounds of the factories and the docks now thrummed with a different kind of vitality. This was an opportunity to forget the war that had killed so many and cost others their homes. Instead of the conscious awareness that the air-raid sirens could sound at any minute, the hardworking East Enders felt unusual excitement. Men and women who had risen early to work in the factories and shipyards now stood shoulder to shoulder, their work-worn faces alight with anticipation.

Silvertown children had only seen the king and queen from photographs on the walls of public buildings or on the news at the cinema. Like many adults, they clutched their Union Jack flags. The flags, some faded or frayed at the edges, fluttered like the heartbeat of the community.

Despite the cold air, and many people with coats too thin or boots stuffed with newspaper to keep out the wet, people laughed and chattered to those around them. Elderly veterans who'd earned medals in the Great War wore them proudly on their jackets.

Mothers cradled small infants in their arms, wrapped in shawls to keep out the chill. All constantly looked along the road for their first glimpse of the royal couple.

At the docks, the seagulls had no interest in the royal visitors. They continued flying around, screeching, looking for pickings from the unloading boats.

And then, there it was – an elegant black vehicle, shining so much it reflected everything it passed. The crowd's cheer swelled into a single unified voice, a sharing of national pride, momentarily drowning out the war's relentless undertone. All waved their flags, and some began singing the national anthem.

The king and queen, warm in their car, acknowledged their subjects with their usual grace. They caught the eye of many people as they passed and their regal waves were not just a formality, but an acknowledgement of all that the brave, tough people of the East End had endured.

Even the buildings, bruised and battered by the Blitz, seemed to stand a little taller, their faces momentarily forgetting the pain of conflict. For one brief afternoon, Silvertown was not just another deprived district in London's East End; it was the most important part of the city, alive with excitement.

At last, the car approached the library and slowed. The three librarians stood together on the broad steps, shivering with the cold, so nervous they could hardly move.

'I never slept a wink last night,' Mavis said. ''Ad to 'ave a tipple of brandy what's been in the back of the cupboard for years to get off.'

The car was slowing to a halt. They'd been instructed by the security men to stay where they were. The royal driver would open the door and help the couple out.

Cordelia struggled to keep her nerves in check. Then something Mrs Taylor, the beloved family cook, used to say to her when she'd been a child came to her mind. Whenever they talked about anyone royal or very important, Mrs Taylor said the same thing: 'Imagine them in their pyjamas, dear. They look just like us then!' The memory made Cordelia smile.

The crowd continued to cheer as the royal car door opened and King George and Queen Elizabeth alighted. Before going into the building, they turned towards the crowds in the street, smiling and waving to them.

Queen Elizabeth wore a tailored dress suit in sombre navy. The collar was made of fur and framed her familiar face. Cordelia, who used to buy more clothes than was sensible, noticed that the jacket was sharply cut, with structured shoulders that lent an air of authority. It was fastened with simple yet polished buttons that had an air of military uniform about them. Her skirt fell below the knee, its pleats crisp, allowing room to move. On her feet she wore a pair of sensible but stylish black shoes with a low heel. As always, she wore gloves and had a handbag over one arm.

The couple walked up the two wide steps to the library and the three women curtsied.

'Welcome, your majesties,' Cordelia said, surprised that she could speak at all. The three of them stood aside to let the king and queen and their attendants enter.

Inside, the Newham mayor and the head of the library service were waiting. They bowed as they were introduced and before they had finished, the three women were beside them, ready to be introduced.

The king stepped forward, extending his hand to each of the librarians in turn. 'My wife and I have been informed about the sterling work you have done for this community.' He paused as he often did, catching his breath to overcome his stutter. He looked at the interior of the reading room. 'You are truly guardians of knowledge.'

Queen Elizabeth had been looking around, and Mavis saw her smile at the children standing to attention ready to sing. At the side of them were some veteran servicemen who were regular library users. They wore their best suits, often shabby but spotlessly clean and adorned with medals won during previous wars.

'I can see you provide a service for people of all ages,' the queen said. 'Splendid.'

The mayor stepped forward. 'Before we show you around, our young library users would like to sing for you.'

The teacher who had been training the youngsters lifted her arm and prompted them. They sang 'God Save the King' with gusto, their mouths extravagantly wide, their fidgets hardly suppressed. The royal couple stood attentively watching and listening to them. Then the king thanked them.

'We are delighted to have this opportunity to meet you all,' he said.

The teacher nodded to little Enid, who had been hiding behind the singers. As she'd been taught, she held her head up high, took a deep breath and walked towards the queen. Enid looked proud in her new dress and cardigan, her new shoes tapping on the wooden floorboards.

The fabric flowers were quite heavy, and she needed two hands to hold them in her skinny arms. The three librarians couldn't have been prouder when she curtsied and presented the flowers.

The queen looked at them, her eyes widening. 'Look, dear,' she said to the king. 'They're made of fabric. How lovely.'

She turned back to Enid. 'These flowers are a wonderful gift, thank you so much, my dear.' She held out her hand. Enid hesitated, then held out her own tiny one.

'We have a very active sewing group at the library,' Cordelia said, unsure if she should speak or not. 'They made the bunting around the walls and the beautiful quilt behind the desk.'

The queen and king both looked around and nodded as if pleased with what they saw.

'I am very impressed by the skill shown by the mothers of these young people and the sewing group.' The queen looked again at the flowers. 'I'm looking forward to learning more about your library.'

'May I introduce my colleagues to you, ma'am?' Cordelia said.

The queen looked at the others as if seeing them for the first time. 'Yes, please do.'

For a second, Cordelia wondered if either Mavis or Jane would be offended if she introduced them last. It was a silly thought; they were mature women who weren't oversensitive.

'This is Mrs Kent, one of my very valuable librarians.'

Mavis curtsied and took the queen's hand, which was held out to shake.

'Good afternoon, Mrs Kent. What do you do in the library?'

Mavis looked stunned, none of them having expected Jane or Mavis to have the opportunity to speak to the queen. 'Um... well... I'm a librarian. I issue books, put the returned ones back on the shelves, help people what want 'elp and anything else the boss 'ere wants me to do.'

'Excellent,' the queen said. 'And who is this standing next to you?'

'This is Mrs Wilkins, our other full-time librarian,' Cordelia said.

The queen shook Jane's hand. 'And you do the same tasks as Mrs Kent, I expect.'

Jane nodded. 'I do, ma'am, and I am in charge of the children's section. We believe it is important to get children reading young. I help them find appropriate books and hold story time sessions several times a week.'

'And Tom here, Mr Hudson, is our part-time volunteer. He is

invaluable and helps with the story time and craft sessions as well as supporting the full-time workers.'

The queen shook his hand too, then turned back to Cordelia. 'Perhaps you can show me round the library now. The king will no doubt be looking through your bookshelves for a few minutes.'

While they'd been speaking, the children had gone to one of the back rooms where some of the quilting ladies had laid on some cakes and drinks for them. Their excited chatter formed a backdrop to the library tour.

Cordelia felt proud of their humble library as she showed the royal visitors round. The library volunteers had done a wonderful job of painting, repairing and polishing so she never once felt embarrassed as the queen walked around.

Looking at the children's section, the queen commented, 'I'm very impressed this library offers so much to this area which has suffered so badly during this war. I commend you and your colleagues on your work.'

As they went around the building, the queen said a few kind words to the quilting ladies who had come in specially for her visit. She also very briefly spoke to Bert, who seemed quite at ease, praising the library as 'a godsend to folks like me'.

At the end of the tour and following advice, Cordelia and the others had prepared a small offer of refreshments, just tea and dainty sandwiches. The king, the mayor and the senior library manager all joined them.

As they waited for the tea to be poured by Tom, Mavis picked up the book they had chosen to present to the royal couple. 'Your royal highnesses. I hope you will accept this small gift as a memento of your visit to our library.'

The book they had chosen had an old leather cover as befitting its age, but Tom had treated it so it was supple once more and shone like new.

The king took the book from Cordelia and looked through it.

'This is very interesting,' he said, pausing here and there to look at photographs from long ago. 'My wife and I will enjoy looking through this when we return to the palace.'

The queen noticed the postcard with its tiny ribbon flower. 'How thoughtful,' she said. 'And I'm guessing this flower is another example of the wonderful skills of your readers.'

When everyone had gone, Cordelia and the others couldn't stop talking about the visit, although they all said they couldn't remember a single moment.

'Well,' Cordelia said. 'I think we all did a marvellous job. Why don't we lock up and go to the Essex Arms for a drink to congratulate ourselves?'

35

23 DECEMBER 1941

'Phew, I thought he'd never go,' Mavis said, seeing the last library visitor out and bolting the door with a satisfying thud. She noticed it had stopped raining, although the slate-grey clouds were still heavy and threatening. No sign of a white Christmas.

Jane and Cordelia were already tidying the library, ready to shut down for the Christmas holiday. Usually, the library was hushed, apart from the footsteps of its patrons or the whisper of pages being turned, but they put on the wireless and sang along to the Christmas music being played. The library was cheerfully decked with sprigs of holly and paper chains that fell down every ten minutes.

They chatted and laughed as they tidied, emptying bins and ashtrays, straightening chairs, returning books to their rightful places.

Through the tall windows, Mavis glimpsed people hurrying about their business, wrapped up against the winter chill. It would be a modest Christmas for everyone this year. Most people in the East End were poor all the time and the wartime rationing made it even more difficult to find suitable Christmas gifts.

'What are you giving Helen for Christmas?' Mavis asked Jane.

Jane stopped what she was doing for a minute. 'I got a couple of dresses at the jumble sale. Ladies' ones, worn out but good enough in parts to cut out a dress and blouse for her. It was difficult waiting for her to go to bed to work on them every night. What about you? What have you got Joyce?'

Mavis thought about the children in the children's home that Joyce still lived in. Most of them had no parents or parents who rarely visited. She felt sure the staff would make Christmas as pleasant as they could, but it would still be a subdued day. They'd go to church in crocodile file and come back to their dinner and no doubt a tiny gift.

Thank goodness the home had agreed to let Joyce stay with Mavis for a week. Hopefully it wouldn't be many more weeks before her adoption was formalised.

'I've knitted her a jumper and matching hat and scarf,' she replied. 'And I managed to find a jigsaw puzzle. But I found her a very special gift.'

The other two both turned to her. 'What is it?' Jane asked. With rationing and little money, special gifts were hard to come by.

'Do you remember that lady from the IIP people gave me a tip for how to find something that belonged to Joyce's mother?'

Jane sighed. 'I remember you saying at the time that you could see her arm sticking up through the rubble. It was so sad.'

'It was. Really horrible. But I followed her advice and tracked down her watch. Better still, I found a small silver locket and it's got two photos inside – one of each of Joyce's parents.'

The other two were too surprised to respond for a minute.

Then Cordelia found her tongue. 'Mavis, that's absolutely brilliant. A very special gift. You'd said she had no photos of her parents. She'll treasure that forever.'

Mavis swallowed a tear as she remembered the moment she

first saw them. 'It was the least I could do. I went from pillar to post with different local authority offices, but it paid off in the end.'

Now it was Cordelia's turn to be questioned.

'What about you? Have you got gifts for your parents?' Jane asked.

She had but didn't like to say so. As the only one comfortably off financially, she'd been able to find a beautiful necklace for her mother and cufflinks for her father. But not in Silvertown. None of the shops there sold such things. She'd gone to the West End on her day off.

'Just little things,' she replied.

It was only half a lie. The gifts were small.

'Let's have a cuppa before we go, shall we?' Cordelia suggested. 'We won't see each other for a few days.'

She went to the tiny kitchen area and put on the kettle.

Outside, they could hear a choir singing 'Away in a Manger', more loudly than the wireless, which they turned off. They all stopped and listened, each transported to Christmases in the past, before the chaos of war had altered everything. The three women quietly sang along, then Mavis, not usually known for showing emotion, reached across to her friends and squeezed their hands, holding back tears.

Cordelia poured the boiling water into the pot. 'Been a busy few months, hasn't it? The highlight had to be the king and queen visiting. At least little Tommy didn't get up to any of his tricks, trying to kiss one of the girls. I was on tenterhooks the whole time they were singing.'

'Me too,' Jane said, inspecting a small pile of papers she'd rescued from the back of a drawer under the desk. 'But the queen did seem genuinely interested in what we're doing, and they looked really pleased with the gift we gave them.'

She flipped through the papers, then pushed them on a metal spike. They could be used for scrap.

Mavis grunted. 'Not 'ard to be interested in what folks are doing when you get paid for it, is it? Not exactly 'ard work, is it?'

Cordelia put her cup back in its saucer. 'You're right, Mavis, but you've got to admit their visit was good for morale. Goodness knows we need it. The Blitz may have stopped but the occasional bombing still gives our IIP people enough to do.' She turned to Jane, who was still sorting paper clips and bits of fluff. 'You can stop working now, Jane! You did a fantastic job when you helped them out that day.'

'It nearly broke my heart when I had to give bad news or even when there was no news,' Jane said, brushing dust off her fingers. 'When I think back, one of my highlights was seeing Mavis sort out that black marketeer. You could be hired to be on the door of a nightclub sorting out the troublemakers, Mavis.'

Mavis wasn't sure if that was a compliment or not but decided to take it as one. 'You gotta stand up for yourself. No one else'll do it for ya!'

Bang! Bang! Urgent hammering on the door made them all jump. Mavis scoffed. 'I recognise that knock. It's blooming Bert – bet you a penny to a pound.'

'We're closed!' she shouted. 'Come back after Christmas!'

The hammering paused for a second then started again. 'Open up. It's me, Bert.'

As if they hadn't guessed.

'Let me see to him,' Cordelia said with a sinking heart. She opened the door just a crack. 'We're closed now for Christmas, Bert. I can't let you in.'

He leaned sideways and looked past her at Jane and Mavis. 'Ain't trying to come in, am I? Just wanted to give somethin' to my favourite girls.'

He opened a shopping bag and produced a square, flat parcel wrapped in old newspaper. Cordelia stood still, unsure what to do.

'Go on, take it. There's one each.'

And with that, he spun on his heels and hurried away, shouting 'Merry Christmas' over his shoulder.

Curious, the three women unwrapped the newspaper, which smelled faintly of fish. Inside were three pairs of stockings. The women looked at each other in amazement.

'Little bleeder,' Mavis said. 'I know 'ow 'e's got them. Black market, ain't they?' But she moved fast, grabbing a pair and tucking them under her arm. 'Never look a gift horse in the mouth, that's what I say.'

'Well, we can't give them back, can we?' Cordelia said, taking a pair. 'And it's good to know that Bert values us so much. He's a funny old stick, but inside there is a heart of gold. It would offend him if we gave them back.' She put them on top of her case. 'Now what were we talking about?'

'I wanted to say one thing I remember every day is how smart the library looks now,' Jane said. 'Painted, polished, cobwebs gone and that lovely quilt behind the desk. It makes me feel proud every morning when I come in. And I was thinking how lucky we are. Not like some people around here who've lost their homes or their loved ones. I've got George coming for Christmas and Helen has really settled back home.'

'And I'll be collecting Joyce tomorrow,' Mavis joined in. 'I think the adoption will be going through soon. She's staying for a whole week this time. I'm really looking forward to it.' She picked up one of the biscuits Cordelia had provided.

'What about you, boss? What're you doing? Don't suppose your man can get home?'

Cordelia shook her head, wishing that Robert could be with her more than anything else in the world. 'No. I'm going home to my parents. My case is ready. As soon as we lock up, I'll be heading for the station. It's a pity Tom couldn't be here today,' she said. 'I've got a little gift for him. He'll have to have it another day.'

'Oh, that reminds me! I've got one for each of you!' Mavis squealed like a child, excited to have something to offer.

She reached under the desk where she had hidden two small parcels, each wrapped in colourful magazine pages.

'Can we open them now?' Jane asked excitedly.

'Course you can.' Mavis was a bit nervous. She'd managed to get two cigar tins and had painted flowers all over them. She was no artist, but she thought they looked okay.

Jane and Cordelia unwrapped their gifts and exclaimed with pleasure.

'That's beautiful,' Cordelia said, looking closely at the painting. 'I have just the use for it. My hairpins. I'm always losing the darn things.'

'And I'll put sewing needles in mine,' Jane said.

By the time they'd finished exchanging gifts and doing a final tidy up, it was nearly time for Cordelia to leave to catch her train.

'Well, girls. We'll meet each other before new year, but I wonder what 1942 will bring? As long as I've got you two by my side, I feel I can cope with anything.'

She reached behind a cupboard and produced a bottle of sherry with all the aplomb of a magician. 'Hey, presto! Let's have a drink before we go.'

She fetched three small glasses she'd got at the market and poured them each an extravagant splash.

'We've weathered some storms, all of us, literal and of the heart. We can't predict the future, but we can enjoy now, this minute, the three of us together.' She raised her glass. 'Here's to us, three brave librarians, and all we've achieved.'

ACKNOWLEDGEMENTS

I'd like to give my thanks, as usual, to my husband Rick. His patience and plot ideas are invaluable. Also, thanks to my wonderful friends and writing buddies Fran Johnson and Maggie Scott. And last, but by no means least, my wonderful editor, Emily Yau.

ABOUT THE AUTHOR

Patricia McBride is the author of several fiction and non-fiction books as well as numerous articles. She loves undertaking the research for her books, helped by stories told to her by her Cockney mother and grandparents who lived in the East End. Patricia lives in Cambridge with her husband.

Sign up to Patricia McBride's mailing list for news, competitions and updates on future books.

Visit Patricia's website: www.patriciamcbrideauthor.com

Follow Patricia on social media here:

facebook.com/patriciamcbrideauthor
instagram.com/tricia.mcbride.writer

ALSO BY PATRICIA MCBRIDE

The Lily Baker Series

The Button Girls

The Picture House Girls

The Telephone Girls

The Air Raid Girls

The Blackout Girls

The Bletchley Park Girls

Christmas Wishes for the Bletchley Park Girls

The Library Girls of the East End Series

The Library Girls of the East End

Hard Times For The East End Library Girls

A Christmas Gift for the East End Library Girls

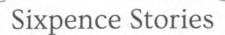

Sixpence Stories

Introducing Sixpence Stories!

Discover page-turning historical novels from your favourite authors, meet new friends and be transported back in time.

Join our book club Facebook group

https://bit.ly/SixpenceGroup

Sign up to our newsletter

https://bit.ly/SixpenceNews

Boldw👁👁d

Boldwood Books is an award-winning fiction publishing company seeking out the best stories from around the world.

Find out more at www.boldwoodbooks.com

Join our reader community for brilliant books, competitions and offers!

Follow us
@BoldwoodBooks
@TheBoldBookClub

Sign up to our weekly deals newsletter

https://bit.ly/BoldwoodBNewsletter